PROUD PADA

THE LAST LUMENIAN SERIES

BOOK III

S.G. BLAISE

info@thelastlumenian.com.

First paperback edition December 2022

Book design by Tim Barber from Dissect Designs
Map Illustrated by Clif Chandler
Edited by Julie Tibbott and William Drennan
Publisher: Lilac Grove Entertainment LLC

Paperback ISBN: 978-1-7347605-7-6
E-Book ISBN: 978-1-7347605-8-3

www.sgblaise.com

To receive exclusive content sign up for the S.G. Blaise newsletter at sgblaisenews.com

To Alex:
your support and encouragement keep me going.

To Gabe:
who made quite a few good points regarding this story.

To My Mom:
who can't wait for this series to be made into a movie (or TV show; she is not picky).

To all of you, Dear Readers, who asked for more. It's my pleasure to oblige!

CHAPTER 1

"You are so beautiful, Lilla," Callum says. He looks striking in his form-fitting, black military uniform, which emphasizes his tall, muscular body. The lapels of his jacket, turned to the side, reveal dark gray lining in a V shape. Colorful triangular buttons line up on the inside of the lapel in three rows. Tight black pants show the shape of his muscular thighs. Knee-high black boots complete his outfit.

I can't look away from his blue eyes. They shine with so much love and happiness on his tanned face, framed by short black hair. A thin, jagged scar runs from his eyebrow to his strong jawline—evidence of the dangerous life he's lived in his twenty-five years. A lopsided grin appears at the corner of his mouth.

Behind Callum, an orange-red sun ascends above the horizon. Along with it rises the already humid heat. It will become overbearing in a few hours. Small purple birds burst from the evergreen tropical trees, soaring across the cloudless, green-tinted, blue sky. They chirp and twitter, adding to the cacophony of the waking jungle.

Excitement raises goose bumps on my arms. I can't believe today is the day our life together begins. The day I've been waiting for, ever since I invoked the Teryn traditional marriage proposal called Bride's Choice on Callum.

With shaking hands, I smooth the front of my gray, sleeveless dress, ending in a wide skirt that does not reach my sandaled feet. So many feelings wash over me. Excitement. Worry. Joy. How I wish for the impossible that my mom and brother could be here.

I shiver.

Callum reaches for my hand, the calluses from wielding his longsword rasping on my olive-toned skin. "Are you nervous?"

I glance at him and raise my eyebrows. "Have *you* changed your mind?" We've only known each other a few months. During that time, we fought an archgod and survived; became separated for days; and learned that not all his family members were supportive of our pending union.

A soft breeze, scented with sweet flowers, tangles with my dark violet tresses, blowing them across my face and into my dark violet eyes.

He touches my cheek, his thumb rubbing a circle. "You didn't answer my question."

How do I find the words to explain that I am bursting with so much happiness, like I've never felt in my nineteen years? That I can't wait for my Bride's Choice claim to be honored by his father, Caderyn, praelor and ruler of the Teryn Praelium—the most dangerous empire in the Seven Galaxies? Yet I fear that something will happen to prevent us from getting married. "I'm not nervous. You?"

"Nothing could make me change my mind," Callum says and tucks the loose strands behind my ear. "I am sorry your father couldn't be here."

I look away, trying to sort through my warring emotions.

My friends mingle among thousands of black-clad Teryn warriors who are getting ready to line up for our wedding ceremony, held on this orange-green planet in Galaxy Seven named Cathal. The location of my next mission as sybil, right hand and general to the Archgoddess of the Eternal Light and Order—one of the ruling archgods of the Seven Galaxies—or The Lady, as I like to call her. We've been stationed here for more than a week now but nothing has happened. Not. A. Single. Thing. That was the only reason Callum and I were able to wear down Caderyn's resistance against this ceremony and convince him to officiate it now. We all needed a change from the monotony of, well, boredom. Hence the impromptu wedding, announced yesterday.

"I wish Father could have joined us," I say, "but he could not have made the journey in time. He did send his best wishes and blessings when I talked to him this morning." Our relationship will always be complicated, but at least we're talking to each other.

"I'm glad to hear that." Callum pulls me closer to him with a quick motion. I brace myself with a hand on his rock-hard chest.

I crane my neck to look him in the eyes. "Impatient, are you?"

He leans down and kisses my nose. "Very." He places his hands on my waist and studies my face, drinking in my features. "I know this is not how you must have imagined your wedding—"

I press a finger on his lips. "I never wanted the pomp that came with the royal court even when I was a princess. Now that I am a princess only in name, I have even less need for it."

We could not have picked a more perfect place for the ceremony even if we had tried. The clearing we've gathered in, not too far from the imposing black Teryn warship, is bursting with life. Flowers in all colors and shapes bloom around us—on branches and vines that snake around the thick trunks of yellow-tinted trees. Critters rush by, rustling leaves of the thicket that covers the ground in orange-brown patches. Pink-hued steam puffs from cone-shaped mounds from time to time. Sunlight sparkles on drops of water clinging to the wide leaves of the native plants. Three moons, each smaller than the next, line up in the distant sky in a half circle. Peace and calm saturate the atmosphere of the otherwise uninhabited planet. I wonder anew why The Lady sent me here with the whole Teryn armada, when there is nothing happening here.

I turn back to Callum. "Where is your family? They should have joined us by now."

He kisses my cheek, then frowns in the direction of the black warship, the size of a small city. "They are late. More importantly, *he* is late."

I stifle a sigh of worry. "I'm sure Caderyn will be here any moment."

Callum shakes his head. "He's always punctual. This is not like him."

"Maybe if we wait a bit longer . . ." My voice trails off. Even I don't believe Caderyn will show.

Callum growls. "I'm done waiting." He reaches for my hand and adds, "We'll drag the praelor here, whether he likes it or not."

CHAPTER 2

Glenna, my petite best friend and healer, falls into pace with me. "What's happening?" We cut a path through the remnants of the crowd. She shoves a white strand of hair—a clear sign of the corruption growing in her—off her shoulder.

I open my mouth to answer my friend's question when Moira—the fabled queen of the original Teryns, my melded spirit, and the Heart Amulet herself from the Teryn tales—interrupts me. *What did I miss?* she asks in my head and yawns, showing off white fangs in a wolfish face framed by black lyon mane and covered with tiny scales that glint with a multihued light. She clasps her lyon-like paws in front of her long red dress, which accentuates the athletic curves of her bear-like body in a flattering way. Ever since we joined, or melded, the two of us can communicate in thought, share my body equally, and transfigure into a unique battle form no other Teryn has.

"Caderyn never showed up," I say to both, staring at the humongous black warship that seems to swallow the sunlight with its darkness. For a second, I despise that ship. It reminds me how cold, ruthless, and close-minded the Teryns can be to outsiders—a lesson I learned the hard way, almost dying in the process. All they care about is their weapons and fighting, and oh, yes, how could I forget? Their honor. The problem is that they seem to have a different description of what honor means than I do. Case in point: Caderyn going back on the promise he made not even a day ago. I push down my rising irritation.

Callum glances at me. I detect the same anger in his eyes. He just hides it better.

Glenna pats my arm in comfort, then glares at Ragnald, a two-hundred-forty-year-old battlemage and friend, who hurries to catch up with us.

"What do you mean he 'never showed up'?" Ragnald asks. He reaches into the pocket of a black mage robe he wears over a gray suit and black shoes. He takes out a leather string and pulls his long silver hair into a ponytail. A colorful circular emblem, embroidered with all six light elements, stands out on the black fabric, showing: azure blue A'qua for water, dark brown T'erra for ground, ruby-red Fla'mma for fire, sky-blue A'ris for air, straw-yellow A'nima for all living souls, and golden-white Lume for light. "This reminds me of the time when the Academia of Mages sent me to the Monarchy of—"

"We don't have time for your tales," Arrov, my seven-foot-tall, ex-rebel friend says. He wears an all-white outfit that makes his light-blue skin tone, midnight-blue hair and eyes even more striking. Plenty of Teryn warrior women eye him as he passes by.

Marauder crown princess Intonia Varia Yanna, aka Ivy, elbows Arrov to the side. "Did you poison him like I taught you?" She chews open-mouthed on a purple mass of gum. She swipes a hand through her long blond hair and arranges her boobs in the tight, teal-colored minidress that has more holes in it than material. Her green eyes flash with mischief and intellect.

Belthair, my ex-boyfriend and ex-rebel captain, wave his six hands in agitation. "Of course she did not poison him." Dressed in a leather jacket with pants tucked into black boots, he looks menacing. He raises a black eyebrow in question. I shake my head, indicating that I did not poison Caderyn. It had never occurred to me, but now I find the idea tempting.

Arrov nods toward Ivy. "Why is she still here?"

Ivy pouts. "You know I can't go back to the Marauders Syndicate. They will kill me for failing the dowager queen's command. Probably." She tilts her head at Callum. "Though he is still up for grabs."

I slice out a hand. "There will be no poisoning, or grabbing—outside of mine, that is." Even if it's the last thing I do.

That's the spirit, Moira says, then laughs. *No pun intended.*

Ivy asks around her gum, "What's wrong with poisoning? It's the Marauders' way."

Isa and Bella, twin princesses from the scientific world of Barabal, my good friends and best hackers in the Seven Galaxies, giggle. "There are a lot of things wrong with poisoning," Bella says and shakes her black hair styled in a bob. She wears a yellow jumpsuit on her petite and slender body, along with ankle boots.

5

"We discussed this, remember?" Isa asks, looking almost identical to Bella, elegant and stylish in a similar jumpsuit.

Ivy eyes the twins with a frown. "I thought you two were joking."

Arrov crosses his arms, making his bicep bulge in his white jacket. "That's just great. What if Ivy decides to poison all of us in our sleep?"

"If I wanted to poison any of you, it would have been Lilla for stealing Callum from me—"

Callum scowls at Ivy. "Lilla did not steal me from anyone."

Ivy pulls her skirt lower, which keeps riding up her legs. "But I am a much more forgiving soul than that."

Arrov blinks at Ivy. "In what reality are you a forgiving—"

Belthair smiles at the Marauder princess. "You are so humble, too."

Ivy blushes. "I know."

Glenna and I exchange a look. Neither of us has missed the fact that Ivy hasn't answered Arrov's question. Her life in the court of the Marauder Queen was anything but easy. She survived assassination attempts from her family by becoming a spoiled and superficial princess, someone who was not a threat to the queen's throne.

We enter the enormous black ship and stride onto a narrow and windowless corridor, taking one hallway after the other until they all blur. Angled panels with a fur-like texture make up most of the wall. Soft light comes from around the perimeter of the rectangular panels but fails to make the ship feel warm. Under my feet, a metal grate covers a tube full of yellowish gas fuel. In the gas, long beaked-salamanders swim, cleaning it from space particles as they feed on them.

I should have known the wedding wouldn't happen. Neither Caderyn's wife Sorcha, nor Callum's sister Rhona, nor his two older half brothers, Sachary and Sawney, were present in the clearing. Caderyn probably told them not to bother.

You cannot know that dear, Moira says. *They could have a legitimate reason for their absence.*

Like what? I cannot think of any.

Something, uh, important, Moira says, then winces.

We take another turn and run into Caderyn.

Caderyn—an older image of Callum with his wide shoulders and similar height but with gray hair and beard—stops and stares at us for a second, looking lost. He clears his throat. "There you are. I was looking for you."

Callum narrows his eyes. "What do you mean you were looking for us? You know we were outside, getting ready for our wedding—"

Caderyn dismisses his son's comment with a flick of his wrist. "That's not important now."

I take an involuntary step back. I have long suspected that Caderyn didn't like me from the moment we met, but to dismiss my wedding as something unimportant hurts like a deep cut from the prickliest seashell.

Moira shakes her head. *Don't let him see how much he hurt you, dear. We've proved him wrong once; we'll prove him wrong again.*

Callum takes a step forward, but I stop him with a hand on his corded forearm. He cannot challenge his father on the ship, or he'll break one of the Ground Rules that govern all Teryns.

An orange-reddish light flashes in Callum's eyes, a clear sign of his anger. "Would you care to explain to us what was more important?"

"It's best if you see for yourself," Caderyn says. Something akin to pain crosses his face, making him look older than his age of fifty-five. "Follow me."

CHAPTER 3

Caderyn stops at the entrance to one of the ship's living quarters. He waves his palm on the raised panel, and the inward-angled door opens with a quiet swish.

For a moment I don't see anything wrong in the spacious room. On the left, a floor-to-ceiling glass wall opens to verdant green vegetation. On the right, a light gray bed, attached to the wall, and two chairs with a table complete the furnishing. My gaze lands on a tall, dark-haired woman wearing a black military-style uniform. Sorcha, Caderyn's second wife and Callum's mom, with haunted eyes in her pale face, stands in the middle of the room with her daughter Rhona hugging her shoulders. A bald Teryn warrior with a green medic ribbon on his pocket waits next to them, a forlorn expression on his face.

Rhona, dressed in the black military uniform, drags a hand through her black hair, a motion I've seen Callum do a hundred times. When she looks up, her blue eyes look pained.

Dread spreads from my belly all the way up my spine.

Callum stops, his body rigid.

The women move back as I enter, and that's when I see it.

Blood—spreading in a widening pool on the gray carpet around a prone and black-clad body behind the table.

Inhaling the air, scented with copper, I cover my mouth with a hand. My heart drums in my ear.

I recognize the body with his dark brown hair. Sachary—Callum and Rhona's older brother from Caderyn's first marriage—lays on the carpet, lifeless.

Glenna rushes into the room and kneels by Sachary. She threads transparent ribbons of A'ris magic into him, attempting to heal him.

For a second, I see a different dead body floating facedown in the shallow water of Frida's Bay back in Uhna. A young woman with fake, dark violet hair, wearing a torn and bloodstained evening dress that drifts around her, while the waves push at her slim body with small blue crabs crawling all over her.

"I just talked to him yesterday at dinner," I say and my voice quivers as I try to come to terms with the thought that he will never join us again. How can he be dead? Who would want to kill him and why?

Callum squeezes my hand, his mouth in a thin line. He looks at me with eyes pained, then strides to his mother and hugs her. Sorcha buries her head in his shoulder, her wails muted.

Glenna shakes her head. "His body is still warm. I estimate the time of death to be less than an hour ago. Cause of death is a single puncture wound to the heart."

Caderyn grinds his teeth. "That's what the medic said."

"I wonder . . ." Ragnald's voice trails off. He closes his eyes, then moves his hands in a circle, mixing transparent red ribbons of Fla'mma with brown ribbons of T'erra before blanketing the room with the magic mix.

Every inch of the living quarters lights up, with dark footsteps around Sachary and a single line of footsteps leading out of the room.

Ragnald opens his eyes and puts on the yellow glasses that allow him to see magic. He relays the magical pattern he sees for the others then adds, "There is no sign of struggle. Only one attacker."

I study the magical marks. "Nor is there a sign that Sachary tried to transfigure to defend himself."

Moira nods. *I don't detect any shimmer sparks left over from a transfiguration.*

Caderyn sighs. "That's what I concluded as well."

Rhona crosses her arms, looking more like her old self. "Whoever attacked Sachary was someone my brother must have known. He trusted this person enough to let him or her into his room. I wonder if it was one of Sachary's old enemies. We all know that my brother's temper can, I mean, *used to* get the best of him—"

Caderyn snaps, "Yes, we do know that. I issued a command to prevent anyone from leaving the planet. All the reports coming back state that no one managed to escape via shuttlecraft or left my ship. I know that much. The killer is still here."

"Have you issued a search yet?" Callum asks.

Caderyn pales. "I, uh, ordered everyone to get back and put the ship in a lockdown, but I, uh, haven't thought of . . . I can't believe I haven't thought of . . ."

Sorcha, with tearstained face, hugs him. "You were too distraught, my love, but it's not too late now."

Callum hits his fist in his open palm. "The killer has nowhere to go. Have your most trusted warriors search for anyone who is not at their station."

Caderyn nods and presses on his earlobe to use his k'bug—the Teryn communication device that is a living insect attached to the back of his ear. Activating the long, thin hairs on its legs, the sound waves created can reach other k'bugs. He barks the order, then looks at Callum. "Anyone can be the culprit . . . how will we . . ."

I never thought I'd see the praelor so bewildered, dear.

My heart aches for Callum's family. I cannot know what they are going through, but having lost my brother Nic, who was murdered in front of me, I can imagine their pain all too well.

Callum strides to the door. "I will find whoever did this, Father."

Ragnald raises a hand. "If you could wait for a second." Then the mage steps outside the room, ahead of Callum.

We follow Ragnald. There he uses Fla'mma magic to highlight a trail of dissipating footsteps heading to the right. "At least I can help you with a direction to start your search. May the Archgoddess of the Eternal Light and Order guide you."

Belthair cracks his twelve knuckles. "We're coming with—"

"I'd rather you stay," Callum says, interrupting him. "I need you to protect my family." Then he turns to his father. "I'll find the killer."

I clasp Callum's hand. "I'll help you." He hesitates for a second, then nods.

Together we hurry down the corridor.

CHAPTER 4

Callum and I head right on the twisting, narrow corridor. The low hum of the engines is the only sound that can be heard outside our footsteps.

I glance at Callum, his tanned skin stretched tightly on his sharp cheekbones.

My eyes well up but I swipe away the moisture. I cannot give in to the sadness. Not now.

The time will come for that, dear. Later. Now Callum needs you to stay strong.

I nod and hug my middle as shivers try to break out over my body. Someone has managed to deceive one of the most lethal warriors in the Seven Galaxies and commit this murder without detection. They attacked Sachary before he could act in self-defense and transfigure into his powerful battle form. A battle form that comes from melding with a Spirit Warrior—one of the original inhabitants of Teryn world before they were killed in the previous Era War—giving the warriors superior skills, strength, and a high level of magical resistance.

I doubt the attacker was someone Sachary knew, dear, says Moira. *There would have been more signs of a struggle, as that kind of attack is usually the result of passion or hurt emotions and often ending in dozens of stab wounds, not a single precise strike. I saw many such cases when I was a queen. There is a certain level of brutality to those attacks, not cold and premeditated like this one. Not to mention that at the first sign of a weapon, Sachary would have fought back with all his might.*

I nod. *This does feels more like an assassination. Sachary must have underestimated whoever entered, or was tricked into believing that they presented no danger to him; thus the attacker was able to kill him with a single stab.*

A lone crewman, dressed in dark blue overalls, approaches us from the right corridor, without looking at Callum or me, almost cowering.

I shake my head seeing the crewman's distress. In Teryn society the hierarchy goes from the melded warriors at the top, to consuasors, or senators, who are responsible for governing the empire. They've earned the despised nickname "Brainiacs" from the warriors because they failed their trial and did not acquire a spirit. At the bottom of the hierarchy are the Teryn civilians. They are nonmelded but contribute to society in other ways, such as being crewmen on spaceships or having a trade skill they use on the Teryn home world. Anyone who is not a melded warrior is looked down upon by the warriors, thanks to the Ground Rules on which they base their honor system. These Ground Rules are also a sort of constitution that regulates their lives, especially when it comes to fights.

Callum eyes the young man, though not for being nonmelded. I haven't seen Callum regard other Teryn civilians with anything but cordiality. He scrutinizes the crewman for the same reason I do—we both wonder if he is the killer. The culprit could have hidden anywhere on this colossal ship.

"We should have enlisted the help of my friends," I mutter to Callum. "How are the two of us going to search every nook and cranny?" Even with those warriors Caderyn trusted, we are not enough to carry out such a massive pursuit.

"I can't risk the safety of anyone else. I can protect you, since you are with me, and those warriors know how to take care of themselves, but I can't say the same for your friends."

I open my mouth to argue that he underestimates my friends, but he shakes his head and I stay silent. The crewman stops in front of us, gawking and rooted to the spot. His tanned face pales a shade. He hunches his shoulders that tremble the tiniest bit under our inspection. His posture reminds me of the Uhna palace servants—they did their best not to attract any attention. Staying invisible was vital to them.

Callum mutters a curse. "As you were, crewman."

There is so much in his expression that I relate to. Sorrow and anger. Concern and frustration. All because of a regressive and pitiless society.

I watch the crewman turn left, remembering how stifled and restricting the Uhnan court was until the fall of the monarchy that happened after my battle with DLD. My father, the ma'ha and king, ignored signs of unrest from his

12

civilians. He treated the refugees on our world like another source of labor. He bribed his way to be the leader of the Pax Septum Coalition, much to the chagrin of other worlds in the nineteen-planet-strong alliance. They were accustomed to democracy, which my father interfered with. Many of those worlds also financed the rebellion that was the last straw against the monarchy. Of course, the archgod hiding on my world and devastating it did not help.

"Lilla!" Callum shouts.

My head snaps up, only to find him running toward me.

Where did he come from? He was next to me a minute ago.

"You took a wrong turn," he explains.

Oh. "I was lost in thought."

Together we retrace our steps and head right.

At my questioning look, Callum says, "My instincts urge me to keep going right, toward the storage areas. It's the perfect place to hide. I think the killer will try to wait out the search, even if it takes days or weeks. That's why we're not heading left, toward the space shuttles, where Caderyn set up guards."

"I guess that makes sense. As much as anything can in this surreal situation."

I'm glad he listens to his instincts. I learned to trust mine, dear.

"I keep trying to figure out who would want my brother dead and why," Callum says. "Rhona was right. His temper often got him into trouble, but I never thought someone would go this far."

I touch his hand. "I am so sorry."

Callum nods. "I don't understand why my brother didn't fight back. That's not like him."

"What if the killer used some kind of magical disguise to blend in?" The Teryns prefer biology-infused technology, which may not be strong enough to detect magic-infused technology. This could explain how the killer was able to stay undetected—by using a magical camouflage.

We stop and look at each other. "I should ask Ragnald to look for any dark elemental magic taint," I say, and then do so with the help of the k'bug.

"I didn't notice anything," Ragnald's voice comes through my k'bug, "but I wasn't looking for any dark elemental magic either. I have to do some preparations, as dealing with dark elements does not come naturally to me. I'll get back to you soon."

I convey the mage's words to Callum.

"Good," he says as we resume our walk. "Now stay close. I can't protect you if you're not with me."

"I don't need protection," I insist.

Callum raises a placating hand. "I agree. I meant to say, 'I won't be able to keep you from getting lost.'"

You do have a tendency to get lost, my dear.

I duck my head.

We take the corridors in silence.

Wait. What was that? Moira asks.

I slow my steps. *What do you mean?*

On your left.

I look to the left but see nothing out of the ordinary.

"There. Can you see it, dear? There is something in that corridor. May I? Moira indicates her need to use my body.

I nod. An odd sensation envelops me as I become the observer. I shove the rising panic aside—I trust Moira. This is not the first time she's taken control of my body temporarily when it was needed.

Moira drops down to my knees, leans forward, and sniffs the ground.

Something repulsive and acrid hits my nose.

That! Moira says. *That's what I detected. I think it's best to follow it.* She relinquishes control over my body, and I get to my feet.

I turn to Callum to let him know what Moira and I have discovered, but he is nowhere to be found. We're separated. Again.

CHAPTER 5

I chew on my lower lip. *I should call for Callum and wait—*

There is no time to waste, my dear. Just go, before the track disappears.

Picking up the pace, I rush down the corridor. The grated floor over the gas tube gives way to smooth, dark-gray carpet. The deeper we go, the more that acrid and repulsive smell bothers me. Suddenly I realize why.

It's Acerbus, the dark element of DLD. In the beginning, the Omnipower created only one archgod to govern the Seven Galaxies, who ruled over twelve elements: A'ris and Dusky A'ris, A'qua and Murky A'qua, Fla'mma and Black Fla'mma, T'erra and Barren T'erra, A'nima and Diseased A'nima, Lume and Acerbus. These elements were later separated and grouped into six for light and six for dark; one group for each archgod to rule over, for balance. These elements, such as Acerbus to Lume, are each other's antithesis.

Though its presence explains why no one could detect the attacker hiding on the ship. The killer must have used Acerbus to disguise himself, which must have been why poor Sachary didn't react in self-defense. This is perhaps another reason Ragnald didn't sense it, as it is not a light element, one that the mage has an affinity to. The dark elements are the territory of Turned— magic users who have abused their magic, becoming corrupt aberrations that desire destruction and killing in the name of DLD.

But why kill Sachary? Who benefits from his death? None of this makes sense.

We can ponder it later, dear. Now hurry.

Fighting my repulsion, I sprint down the corridor when the Acerbus trail stops.

I halt, looking around.

Can you sense it, Moira?

Moira shakes her head in frustration. *I think the attacker covered up their trail. I smell nothing.*

Buckets of fishguts!

You have magic too, dear. Maybe it's time to use it?

Right. I keep forgetting. Most of my life I did not know I had magic. I had a natural and instinctive aversion toward it, because whenever Glenna tried to heal me with her A'ris magic, it always backfired. Then I recalled a suppressed memory of how my mom tried to teach me magic, all the while making sure that I would keep that a secret to protect me. I realized that the trauma of her death made me forget my magic. Now I know that all six elements of the light reside somewhere in me, given my heritage as a Lumenian. All I need is Lume to find the Acerbus.

Closing my eyes, I reach for the pulsing bright orb, covered in millions of threads of elemental magic. My magic. I engage a thin thread of Lume and probe the ground in front of me.

The trail lights up for just a few steps. Then it retreats, backtracking until it takes another right-branching corridor.

Keeping my Lume thread engaged, I follow the trace of Acerbus, taking a sharp turn only to come face-to-face with a crewman covered in Acerbus.

CHAPTER 6

A light flickers on top of the panel behind the scrawny crewman, as if reacting to the Acerbus emanating from him. Even the air smells stale here.

The killer backs up until his heels hit the wall of the dead end. We both know he has nowhere to go but through me.

He glares at me but makes no move otherwise.

I take a step back and lift my arms with palms out, a posture that looks nonthreatening yet is easy enough to shift to use either my elbows or my fists for an attack. Belthair taught me this when I joined the rebellion on Uhna.

I study the man. He looks unassuming, wearing the usual dark blue overalls of Teryn crewmen. Short, black hair frames a tanned and angular face with no marks on it, not even a mole. A straight nose perches above his thin lips. Dark brown eyes glint with malice as he sneers, showing off perfect white teeth.

If not for the Acerbus tainting him, I wouldn't have thought twice passing this crewman.

The hair stands up on the back of my neck from the menace radiating from him. I resist the urge to rub my arms, knowing it would not get rid of the repulsion I feel toward the dark element.

I open my mouth when Moira interrupts me. *Best not to rile him up, dear.*
I wasn't planning to.

"Who are you and what are you doing on this ship?" I ask in a voice designed to keep him calm.

He spreads his grease-spotted hands, though malice glints in his eyes. "I am nobody, just minding my own business. I should get back to my duties." He smiles and takes a few steps forward, but I block his way.

He can't fool me so easily. "Who are you? Why did you kill General Sachary? Who hired you?"

The smile slides off his too-perfect face. "He deserved to die for failing her."

Now we're getting somewhere. "Who is this mysterious 'her'?"

"You know who she is."

I have no clue. "It would be nice to narrow it down. Care to elaborate?"

He just glares back in answer.

Let's try something else. "Where did you get this Acerbus-infused disguise?"

"You're wasting your time," he sneers, and lunges at me.

CHAPTER 7

I ready to tackle the attacker when a laser shot pierces the fake crewman's chest before he can reach me. He stumbles, looking shocked. Black flames engulf him, burning him to smithereens in an instant. A small pile of ash settles on the floor.

I whirl to find Callum lowering his laser gun.

"I had it under control," I grind the words out.

That's one way to put it, dear.

Callum holsters his weapon, then steps close to me. He runs his hands down my shoulders and arms, checking for injuries. "I am sure you did, my love. However, I did not want to take any chances when your life was at stake."

I bat his hands away. "I'm fine. But now we can't ask him any more questions."

"He wouldn't have talked," Callum says, then grins. "You look adorable when upset."

Ugh. "It would have been nice to at least *try* to get some information out of him."

He reaches out and clasps my hand, pulling me close. He cups my cheek with his other hand, his callouses rough on my skin. He slowly rubs my cheekbone with his thumb. "I would do it again even knowing that it would upset you. Your safety is always paramount to me, Lilla. I care for nothing else." He leans down and kisses my lips, sealing his promise with such passion that it threatens to burn me up.

I return his kiss, rejoicing at his closeness, wanting more, almost forgetting about everything else.

My k'bug clicks and Ragnald's voice comes through. "You're not going to believe what I've found. It was—"

With a sigh I pull back and activate my k'bug. "Acerbus."

"Oh," Ragnald replies. "You already know."

I turn to Callum. "All I got out of the killer is that 'Sachary deserved to die because he failed her.' I am not exactly sure who he was referring to."

Could be the dowager queen of the Marauders, dear.

That's one possibility. "Moira thinks that the 'her' could be the dowager queen of the Marauders."

He lets me go. "That would make sense since she didn't get the alliance with the praelium. It's her retaliation." A muscle jumps in his jawline.

I wrap my arm around his waist. "We'll find a way to make her pay."

Callum kisses the top of my head. "For Sachary."

Not to be the bringer of bad news, but we must be sure that the Marauder Queen is the one who hired the killer. There might be others who had the opportunity and/or motive. We need proof.

There is only one place left where there might be any clues.

I step away from Callum and squat by the pile of ashes that once was the killer, searching for any signs. It still emits a sickening pungent smell and a faint wave of repulsion.

Callum squats by me and covers his nose. "What are you looking for?"

I lift a shoulder. "I'll, uh, know it when I see it."

The light above me flickers.

Something sparkles faintly in the ashes.

CHAPTER 8

"There." I point at the pile of ash. "Could you please get whatever sparkled?"

"With pleasure," Callum says without hesitation.

He pulls two square, palm-size mirrors from the pocket of his black uniform jacket. He uses one of the mirrors to sweep the ashes to the side, until it hits something with a tinkling. Then he scoops the objects up with the other mirror, lifting it up for me to see.

Minuscule purple rocks glitter on top of the mirror, smeared with black ashes.

I lean closer to study them. They look familiar. "I know those. I've seen them around the Pada monastery and in their fountains."

"Now that you mention it, I recall seeing them too. These rocks only prove that the killer was on Pada, not that the dowager queen employed him."

I concur with your, uh, boyfriend, dear. Or do you call him your fiancé? Or your "almost husband"? Since the wedding hasn't happened yet . . .

Funny.

I nod toward the rocks. "Technically, this could also mean that whoever hired the killer may have been on Pada as well. We know that the Tier One factions must report to the Teryn consuasors, including the Marauders." All the conquered worlds must fulfill their assigned quota to the Teryn Praelium and report back to the consuasors during a check-in summit that is held on the monastic Pada world. These worlds are grouped into tiers based on when they were subjugated. Uhna would have been in the fifth tier, but my Bride's Choice prevented Caderyn from conquering my world outright. He had to make an alliance with Uhna. I suspect that was one of the other reasons why he wasn't so happy with me.

Callum pulls a small transparent bag out of his pocket and places the mirrors and the rocks in it before putting them away. "That's true."

He gets to his feet and helps me up too. He steps to the closest wall panel and taps on its lower corner. A round plate pops open; it features rune-like writing on triangular buttons. He presses a button. A narrow board flips open at the bottom of the wall, near the pile of ashes. Hissing noise sounds and all the ashes, including the purple rocks, get sucked into the wall, leaving behind a clean floor.

When he is finished, I say, "Which means, we need go to Pada to search for the real culprit."

He nods. "Let's tell the praelor that—"

"No!"

Callum raises both of his eyebrows. "What do you mean, 'no'?"

That's a good question, dear. Why not?

I put a hand on the wall, digging my fingers into the fur-like texture of the panel, trying to explain why my instinct demanded such vehemence. "We cannot tell Caderyn any of this. He will tear apart the Tier One factions, looking for whoever hired the killer. That could result in an intergalactic war. The Lady needs the Teryn armada to win the Era War. Without Caderyn, there is no army for the archgoddess. We cannot afford that." I made a promise to my mom when we visited the refugee camps to always protect the innocents who cannot protect themselves. That was the reason why I accepted the Sybil role—not because of duty but because of the promise I made and intend to keep. "I also have to find out who supplied them with Acerbus and to ensure that won't happen again."

Callum crosses his arms. "Are you asking me to lie?"

I cringe. "That's a harsh word to use. More like omit a few details when we talk to your father. You and I could do a better job investigating and with less attention on us. We must go to Pada now, without Caderyn, and take care of this mess."

"What about The Lady? She ordered you to be here, on Cathal."

I successfully completed my first mission as a sybil, which was to acquire the Teryn armada. The second mission, which was to bring the Teryn armada to Cathal, is technically completed too.

"True, but my next mission hasn't quite started yet, and The Lady did not provide any more instruction to go on. I don't know how much time there is left before She orders me to do something else. We must bring justice for Sachary's death, now. Together."

Callum uncrosses his arms and drags a hand through his short hair. "Logically I agree with you, but I still don't like lying to him."

"You can tell him everything once we have the culprit. Then it won't be lying. You simply waited to have all the facts in hand."

Callum looks to the side, considering my words.

You can be quite convincing, dear.

I don't like lying to Caderyn either, but I have no other choice. He would ask even fewer questions before attacking the factions, scaring away whoever is behind this assassination. Then we won't know why Sachary had to die. No, I must prevent an intergalactic war between the Tier One factions and the Teryn Praelium. We are better off without Caderyn's interference; I just know it.

Those are valid reasons. Caderyn does underestimate others often, even if it's to his own detriment. Like he did with you, dear.

Callum looks back to me. "Fine." He touches his ear, activating his k'bug. Subvocalizing, he sends a message to someone. Finished, he says, "We better go and make our 'report' to my father before he comes looking for us."

CHAPTER 9

Callum and I stop in front of inward angled double doors, leading to the command center of the ship.

Callum taps the side where the control panel is, and the doors slide to the side, disappearing into the wall with an audible swoosh. He strides in.

I move to follow him, but two Teryn warriors bar my way. Callum whirls around with a furious look on his face just as the door shuts in front of me.

I huff out a frustrated sigh, then turn around. Inhaling, I force calm on my nerves. I don't understand why Caderyn still won't let me in his command center after all these days.

Don't take it to heart, dear. He likes everyone to know their place. Evidently yours is outside his command center.

A few warriors enter the narrow corridor, striding past me with knowing smirks on their faces.

I grind my teeth at the humiliation but refuse to look away from them or give any indication how much this upsets me.

I'm sure they are not allowed in either, dear.

I stifle a sigh. *Small comfort.*

Muffled voices sound from the other side of the doors. Then Callum steps out, followed by an irritated-looking Caderyn.

Callum, facing his father, stops next to me.

I hide my surprise at this turn of events.

If the fish won't swim into your net . . . Moira says with a chuckle.

Caderyn glares at us. "I'm here. Now make your report."

"Lilla and I found the killer and took care of him, ensuring that Sachary's death met justice, bringing him honor in the afterlife. It was just, uh, an unfortunate scuffle that got out of hand in the flare of tempers."

Caderyn studies Callum's face and then mine. "Is that so?"

We don't answer him, just wait.

After a long moment Caderyn inclines his head. "Sachary always had a way to get the worst out of his fellow Teryns. We will have his last honoring ceremony on Teryn, after we're done with this mission. Now if there is nothing else . . ." He turns to leave.

"Before you go," Callum says, stopping Caderyn in his tracks, "Lilla and I would like to go to Pada."

Caderyn turns back to us, glowering. "Absolutely not."

CHAPTER 10

Callum returns his father's glare in a calm manner, while I gape at Caderyn. The praelor didn't even consider it for a second.

"Why not?" I manage to say into the uncomfortable silence.

Caderyn narrows his eyes on his son. "We are in the middle of your mission, Lilla, which your archgoddess ordered us to accomplish. Though what this mission entails, other than wasting my time staring at the jungle growing a few feet each day, is beyond me. My armada and I could be stomping out corruption, but we are stuck here, on this godsforsaken, green and humid planet. A planet with nothing but overzealous plants and bizarre animals as our companions. If I can't leave, then you can't either."

Callum crosses his arms. I close my mouth.

Caderyn has a point, dear.

I understand that but I can't tell him the real reason why Callum and I are the ones who have to go. I must follow the corruption. Someone supplied the killer with Acerbus-infused technology. The existence of such technology is more than dangerous; it could affect the outcome of the Era War. I must find its source.

What about your wedding, dear?

I sigh, holding my emotions in check. *It has to wait until we take care of the mysterious "she" who hired the killer and dabbled with Acerbus-infused technology.*

Forceful footsteps approach us.

We all look to the left.

Teague, dressed in the Teryn black military uniform, strides into the corridor. He winks at me as he pushes dark hair streaked with scarlet, white, and blond strands out of his face. His dark brown eyes glint with mischief as he halts in front of us.

Callum acknowledges the other man with a small nod. He must have sent that subvocal message to Teague, knowing Caderyn would not approve of us leaving for Pada.

"Sir, here is the report on the Tier One factions," Teague says, and hands a palm-size device with a transparent screen to Caderyn.

The praelor takes the device. "I did not ask for any report, Colonel."

Callum points at the device. "You should read it."

Caderyn sighs. "Why not? I've wasted enough time standing here chattering with you two. What's a few minutes more?"

Moira laughs. *He is a rancorous—*

Moira.

Don't act so dignified, dear. After all, like recognizes like.

I smile, recalling Moira's hospitality in the spirit realm when we first met. She sent attackers to repel my friends and me. She then lied about the Heart Amulet, trying to mislead me about its whereabouts. After that she threw us in prison, where I'd discovered she lied. Her mood changed from welcoming to downright hostile in an instant.

Glenna and Ragnald appear in the corridor, followed by Ivy, as well as the twins, Arrov, and Belthair.

"This is unacceptable," Caderyn says and looks up, noticing my smile. "It is not a laughing matter, Lilla. I have not seen such underperformance in a long time. They are getting lazy because I am not there supervising them."

"I, uh, wasn't—"

Caderyn shakes his head with growing aggravation. "This changes everything. I must go to Pada now and take care of this matter personally for the good of the Teryn Praelium." He hands the report back to Teague.

He wants to do what? "You cannot take the whole Teryn armada with you to Pada. That would defeat the purpose and disobey The Lady's—"

"I wasn't planning to take my armada. All I need is a shuttle."

Callum shoves black strands off his forehead. "Lilla and I are going with you."

Caderyn eyes my friends. "Let me guess. You want to tag along as well."

They all beam.

Caderyn pinches the bridge of his nose. "For the record, I like Fearghas and no one else. That battle horse is always welcome to join me."

CHAPTER 11

I look around the cramped spacecraft we boarded a few minutes ago. From the outside, the Teryn ship looks like an aggressive black star with all its obnoxious armaments, sticking out in the dripping jungle like an incorrect knot on a sail.

At the helm, Caderyn and Sawney prepare the craft for takeoff. The viewscreen shows vivid green vines and orange plants, looking almost like a landscape painting with its lush variety and brightness.

In the back is a rectangular and windowless compartment with seats in a single row running on each side of the ship, where my friends and I sit. Above us, near the inclining black ceiling, ropes secure our belongings.

In the middle of the dark blue floor, a sunken and padded area holds a kneeling Fearghas, who looks content, neighing. The weak yellowish light that comes from the edge of the ceiling makes the black hide that covers his robust muscles shimmer like silk. But there is nothing soft about this beast, which can withstand laser shots and cuts from most bladed weapons. Fearghas was bred to be a battle horse with his thick hide, coarse black mane, webbed claws, sharp fangs, and fierce disposition. Many stable boys bear scars from said disposition. After the wars ended, there was no more need for battle horses. Fearghas became an unwanted orphan, starved and beaten. The Uhnan captain of the guards rescued him, then gifted Fearghas to me when I was eight, three years after my mom died when I was still struggling with grief. The good captain paired us, two injured souls, to heal each other.

If my claustrophobia wasn't clamoring at me, I would laugh at the excitement that radiates from Fearghas at the prospect of another adventure. I swear he loves space travel more than riding on the beach—his old favorite activity.

I gasp for air and close my eyes, fighting the urge to flee. Cold sweat breaks out on my forehead.

A callused hand touches mine. "You're safe," Callum says. "Focus on your breathing, as you practiced." He adjusts the restraints of my seat until they don't cut into my body so much.

I manage to nod.

Inhaling the air tinted with metallic scents, I concentrate on feeling safe and calm, then exhale to the count of eight. I repeat this over and over until I can open my eyes.

Callum smiles at me. "That's it."

My cheek stings. I turn to the left to find Sawney glowering at me. It's clear in his eyes what he thinks of my "weakness." A weakness that dates back to the day my mom was murdered. She tried to hide me away in a small, dark cubbyhole, which triggered my first attack of claustrophobia. Growing up, I had to hide this from the court, knowing they would hold it against me, as Sawney does right now, although Callum, and even Caderyn, have been understanding.

I frown at Sawney until he turns away.

The spaceship tilts skyward and takes off with a high velocity that plasters all of us to our seats. Caderyn lays out our course, using CWP, also known as the Cosmic-Web Propulsion system. Using hydrogen atoms, it allows us to travel at light-bending speed along the cosmic highway. We slingshot to our destination, the Pada world.

CHAPTER 12

The viewscreen turns white as the stars streak by from the high velocity of the spacecraft.

Caderyn swivels his seat toward us. "We'll be on Pada in sixteen hours," he announces, "arriving in the evening, right when the check-in summit starts with a dinner reception. We'll stay until the summit is over, seven days, but not a minute longer."

Seven days should be enough time for Callum and me to determine who hired the killer and how they got their hands on Acerbus-infused technology. I hope.

Belthair turns away from the rushing white space. "All this whiteness reminds me of the snowcapped mountains of my home world, Judoc."

Isa looks at him. "We didn't know you were not from Uhna."

Belthair shrugs. "I was adopted after a cave-in killed my parents and my three sisters and two brothers in the mine. A handful of us, including me, were the only survivors."

I glance at him. "I had no idea . . . You've never told me any of this."

Belthair pulls out from his pocket six small pieces of wood that he's been working on. "There was not much to tell. We've lived the simple life of miners. My fondest memories are playing in the snow with my siblings after our shift."

Isa points at one of the miniature wooden sculptures in Belthair's hand. "Is that Lilla in a princess dress?"

Belthair blows on the tiny figurine that does look a bit like me and nods. "I'll never forget the day I met Lilla. I will always see her like that—elegant, regal, and beautiful."

My cheeks heat, and I fidget in discomfort.

Callum crosses his arms. "You better forget it and fast."

Belthair chuckles and goes back to whittling the little figurines. The other one looks a lot like Glenna with her hands on her hips when she is upset.

Rhona stands up and pulls two ancient-looking leather-bound tomes from her bag. She sits back down, looking from one book to the other with a frown.

I tilt my head, trying to read their titles when Rhona asks, "What's wrong with your neck? It looks strange."

My neck doesn't look strange. "I'm just curious about your books."

Rhona beams. "Oh, I'm glad that you're interested. I can't decide which one to read first." She lifts the first one and says, "This one is my favorite: *Tactics, Strategies and Stratagems—How to Win Any War.* But I also like the other one: *The Punisher—The Adventures of the Seasoned Warrior Who Can Sense Those Who Failed Their Trial but Pretended Otherwise and Now He Punishes Them.*"

"That's a bit of a mouthful," Glenna mutters. "Doesn't leave much to the imagination."

Rhona ignores my healer friend's comment and asks me, "Which one would *you* read?"

Neither. "Um, probably the latter. It sounds like a great action adventure."

Glenna nods. "Good choice. You were always partial to those stories. I seem to recall a large tome you carried around with you for weeks. You were obsessed with that story. What was its title?"

I shake my head at Glenna, but she is too lost in her thoughts as she continues, "Oh, yes. I remember. It was: *Grey Beard's Escapades of Treasures, Looting, and Women.* Though that was more of a romance than adventure, wasn't it?"

All eyes turn to me, including Callum's.

I spread my hands. "It was, uh, a long time ago."

Teague winks at me, then takes a thin red jerky from the pocket of his black jacket and tears into it with gusto. "My Steaphan, he likes reading his speeches out loud to me, testing them out before he'd have to present them before the Senatus. If my eyes glazed over, he'd change the pace or add a passionate exclamation to regain my attention. He is such a master of words. I miss those nights." He looks at the last piece of jerky, and sighs as he adds, "I miss him so much."

We all murmur comforting words to Teague.

The twins dismantle a palm-size Teryn device with a transparent screen. "We loved reading, just like Lilla," Isa says, and Bella adds, "We read everything we could get our hands on just to escape studying physics or anything that involved technology and invention. We even went skiing to recreate one of the adventures we read about, only to crash into a boulder and end up with a broken arm and leg."

Glenna points at the scattered pieces of wires and other knickknacks. "What changed your mind?"

Isa looks up with a grimace. "After that accident, we were told that it was for the best that we skip school, since we'd never be as good as the other students." Bella adds, "Or as good as our siblings. We decided to prove everyone wrong."

"That explains why you stole your inheritance," Glenna says, and raises a hand when Isa's eyes glint with happiness. "Not that I approve of your actions."

Isa shrugs as she drills a hole into a small panel with a pencil-like tool. "Your disapproval will haunt our dreams." Bella giggles and hands a bunch of screws to her sister.

Ivy pops a purple piece of gum into her mouth and chews it. She blows a hexagonal spikey bubble. "I can't believe how spoiled you *princesses* are," she says. "It was a death sentence for me to get caught with any reading material that was not a fashion catalogue, lest I develop some brains and become ambitious for the Marauder throne. I had to hide any tome I managed to smuggle in, and burn it once I finished reading it."

Arrov shakes his head. "Gods, no wonder you don't want to return to the Marauder's court."

"Don't you dare pity me," Ivy snaps, though her face contains a mix of emotions—excitement and nervousness—betraying her bravado.

Arrov gets to his feet. He takes out his three-tiered crossbow from his bag. "At least, Mathilda, you won't ever argue with me," he mutters as he adjusts its drawstrings. "You were there when I left A'ice. I don't need anything else in life—not any throne, or any useless knowledge—"

Rhona glares. "That is exactly why you should read books—for knowledge."

Callum bursts into laughter. "Did you just call your crossbow 'Mathilda'?"

Belthair chuckles. "Are you going to kiss 'her'?"

Arrov runs his finger over the top limb, ignoring the other men. "Don't mind their mocking, Mathilda. You've never failed me."

"Why is it a 'her'?" Glenna asks and tucks a white strand behind her ear.

Arrov gets a rag out of his pants pocket and wipes the foregrip. "What else would Mathilda be? She is precise and temperamental."

I cover my eyes. "I can't believe you just said that."

"What?" Arrov asks with an oblivious expression. "What did I say?"

The other men laugh even louder.

Ivy grins. "We'll let your future girlfriend deal with you. I just hope I get to witness that drama."

Oh, dear. He truly has no idea.

Glenna pats his forearm. "I'll explain it to you later, sweetie. How are you feeling? Any signs of, uh, your, um, change?"

Arrov shivers. "Please don't remind me. I still have nightmares of turning into a monster. I have no idea what made me change back, which means that any second, something could trigger that change and then I'll have no control again . . ." He swallows with a nervous expression, his fingers holding the crossbow in a tight grip.

"We will help any way we can," I say and look at my friends. "Won't we?"

Everyone mutters an agreement; even Callum nods reluctantly.

Ragnald clasps his hands in his lap with a thoughtful expression. "I've never relied on any weapons outside my own magic. Not when the Academia of Mages sent me to handle a herd of frost trolls attacking a village. Now let me tell you, those frost trolls really don't like Fla'mma magic. I've never seen them run so fast."

Glenna frowns at the mage. "That's just horrible. How could you scare those poor things like that? Is that what makes you happy? Hurting innocent creatures with your magic?"

Ragnald gapes at her. "Of course it doesn't make me happy."

Rhona glances up from her tome. "This doesn't look good for you, mage."

Ragnald stammers as he says, "When the herd gets too large and they have no other food source, they steal children. Why would anyone want to protect them?"

Glenna crosses her arms. "All creatures have the right to live."

"I disagree," Rhona says and turns a page. "I would have cut them up into tiny, bloody pieces if they neared any of our children. Whether they lacked food or not would not have mattered to me."

Glenna glares at Ragnald, then turns her head away from him with a huff. Everyone turns quiet and busies themselves.

Fearghas finds a leather feed pouch and digs in. He seems happy and refuses to part ways with me. Not for lack of trying to find him a new home. He escaped from a village back on Uhna and nearly attacked Caderyn in an effort to follow him. Then on Teryn, Caderyn gave my horse a stall behind his residence, but Fearghas broke free. When we were getting ready to leave for Cathal, my horse showed up, practically standing in line with the other warriors waiting to board.

Moira yawns in my head. *I'm going to take a well-deserved nap, dear.*

Leaning my head back, I close my eyes too, trying to fall asleep, but my mind keeps replaying the events of the past few hours. It's hard to believe how far I've come from Uhna, with its pirate past and failed monarchy. I never thought I would leave that planet. Then I ended up on Teryn, Callum's world. Its red hues and desolate desert landscape hid secrets that the Teryns were prepared to kill to protect, but my friends and I uncovered them and survived to tell that tale.

"I don't understand why she has to come with you," Caderyn grumbles. "She always brings her friends with her, like they are some sort of package deal."

I don't show any reaction to his words, nor do I open my eyes. Caderyn shouldn't be so surprised. My friends have been through so much with me. They are my trusted allies. I cannot imagine embarking on a mission without them by my side.

Callum's arm brushes against mine. "She is my love and life, Father. That's why we tried to honor her Bride's Choice claim this morning. Remember?"

Love warms my heart. I cannot get enough of hearing Callum declare his feelings for me. The old tradition of Bride's Choice originated from having fewer women on the Teryn world than men. Its purpose was to prevent unnecessary fighting, and it evolved into a marriage custom that Caderyn refused to honor until today.

"She may have managed to find the Heart Amulet and meld," Caderyn says, "but she will never be like us."

The Heart Amulet, also known as Queen of the Spirits, the ruler of the old Teryns, or as I like to call her, Moira, snores in my head.

"She is nothing like an honorable Teryn," Sawney says. "She should stop pretending otherwise."

I've tried to fit into the Teryn society, into Caderyn's family, but it seems I've failed.

"You are one to talk about honor," Rhona snaps, her voice full of banked anger. "Don't think I didn't notice Sachary limping, and you missing your other—"

"You have no idea what you're talking about," Sawney says, interrupting her. There is a hint of panic underlying his anger.

"The games *you* have been playing," Callum says in a low voice, "did not go unnoticed, brother."

Teague bursts into a violent coughing fit.

"What games?" Caderyn asks, and I wonder the same.

"Nothing important, Dad," Rhona says.

"I assure you that I have it under control," Callum says. There is a trace of violence in his voice that makes no sense to me. I wonder what Rhona, Callum, and Sawney are hiding.

I open my eyes to ask Callum what he meant by his cryptic comment when I find myself in a beautiful meadow.

CHAPTER 13

"Not now," I say with a groan. I look around at the peaceful and gorgeous meadow with long grass stalks that bend in the spring breeze. For some reason, The Lady loves transporting me to this meadow whenever She wants to speak to me.

"What did you say, my child?" the Archgoddess of the Eternal Life and Order asks from behind me.

I jump and face Her. Long golden blond hair, so bright that it's as if sunshine is infused into each strand, frames a beautiful face. Molten-gold eyes glint with kindness. Lush pink lips stretch to a welcoming smile. The Lady stands a head taller than me, like benevolence personified. The breeze tugs Her white wraparound dress, which reaches the top of Her bare feet.

Next to Her waits Acolyte Aisla, like a petite replica of the ethereal archgoddess. She scowls at me in disapproval.

"Nothing," I say. "What is it now?" I do my best to hide my worry that She'll order me back to Cathal.

Love and joy cascade down my spine in punishing waves from my sybil talisman. The finger-long oval and transparent talisman, lodged in my spine by thin gold filaments, cannot be removed without killing me. It can be the source of some healing magic or a direct line for The Lady to punish my insolence, like now.

Moira screams in my head, mixing with my own agonized cries as I drop to my knees, grasping my head from the pain. "Stop . . . this . . ."

The unbearable waves of love and joy recede.

I scramble to my feet. I should have known better than to antagonize Her, but I can't help it. I refuse to prostrate myself in front of the archgoddess. I have not forgotten how She tricked me into wearing the talisman or how She lied about DLD killing my mom.

The back of my neck itches and I scratch it. A painful electric zap stings my fingers before they touch the talisman. I swear that thing hates me.

"I noticed that you are not on Cathal, my child."

Did She now? I swipe at the moisture leaking from my eyes.

The Lady tilts Her head to the side in an unnatural and predatory way that raises goose bumps on my back. "Explain yourself, my child."

I grind my teeth at the moniker of "my child." The Lady created the magical race of Lumenians to fight against the corrupted dark servants and dark fiends, DLD's underlings. I had not known about my heritage of being a Lumenian until seven months ago, when She'd burst into my life on Uhna, upending it, never telling me that I was the last of my kind. The other Lumenians were hunted and killed by DLD. She gave me no rest until I joined Her side in this Era War.

Dear, please don't agitate the archgoddess. I can't stand the horrid method of punishment She unleashes on us.

I sigh. "I am following a trail of Acerbus-infused technology."

The Lady raises an elegant eyebrow. "There is no such technology in existence. The archgod never attempted to infuse His elements with technology."

"Well, someone did it." I explain what happened with Sachary's killer on Cathal.

The Lady frowns, but even that looks gorgeous on Her face. "That is, indeed, curious. I allow you to veer off your mission, my child, for five days."

"That's not nearly enough."

The Lady smiles. "Make it enough, then return to Cathal. It is crucial that you are back there with the whole of the Teryn armada."

"But what is so—" I say, only to realize I am back on the spacecraft with the others staring at me as if I'd grown a lobster head.

CHAPTER 14

DAY 1

For the love of turtle. Why does She have to do this to me all the time?

The others look away, getting up from their seats.

Callum helps me up from the seat. "We've landed. You were unresponsive for sixteen hours."

I cringe. I can imagine what the others must have thought of my frozen state. "The Lady paid me a visit."

Callum nods and jumps off the ramp, which has stopped two feet above the ground. "That's what I thought." He reaches up with both arms extended to lift me off the ship. I squat to make it easier. He hugs me to him for a second before placing me on the grassy ground. Then he assists the twins, while Teague helps Glenna and Ivy.

The others leap off the ramp, carrying our belongings in sacks, except for Caderyn. He steps off the ramp as if it's flat on the ground and surveys our surroundings with a stern look.

Fearghas jumps down and shakes his black mane, prancing around before coming to nuzzle my hair.

I pat his warm neck. "The Lady never held me this long before."

"Maybe She had difficulty putting you back onto a spaceship that travels with, uh, CWP," Glenna says.

That would mean The Lady is not so powerful as She likes to pretend. "Could be." Or She just did it because She could.

Either way, dear, it does not change the end result.

With a cleansing exhale, I turn to face the majestic and fortress-like gray monastery that towers a few hundred feet in front of us, on top of a verdant hill. The twenty-story monastery reaches for the blue sky with peaked roofs on its narrow towers. Evergreen trees surround its thick walls, which have T'erra magic clinging to them like a second layer. Siege towers pop up from among the trees on the wall. Hills roll in the background, covered with bright green forests. On top of the hills, more fortresses nestle. The light gray brick structures cluster in a circle, grouped in six, with the largest one in the center. They remind me of cities, with their cobblestone paths leading to the middle.

The air smells fresh, with hints of flowers and pine needles. I pick up my bag, but Callum takes it from me, and hoists it up next to his.

Fearghas claws the ground and bobs his head.

I laugh seeing his enthusiasm. "I can walk, Fearghas. I promise we'll go riding later."

Fearghas neighs and I can't miss the disappointed tones.

So, this is Pada, Moira says with awe. *It looks even better than in your memory, dear.*

I nod. *Last time we were on the Pada world, a welcoming committee met us, bringing delicious treats served artfully on small plates. Each plate was personalized to its recipient. Mine was a young woman with dark violet hair, on top of Fearghas, and made of sliced vegetables and cuts of meats.*

How marvelous, dear.

I eye the double doors of the monastery, but they remain closed as our group approaches. "I don't understand. Where are the welcoming monks?"

Belthair frowns. "Where are those tantalizing appetizers? I'm hungry."

The others murmur.

Teague's stomach makes a rumbling sound, and he rubs it. "I don't even mind the flowers that they add to their cuisine." He's told me before that most Teryns consider many flowers poisonous and refuse to eat them. Except for Teague, of course, who is not so picky.

Ragnald wipes dirt off his black robe's sleeve. "At the Academia of Mages, every guest gets a luxurious reception and—"

Belthair scoffs. "Not now, mage. Save it for when we're bored and in desperate need of entertainment."

Ragnald mutters a curse.

With my friends busy and not paying attention, Callum and I approach the monastery. At the base of the building, I notice purple-hued sparkles. We squat to get a better look.

Callum takes out the transparent bag with the purple rocks. He puts it on the ground, next to the others.

I look at him. "They are a match." The same tiny rocks we found on the ship after the killer was consumed by Acerbus flames.

Callum pockets the bag. "We are on the right track." Then we rejoin the others.

The double doors open. A familiar, dark-haired, lanky monk, wearing a red robe with two sashes on its front—straw-yellow for A'nima and sky-blue for A'ris—hurries toward us with an apologetic smile.

"Praelor," Devotee Zimon says, out of breath. "We, uh, were not expecting you on Pada for this check-in summit."

CHAPTER 15

Led by Devotee Zimon, Caderyn and our group march through corridors inside the monastery. On our left, brick walls alternate with closed wooden doors. On our right, a low wall runs no higher than my knees, with archways that open to rectangular courtyards.

In one of the courtyards, disciples wearing beige robes and dark headcovers that hide their faces busy themselves harvesting pink fruits into woven baskets. In another courtyard, a few disciples shear red- and beige-colored sheep. In the next courtyard, three disciples tend dark green, leafy vegetables. The last courtyard is in disarray, with weapons piled in no apparent order.

These Pada monks are so self-sufficient, dear. Except when it comes to blacksmithing.

They are not weapon-makers by choice.

We pass through another door into a wide foyer with stone tiles and a steep stairway leading to the second floor. The walls are covered in numerous paintings, tapestries, and metal decorations.

Glenna touches my arm. "I thought the Pada monks always knew when they were getting guests," she says.

Dear, I'm not surprised that they didn't know we were coming. There were only twelve of us on that small spaceship, while last time you visited, you were traveling on the larger vessel. It's highly probable, dear, that the Pada monks have a spy on Caderyn's ship.

I doubt Caderyn would let that happen, but you are right; it is a possibility.

Belthair pokes his head next to Glenna. "I second that." He drapes his dark brown, leather jacket over his shoulder, holding the garment with his top left hand.

Ragnald closes his black mage robe over his light gray suit. "Don't worry. I am sure we'll have a chance to indulge in the monks' culinary masterpieces."

Caderyn grunts. "I am glad they forgot about those annoying plates. Food is not art. The Pada monks are always so pretentious. Just because they know magic does not make them better than we are, Teryn warriors. Well, not you, Lilla, or your ragtag friends. Or even you, Ivy."

Arrov raises an eyebrow. "I can live with that."

"Nobody asked you, giant boy," Caderyn says.

Arrov glares at Caderyn. "It's not like I had a choice. DLD's corruption triggered that unfortunate change. I'm just glad I turned back to me. I would appreciate it if you would stop bringing it up."

Caderyn snorts. "I bet you would, *giant boy.*"

"We don't want to be Teryns," Isa says, and Bella adds, "Too much posturing."

Ivy flicks her hair back. "I prefer the Marauders' way. Poisoning is so much more straightforward than this 'honor' thing." She pulls at a loose string of her white minidress and asks without looking up, "Do you think the, uh, dowager queen will be in attendance?"

The monk nods. "Most of the guests are already seated in the Banquet Hall. You are right in time for the dinner reception."

Ivy pales and stumbles, but Belthair catches her. He pats her shoulder with his top right hand in comfort. He smiles at her. "You're with us now."

"That's right." Ivy raises her chin as we enter the cavernous Banquet Hall, but her gaze remains full of dread.

A wooden coffered ceiling and walls covered in brown and gray stones make up the spacious hall. Alcoves and balconies jut from among intricate adornments and art pieces. A'ris magic sparkles on their clean surfaces, keeping them dust-free. Half a dozen wooden, circular chandeliers with Fla'mma-infused candles that never burn out provide ample light as the sun sets outside the balcony doors. More T'erra magic coats the rectangular bricks inside, than outside. The warm, inviting room—full of circular tables with white silk tablecloths and matching high-back chairs—goes silent as the guests notice our group.

All the warmth and welcoming air gets sucked out of the hall, replaced by a fearful atmosphere.

That is a peculiar reaction to Caderyn, dear.

No one is happy to see him. Why should they be? The seven worlds that make up the Tier One factions were conquered in the name of the Era War, then forced to meet quotas the Teryn senators impose on them to supply the ever-growing Teryn Praelium and its armada, free of charge. And one of the factions did not meet its quota.

A slender man with dark brown eyes, Consuasor Steaphan, Teague's husband, smiles at our group in welcome. Once his gaze lands on Caderyn, however, Steaphan's smile disappears.

Caderyn touches his ear to activate his k'bug and sends a message using subvocal tones. Then he points at a young Teryn consuasor. "You, get the screen up."

What is happening, dear?

I am not sure.

The young consuasor stumbles to his feet. With shaking fingers, he projects a large holo-screen onto a half-moon-shaped platform located at the back of the hall.

Devotee Zimon frowns, looking confused, but clasps his hands in front of him without a word.

For a few seconds, the screen crackles with grayness, then an image of a haphazard-looking space station, near a white and blue moon, comes into view.

An older woman with gray hair and wearing a simple red dress rises to her feet. "What is the meaning of this?"

Caderyn crosses his muscular arms. "Keep watching."

The space station explodes into smithereens.

Moira gasps. *No!*

I take a step back, with a scream lodged in my throat. Were its occupants able to escape or evacuate? Did they even get a warning?

When I look at Callum's face, wearing an angry expression, I know the answers to my questions.

No one has survived.

I cover my mouth. My friends look just as devastated as I feel.

Stunned silence rules the hall.

Representatives from each faction jump to their feet, shouting and yelling. Only the appalled Teryn consuasors and nonchalant warriors stay seated.

Caderyn narrows his eyes. "If you don't sit down and be quiet, your space station will be next."

As if someone pushed a button, they all fall back to their seats, fuming and glaring at the praelor in silence.

Caderyn looks around the room. "Hear me and understand when I say that you have one job: meet your quotas or else be punished. We must win this Era War at all costs."

Then he whirls on his heels and marches out of the hall.

CHAPTER 16

"How could you—" I yell at Caderyn when we exit the Banquet Hall, but the praelor interrupts me. "Not here."

Two disciples, one petite and one tall, wait next to our group. They gesture to us in silence, indicating that we should follow them. They are not allowed to speak until they graduate to devotee status.

I am speechless, Moira stammers in my head with sorrow.

Grief and anger make my muscles shake as my friends and I follow the disciples until they stop in front of a row of rooms at the far end of the monastery. With a bow, they scramble away.

Caderyn opens the door to his spacious living quarters. We pile into the room to his chagrin.

The second that Caderyn closes the door, Callum and I turn to him.

"How could you kill all those innocents?" I demand.

"I did not make that report so that you can go on a killing rampage," Callum snaps at the same time.

Glenna, sitting on a white sofa, covers her mouth. "Are you telling me there were people on that space station? That it wasn't empty?"

Ragnald pats her thin shoulder in comfort and drops down next to her. Glenna leans closer to him, looking like she's fighting back tears.

I know how she feels.

Teague leans on the wall and stares at a handful of nuts in his palm before deciding to shove them in his mouth. He chews slowly, wearing a melancholic expression.

Ivy settles into a white chair. "The dowager queen was sure impressed with your show of power. That's the only language she understands." She shivers.

Belthair takes off his jacket and drapes it over Ivy's shoulders. She looks at him in surprise but accepts the jacket and puts it on.

Arrov shakes his head, closing and opening his fingers as if he wants to hit something or someone.

Before anyone else has a chance to say more, Caderyn crosses his arms. "I told you this before, Lilla, that to run an empire this vast takes an iron fist. I wasn't being flippant about it."

He does believe, dear, that what he did was justified.

It takes all my effort to hold back the rage that wants to burst out of me. "Do you not see the wrongness of what you did to the Farmers Partnership? All because they failed to fulfill their assigned quota. You slaughtered innocent people in cold blood. They were not responsible for their governing body's failure."

"The citizens are indeed responsible for the actions of their governing body," Caderyn says, then looks at Callum. "To be clear, son, it is your job to deliver these reports to me, not when they suit your case but when they actually happen."

Teague bursts into another coughing fit.

Arrov smacks Teague's back. "Are you getting sick?" Arrov asks Teague as he smacks the colonel's back. "These coughs don't sound right. Glenna, maybe you should check him out."

Glenna gets to her feet, but Teague waves a hand, stopping her. "I'm fine. The food went the wrong way is all."

Callum points at his father. "You've never gone this far."

Caderyn spreads his hands. "There is always a first time, son. I did what I had to do for the sake of the Teryn Praelium. Now I'd like to retire. I've had enough of all this chatter."

When no one moves, Caderyn barks, "That means leave. Now."

We scramble to our feet and exit the room.

The door slams behind us.

CHAPTER 17

Twisting and turning, I try to fall asleep in my room, but my mind is too preoccupied. Moira mutters in her dreams and I envy her ability to sleep.

After Caderyn kicked us out, we returned to our own rooms. Callum and Teague felt responsible for the whole tragedy. There was nothing I could say to assuage their guilt.

Sighing, I sit up. I look around the sparsely furnished guest room with its one narrow window covered by beige curtains. The living quarters holds a single bed with a wooden frame; a small wooden table with one drawer and one open shelf at the bottom; and a single white chair. No decorations cover the walls. A few books on the table, with titles such as *Sacred Pie Recipes to Nurture the Magic-Hungry Soul*, *What to Eat to Achieve Enlightment in Your Magical Elements*, and *Everyday Reflections—The Cornerstone of Every Great Pada Monk* are my only entertainment.

I pick up the top book. Its leather cover feels cool in my hands, the pages soft and rustling as I turn them, reading a random section dedicated to gratitude and cocoa, of all things. After a few seconds I realize I've reread the same sentences over and over, and I close it. My mind keeps conjuring up images of the terrified and innocent occupants of that space station.

I put the book back on the table. "We are made of Lume, and when we die, we return to Lume," I whisper the traditional prayer for them, one that is aimed to the Archgoddess of the Eternal Light and Order, who guides souls into the Lume.

Just when I start to think that Caderyn is not the merciless brute he seems, he does something like this to prove me wrong.

Closing my eyes, I take a breath and lie back down. I cannot let this distract me from my goal of finding out who is behind Sachary's murder and the Acerbus-infused technology. I should get some rest. I have only five days; better make it count tomorrow.

"Help!" a deep male voice shouts.

My eyes snap open and I sit up, listening.

"Help!" the voice shouts again. This time his plea echoes in my mind.

What is happening? Moira asks, waking up. *Who is shouting?*

I am not sure. I shove the blanket to the side, propelled by the urgency, and change out of my sleep shirt into a black tunic and leggings tucked into boots.

Something bangs on my door.

Now what? Moira says with a growl.

I open the door.

Fearghas stares back at me with intent, dark eyes, a huge shadowy shape in the middle of the night.

I step out into the corridor. "You scared me." Cold air hits me. My breath comes out in a small puff of cloud.

Fearghas whinnies while pawing the ground, leaving behind scratch marks on the stone tiles from his sharp webbed claws.

"We can't go riding now, boy." I feel for the poor disciple who was assigned to put Fearghas into the animal corral. I don't see blood on my horse's mouth, however, which means no one got hurt when he escaped.

"HELP!"

Fearghas neighs louder, bumping his head into my stomach.

Oof. "Fearghas, stop it."

I think your horse knows where to go, dear.

Maybe.

With a sigh, I jump up on his back and grab ahold of his thick black mane. "Lead the way!"

CHAPTER 18

We gallop through the monastery on silent, clawed feet, taking one stone-tiled corridor after another. There isn't anyone outside—the Pada monks and disciples must go to bed early. My head bobs dangerously close to the Fla'mma-infused candles that hang from the arching stone ceiling. As we ride underneath them, the wooden doors leading to the rooms on my left stay closed; no one pokes their head out to see us.

Cold wind tears into my hair, blowing strands into my face. I shiver and regret not bringing a cloak or gloves in my haste.

We hurry past the empty courtyards. Fla'mma magic clings to the orchards and vegetable plants, keeping them warm against the coming wintertime.

We reach a dead end, with a six-foot-tall brick wall blocking our way on three sides.

Craning my neck, I look for another way around when Fearghas leaps over the wall.

Stifling a yelp, I hug his neck.

Fearghas lands on top of the grassy hill, then breaks into a gallop again, rushing down the slope.

At the bottom of the hill, we enter a dark forest and jump over fallen tree trunks.

Inhaling the pine-scented air with a hint of snow in it, I try to make out a path, but I can't see much farther ahead in the near-pitch darkness, given the blanket of fog rising from the ground.

A branch slams into my arm. I hunch over Fearghas to present less of a target to the forest.

Eerie quiet follows us, the forest staying hushed and still.

I sense danger, dear. Best be careful.

It's too late for that. We are literally *galloping headlong into danger.*

Pine cones shower over me. I curse under my breath.

Could be worse, I think to Moira. *It could have been those wild predators with four pairs of red eyes, attacking me like they did in a different forest, back in your realm.*

Moira ducks her head. *Truth be told, I riled them up a bit, dear. They were harmless scavengers who eat the deceased. Or the weak.*

Something cold lands on my neck, startling me.

Snowflakes.

Great. I love snow but I am not looking forward to getting lost in this forest and freezing to death.

Don't be so melodramatic, dear. If we're running into danger headlong as you think, then I'm sure we'll be dead long before the cold gets us.

Before I can say anything back to Moira, the evergreen trees part.

We burst into a surreal scene over a picturesque clearing saturated with magic.

And with the taint of Acerbus.

CHAPTER 19

Across from me, Guardian Goddess Laoise hovers in midair in the clearing. In front of her kneels a man, projecting ethereal beauty. The man bleeds from many injuries on his wide shoulders, and clutches a broken right arm, but there is no mistaking the defiance of his posture.

The man gets to his feet, swaying. His loose black shirt and pants reveal a multitude of bleeding cuts. His bare and bloody feet grip the ground with straining muscles. His stance reminds me of a skilled fighter. He must have been the one who called for help, and I can see why.

Shocked, I stare at the goddess whom I locked into a Lume prison a few weeks ago. Yet here she is, free and rampaging on Pada. But how?

Unnatural wind plasters the boxy brown dress to Laoise's lean body. Faint hints of Acerbus cling to her, but I can't detect any Acerbus-infused technology on the goddess. Her long black hair whips around her. Anger twists the goddess's angular, grayish-toned face. "You. I will deal with you later."

Laoise gathers teal-colored magic into her palms and focuses on the man. "Guardian God Patra'ch, I am back for your powers. You will find me more prepared now than when I first came to see you. Save yourself the pain and give your powers to me freely. I may consider sparing your life."

Patra'ch wipes blood from the corner of his mouth. "You are still nothing but a pathetic liar. We both know a guardian god cannot survive without their powers. My answer is still no."

Patra'ch glances at me with raised eyebrows.

Better prepare for a battle, dear.

I nod and jump off Fearghas with my heart beating in my throat. I tap my horse's back to get him away from the fighting gods.

Can we transfigure? I ask Moira.

Moira tilts her head to left, then right, and shakes out her arms. *I thought you'd never ask, dear.*

Patra'ch releases a torrent of light blue magic at Laoise.

Now, Moira.

Rainbow-colored shimmer washes over me with power. Power that's not magical but something ancient, before the time of magic.

The transfiguration lifts me a few feet off the ground. I hover in the air in a vertical position, suspended in a cocoon of energy. The next instant, I drift back down in my new Cymmerion battle form that marks me as the true Teryn.

Dra'agon legs support our strong, bear-like body covered in iridescent black scales, standing at ten feet tall. Powerful lyon arms ending in finger-long black claws throb with strength when we raise them. A lush black mane frames a wolfish head with dark brown eyes, baring sharp white fangs. Black feathers coat an eagle head with clear blue eyes and a black beak that lets out an ear-piercing shriek. Multihued scales cover a dangerous dra'agon head with dark violet, slitted eyes that narrow on Laoise. A red forked tongue flicks out from the elongated maw full of fangs.

We roar from three mouths, our voices thundering. "You are trespassing, Laoise. Leave now or pay the price for your insolence."

Laoise drops a few feet in surprise, then blasts us with a teal orb of power.

We bat the magical orb to the side. "How did you get out of your prison?" The magic explodes in the air, showering down bright sparks to the grass.

We spread our leathery wings to their full twenty-foot length and shake our thick scale-covered tail that ends in a scorpion stinger.

Laoise rises another six feet. "It was not difficult. I had help."

Probably from whomever supplies the goddess with Acerbus. "Who?" We lift our stinger, rattling it in her direction.

"No more questions, you dumb beast," she sneers as she lobs teal, light blue, and red orbs at us. "Shame on you, Moira. This is how you show gratitude after I saved you and your people?"

We deflect the elemental magic with our wings. "You locked us into the spirit realm. You are out of control."

Laoise throws her head back in laughter. "Quite the opposite. I know exactly what I'm doing." She pulls out a small black device and zaps us.

Invisible charges bite into our skin, sinking deeply until they sever the connection between Moira and me.

Our battle form disappears from one blink to the next.

Screaming, I plummet naked to the ground and land on my back, with all the air knocked out of my lungs. Pain reverberates in my head, spine, and shoulders as I gasp for air while staring up at Laoise in disbelief.

Warmth trickles down my spine, healing energy from the sybil talisman that takes the edge off the pain, but not enough to completely heal my beaten body.

She used technology to take away our battle form, I say to Moira. *It did not have Acerbus in it, like the killer used to disguise themselves.*

I noticed that, dear. I can't think right now, I'm still reeling from the whiplash.

Can we transfigure again?

Moira groans. *Not anytime soon, dear.*

Patra'ch limps to me and reaches down with his left hand to help me to my feet.

Accepting his help, I get up and try to cover the important bits, while Laoise laughs above us. "You two are nothing but buzzing insects in my eyes, but not for long." She collects more teal-colored magic, but without shaping it.

Patra'ch conjures a simple white dress using A'ris and T'erra magic, and hands it to me. "Here."

I take the garment and pull it on. "She is too strong. She must have cannibalized the powers of other guardian gods."

Patra'ch says, eyeing Laoise, "I agree. Our best chance is to work together."

I nod.

Patra'ch gathers a cloud of sky-blue A'ris magic around him that crackles with lightning. "Get ready."

Reaching for my bright and pulsing orb, I pull dozens of thick Lume threads to me. Hot-and-cold-and-hot-again feelings encase my body. My skin glows golden white as my magic rises to the surface with a pressure pain that threatens to explode out of me. I reel in my magic and shape the Lume threads into sharp vines, tapping into the magical, silver-colored tree marking on my back that I received from the Saage women, one that amplifies my magic.

"Now!" Patra'ch bellows, throwing the lightning cloud into Laoise's face. She tries to bat the cloud away, but it blinds her for a precious moment.

I let the sharp Lume vines burst out of me, flying at Laoise, snapping around her thin body and ensnaring her.

Laoise screams as the magic vines tighten, cutting into her brown dress and leaving bleeding injuries behind.

A yellow-reddish light bursts out of Laoise, clearing both Patra'ch's and my Lume magic from her. "This is not over. I will come back and kill you, *Sybil* Lilla. Then my children will be the new Lumenians."

With a frustrated cry, Laoise escapes into the night.

CHAPTER 20

Patra'ch shakes his head, then hisses in pain. "Laoise could never handle any injuries. Deep down, she is a coward; a bully who cannot stand when others fight back."

Couldn't have said it better, dear.

I sigh. "Yet somehow she escaped. Again." She is nothing if not relentless.

Laoise decided that I was not good enough as a sybil and tried to have Moira take me out in the spirit realm, using both of us for her own agenda. When that didn't work, she came to finish the job herself. She thinks her "new" Teryns will be better as the "new" Lumenians, the leading race in the Era War, but she forgets one vital detail—they don't have Lume magic. It's the only magic that can combat fully corrupted dark servants or dark fiends. However, that didn't stop her from working with someone from DLD's camp—a first when it comes to forming any sort of alliance between the two sides in an Era War.

Cold winter wind blasts over us, blowing my hair into my face, stinging all my wounds. Shivering, I rub my bare foot over my calf.

Patra'ch waves his uninjured hand. "Where are my manners?" Patra'ch mutters and waves his left hand.

From one instant to the next, I find myself in a circular pasture, bright with warm sunlight, surrounded by a shimmering and transparent wall that runs along its perimeter. Pine trees create shaded spots here and there. Short green grass cushions my feet over warm ground. A speckling of white flowers scents the air with a sweet perfume that's pleasing and calming. On the left, a quaint waterfall runs down a mountainside, its top cut off by that shimmering barrier. Glittering motes and pollen float in front of my eyes. Various bird tweets add to the peaceful atmosphere, like the sweetest music from nature itself.

Patra'ch smiles. "My favorite place. I hope you don't mind, but I prefer daytime over night."

I manage to nod. "Uh, sure."

Patra'ch gestures at the ground. "Please take a seat."

Before I can ask where, flat rocks rise out of the grass, forming an inviting semicircle. We sit down across from each other.

I look around. "Where is my horse, Fearghas?"

Patra'ch points to where my horse grazes, hidden in the shade of a large pine tree.

"How did you know to call to me for help?"

"I could sense a presence of someone magically powerful and I reached out instinctually." Patra'ch heals his right arm. The broken bone slams back into place with an audible crack. He shakes out his healed arm, then takes care of the other cuts and wounds. "I am grateful for your assistance."

He nods toward my injuries. "May I?"

I am about to shake my head, since my sybil talisman would take care of it, but then I notice how dormant it has been ever since I've entered this place, probably another pocket realm the gods favor so much. "Please."

He lifts both of his hands toward me, without touching.

Warmth spreads over my wounds until all the aches and pains are gone. I smile in thanks.

"I gather that you were the one who imprisoned Laoise?" Patra'ch asks.

"I did. I thought that The Lady would punish Laoise for her crimes, but She didn't."

"I am impressed that you were able to capture the formidable Laoise, but I can't say I am surprised that archgoddess won't punish her. Laoise has been committing her crimes for quite some time now."

A myriad of small red violet-colored animals, like rabbits, burst out of the trees, surrounding the guardian god. Their long bushy tails, with specks of black among the silver hairs, remind me of the squirrels of my home world, Uhna. Their two-inch-long dark brown pedicles remind me of the female reindeer from Arrov's home world, A'ice. But I've never seen rabbits that have green flower stalks with tiny white flowers entwined around their furry bodies, while A'nima magic clings to them.

A tiny critter hops to me and rises on its hind legs to sniff my hand, its large green eyes glinting with surprising intelligence. Long whiskers move as its nose sniffles, then sneezes.

"I call them szyrilla," Patra'ch says, then gesture toward the little critter. "She likes you. You can pick her up if you'd like."

I reach for her, but she hops into my lap on her own.

Fearghas approaches us and leans down to investigate the szyrilla. He shows her his fangs.

The szyrilla stands up and smacks Fearghas on the nose with a small paw.

My horse rears back, neighing in offense, but leaves the other animal alone.

The szyrilla flicks her long ears back and forth, looking satisfied, then settles down in my lap, promptly falling asleep. "Did you make them?"

Patra'ch glances at the animals hopping around him. He picks one up, placing it in his lap. "No, I didn't. At least I don't think I did. It's hard to tell these days where my powers end. The imbalance between the two ruling archgods has been affecting us guardian gods as well. I have been getting power surges but also experiencing strange hiccups in my magic."

I look up at the guardian god. "What are Laoise's previous crimes you mentioned earlier?"

"Where to start? Laoise first came to Pada to deposit a tribe of highly magical people, the ancestors of the Pada monks. I was puzzled as to why she did such a thing, then I met the tribe. I comprehended why Laoise wrote this tribe off, with their strange duality, as nonvaluable—they had strong magic and even stronger independence, combined with stubbornness and pride. Laoise couldn't influence them or awe them through her Wise Women. She did not anticipate that the tribe and I would bond so well. She regretted her actions and tried to steal them back, but I didn't let her. Thanks to how the Pada monks pray to me every single day, my powers are strengthening even more. I am not an easy target for Laoise to take over. That is probably why she keeps trying after she cannibalized the power of other guardian gods to test her chances."

I remember the magical show Laoise had put up when Moira and I had fought the goddess in the spirit realm. I recall the tortured and pained faces of the victims that flickered over the goddess's face whenever she accessed those stolen powers. "At least Laoise did not use any of her new powers against us today."

"We are fortunate that she did not, but I wonder why. Maybe the assimilation of these powers causes quite a discrepancy inside her. She must have overestimated what she could do, but there is no denying the boost her own power received from whomever she cannibalized. Just a glancing blow from it broke my arm."

Laoise never does anything without a reason, dear. I'm sure she had one for not engaging her new powers. I just can't imagine what that would be.

Looking down, I pat the soft fur of the szyrilla, marveling at how silken it is to the touch, even with the flowers around its petite body. "What is that duality you refer to?"

Patra'ch smiles. "It is not my place to disclose the most guarded secret of the Pada monks, but I have no doubt you'll figure it out on your own."

I get to my feet and place the szyrilla on the rock. "I should be getting back, but before I go, I have one last question. Did you know that technology, like a small device that allows you to have a perfect disguise, can be infused with Acerbus?"

Patra'ch frowns. "That would be an abomination. Though I have detected faint traces of Acerbus on Pada recently."

That means you are getting closer, dear.

"Thank you for your hospitality." I stride to Fearghas, then jump up on his back. For a second I am not sure in which direction to go.

Patra'ch steps up to us. "I can help with that."

I raise a hand to stop him. "No need, since your magic can hiccup—"

He flicks his fingers.

The next thing I see is one of the brick walls in the dead end, back in the monastery.

CHAPTER 21

I turn Fearghas away from the dead end, lest he decides to jump over the wall again. "That could have ended horribly."

He did save us a few hours of wading through the forest, dear, in the cold night.

I huff a cloud of air in response.

Snowflakes fall from the dark sky, like a white lace curtain. Before they can reach the stone-tiled ground, they melt a few inches above it, thanks to the Fla'mma magic that clings to the tiles with transparent ruby-red hues. How genius of the monks to keep their walkways snow-free with magic.

Moira points to the left, into the courtyard, as we trot past. *And many of their orchards and plants are protected by magic too.*

I can't help but wonder if I'll ever reach that level of comfort and trust when it comes to my magic. My first inclination is to use anything but magic. Mostly because I have lost control over it a few times. Once it was Teague's skill—a time-space-displacement pocket that helped to contain one of my magical explosions—that saved many from its destruction.

All you need is more practice, dear, Moira says and yawns. *I'm ready for some sleep. My ears are still ringing from earlier.*

Whatever the goddess zapped us with has taken a toll on my body as well. Cold air sweeps through the open corridor, twirling the falling snowflakes, mesmerizing me as I watch them. I try to keep my eyes open, but exhaustion drags me down.

A loud crash and bang coming from the closest guest room yanks me awake.

"Whoa!" I say and pull on my horse's coarse mane to stop him. Then I jump from Fearghas's back and tear the door open.

Blinking against the harsh brightness of the room, it takes me a second to see what's going on.

Then I find Sawney, lying facedown on the stone-tiled floor, bleeding.

CHAPTER 22

Taking a deep breath, I am about to shout for Glenna when Moira says, *No need to yell. Just use the k'bug, dear.*

Oh. That's better than alerting the whole monastery.

Touching my ear, I active the k'bug. "Glenna, please come to Sawney's room immediately."

After a few seconds, a sleepy Glenna bursts in wearing a long yellow sleep shirt, followed by Ragnald in a white pajama suit. "Why did you wake me up at this ungodly hour?" When her gaze lands on Callum's older brother, all sleepiness evaporates from her face.

She drops to her knees by Sawney. Light blue transparent magic ribbons emerge from her hands, which she threads into Sawney, desperately trying to heal him.

Ragnald frowns. "What happened?"

My throat constricts, but I push down the sadness. "I heard a strange noise and came to investigate. I found him like this."

Ragnald engages his A'ris and T'erra magic, canvasing the room with transparent ribbons of sky-blue and dark brown. "Did you see anyone leaving the room?"

I shake my head, then point at the open window. "They must have escaped by the time I entered."

Ragnald disengages his magic. "Yet again, there are no signs of struggle."

Glenna sits back on her heels and wipes the back of her hand on her forehead, leaving behind a bloody streak. "Single stab wound to the stomach. I was able to stop the bleeding, but my magic won't heal him."

CHAPTER 23

What could stop Glenna's magic from healing Sawney? I ask Moira, fighting a feeling of dread.

Moira sniffs the air. *Just as I thought. I smell the same acrid smell as before on the Teryn ship, dear.*

Buckets of fishguts. *Which means that whoever attacked Sawney must have used the same Acerbus-infused device for disguise. These two attacks must be connected, I just can't figure out how.*

Best to alert Callum and his family, dear. They need to know about this.

Using my k'bug, I call Rhona, Callum, and Caderyn, asking them to come to Sawney's room. I wish I could do more.

Glenna looks up. "We should make him comfortable."

Ragnald steps forward, but I lift a hand. "Allow me." I jump at the chance to be useful, even if it means using my magic.

Ragnald nods and puts on a pair of yellow glasses. "I'm glad you're taking the initiative, Lilla. In the meantime, I'll search for any magic trail."

I know what he'll find but I don't stop him. We all want to do something—*anything.*

Closing my eyes, I engage my bright magical orb. I select a thick thread of sky-blue A'ris and carefully layer it around Sawney. I open my eyes and lift up Sawney with the magical cocoon. Then I move him toward the bed and gently lay him down. Finished, I remove the A'ris layer and disengage my magic.

Glenna picks up the blanket from the foot of the bed and covers him. She arranges his hands by his sides and checks his temperature. She exhales deeply and wipes at the corner of her eyes.

Ragnald touches Glenna's shoulder in comfort.

I look away, feeling helpless.

Something catches my eye.

On the ground, near the dark pool of blood, glints a dagger with a stained wave blade.

With two fingers, I pick it up to examine it. The black leather of the dagger's hilt shows signs of frequent use. There is something about this dagger. It looks familiar to me, but I can't imagine where I could have seen it. I turn it to the side. Its blade shines in the bright Fla'mma-infused candlelight. Dark blood covers the sharp tip of it. I have no doubt Sawney was attacked with it.

There is also that acrid smell clinging to the weapon, dear.

Acerbus.

Ragnald wipes his hands and puts away his yellow glasses. "I've detected Acerbus in two spots. One near the door and one—"

"On the dagger," I say, finishing the mage's sentence.

Ragnald nods. "Which would explain why Glenna is having trouble healing him."

Glenna's head snaps up. "If he is infested with Acerbus, then there is nothing we can do. It takes this mage's magic and mine combined just to keep the corruption from fully consuming me. Since Sawney does not have any magic . . ." She doesn't have to finish the sentence for us to know that he has no chance of survival.

An idea forms in my head and I step to the bed and place the dagger on the nightstand. "Could my Lume magic boost his defenses against Acerbus? I know that the Teryns have some immunity to most magic, which could mean Lume would only interact with the Acerbus stain, helping him heal. Right?"

Glenna looks at Sawney. "I am not so sure. The Acerbus entered his blood, compromising him from the inside. Whatever magical immunity he had is not helping him much now. But I guess we can try it."

Since I don't want to risk an adverse reaction, I select a thin golden Lume thread from my magical orb. With the utmost care, I let the Lume ribbon touch Sawney's right hand.

Sawney's back arches, his feet drumming the bed as he convulses.

"Stop!" Glenna yells, pushing me away.

Immediately, I release my magic.

Sawney's body relaxes back on the bed.

Glenna shakes her head. "It didn't work. I should have known. Your magic didn't help me back on Uhna, right after the battle with DLD, but I thought his case might be different."

The door opens.

Rhona strides in, followed by an upset-looking Callum. They take in the blood on the floor and their unconscious brother. She rushes to the bed and sits down near her brother, with moisture gathering in her eyes as Glenna fills them in on the nature of Sawney's injury.

Callum looks at Glenna, then at Sawney. A mix of emotions—anger, sadness, and angst—crosses over his face.

I hug him. "I am so sorry." There are no words that could ease his pain and sorrow.

After a few moments he steps back, looking collected once more.

"Where is Caderyn?" I ask him.

Rhona wipes her face with a hand and glances at Callum.

Callum curses under his breath. "The praelor is missing."

CHAPTER 24

I blink at Callum. "What do you mean, he's missing?"

I am sure the praelor is fine, dear, Moira says, sounding unsure. I have a hard time agreeing with her.

Rhona joins us. "We couldn't find him in his room or anywhere else in the monastery. That's why it took so long to come back here."

An orange-reddish light flashes across Callum's blue eyes. "We've been searching for him. He won't respond to our hails."

That's strange. "Did you find anything in Caderyn's room?"

Callum shakes his head. "Nothing. This is not like him."

Rhona opens her mouth to say something when her gaze locks on the dagger on the nightstand next to Sawney's bed.

I pick up the dagger. "Do you recognize this?"

Rhona tears her gaze away from the dagger, wearing a nonchalant expression. "No. Why do you ask?"

This is the second time she's acted oddly when it comes to a dagger. First, it was right after someone tried to assassinate me in the spirit realm, and now tonight. What is she hiding?

You know how she likes weapons, dear.

I look at Callum. "Did you check the spaceports?"

"We were about to when your call came in and we hurried here."

Rhona taps on her wrist. "I can access the monks' port terminal now." She activates a small computing device the size of a two-inch square that is part of the hem of her jacket. "The Pada system is archaic, but we've made some improvements over the past few years." Lines flash by in a runic-style language on the otherwise dark screen. Rhona reads it, then turns the device off and it blends back into the fabric. "No one has left yet."

Callum nods. "Which means, the praelor is still here somewhere."

I wave the dagger as I smile at Rhona. "We will find your father before the five days are up."

She glowers. "What do you mean? The check-in summit lasts for *seven* days."

I duck my head. "I, uh, forgot to tell you that The Lady permitted only five days away from Cathal. The archgoddess insisted it's imperative to be back on the jungle world by then."

"Why?" Rhona asks with a puzzled expression.

I shrug. "She did not disclose that information." Or any other information for that matter.

Rhona crosses her arms. "We can't just absquatulate."

What on Uhna does that mean? "What did you say?"

Rhona rolls her eyes. "I meant that I am not leaving until I find Dad, whether The Lady likes it or not."

I don't have such luxury. "Suit yourself."

Callum glances at me. "I can task a few warriors with guarding the space-port discreetly. They don't report to me, and as such their general's orders outrank mine. I cannot guarantee that they will be able to guard it for long, but this could buy us some time. If nothing else, it might give us a warning if someone is trying to leave."

Good idea. "Please do that."

Pressing on his ear, Callum sends a few subvocal messages. "Done."

Then the door bursts open.

CHAPTER 25

Ivy shuffles in, wearing a bright pink sleepshirt that reaches the top of her thighs. She kicks the door closed, then comes to an abrupt stop in her pink fluffy slippers. "Why do you all look so devastated? Who died?"

"Ivy," I snap just as the door opens again.

Isa and Bella enter this time, followed by Teague, Belthair, and Arrov. They crowd into the small room.

Arrov leans on the wall near the window, taking in the scene. "What's going on?"

"I was just about to ask," Ivy says, but her gaze snags on the dagger in my right hand. "Don't tell me Sawney got stabbed with his own dagger."

Rhona whirls to Ivy. "What did you say?"

Ivy gapes. "I, uh, didn't, uh—"

Rhona points at Ivy. "The only way for you to recognize this dagger, which is part of a pair, is if you've seen one before, in the spirit realm."

Realization hits like a crushing tide. "Ivy must have let the assassins into our camp in the spirit realm when I got attacked." The two assailants escaped; one was injured by Arrov in his A'ice giant form, while Belthair suffered an injury from the first attacker, defending me. One of them left behind a dagger that had a blade similar to the one I'm holding.

I told you it wasn't me, dear.

I shake my head. "We always suspected Ivy of sabotage, but could never prove it."

It's hard to believe that Sawney was one of my assassins with the dagger, while it must have been Sachary who was injured. Now Rhona's reference to her brother's limping makes sense. I knew she recognized the dagger Sawney lost in the spirit realm. She discerned that her two brothers were involved but didn't tell me. I glance at Rhona, but she looks away from me with a guilty expression.

Ivy pouts. "You still can't prove it."

Rhona pokes Ivy on the arm. "You have not changed a bit."

Ivy looks around the room for help.

"It's time to come clean, sweetie," Glenna says.

Ivy twists a blond strand around her fingers. "Hypothetically speaking, there was a young woman who was stranded in a strange and *very* scary world. She was so scared. Really, she was. And she was all alone."

Rhona grunts. "Ugh. Enough with the self-pity."

Ivy ignores Rhona. "When she met two handsome warriors who were on a divine mission and who seemed so trustworthy, she believed them when they offered a way out of that strange and scary world. She accepted their help without questioning. She was so naïve back then."

Divine mission? That sounds like Laoise, I say to Moira.

I've told you in the spirit realm, dear, that Laoise wanted to get rid of you.

Arrov snorts but covers it up with a cough. "Naïve, huh? That's one way to put it."

"At first they asked her to do small things. Bring all the food. Get rid of her friends' drying clothes. It seemed fair for her to help any way she could, in exchange for escaping that *scary—*"

Rhona stomps her foot. "For the love of shields, get on with your story already."

Ivy sniffs. "Anyway, the young woman thought nothing of it, until they asked her to let them into her camp in the middle of the night. When she found them attempting to murder her best friend, she heroically sounded the alarm, saving everyone. The End."

Heroically?

Rhona points at Ivy. "I am astounded. You're more delusional than I thought."

"Someone needs a big dose of reality to keep her ego in check," Glenna mutters.

Belthair smiles at Ivy. "It was brave of you to alert us."

Now it's my turn to roll my eyes.

Callum chuckles. On his left, Teague pulls a spikey orange-colored fruit from his pajama pocket, then bites into it with enthusiasm.

"We can't trust her now," Rhona declares.

Ivy looks at each of us, and a red blush appears on her face. "You can't fault me for trying my best to survive. It's the Marauders' way."

Rhona lifts an eyebrow. "This is prodigious. We can use her."

Ivy scowls at Rhona, then turns to me. "What is Walking Dictionary talking about?"

"I told you to stop calling me that," Rhona snaps. "I have no doubt the Marauders are behind all of it."

Callum glances at me. "It does make bizarre sense."

"That mysterious 'she' the killer referred to could be the dowager queen," I mutter. "But why kidnap Caderyn?" It's unclear how Caderyn fits into all of this.

Callum steps toward the door. "We can ask her now."

That would be a disaster.

I stop Callum with a hand on his chest. "We can't just barge into the living quarters of the Marauders and demand answers. What if it wasn't her? Then they would know Caderyn is missing."

My friends argue, creating a cacophony.

I wait until they quiet down. "Yes, you heard it right. Tonight, Sawney was attacked and critically injured with Acerbus, while Caderyn was kidnapped."

Ragnald raises a hand. "I'll check the praelor's room with my magic for any clues." At my nod he leaves, shutting the door behind him.

Rhona glowers at Ivy with aggression. "It fits the machinations of the Marauders. They are without honor and—"

I cut in, "Everyone is without honor if they are not born on Teryn. We need more proof before we condemn them."

Glenna checks on Sawney. "It's understandable for Rhona to be so rattled after what happened. *Anyone* would be in a state of shock."

Rhona's eyes glint with frustration. "I am just splendid, thank you. No need to talk about me as if I am not in the room. Save your pity for someone else."

I need more proof against the dowager queen, and I know just how to get it. "Ivy, I need your help to gather information on the involvement of the Marauders, and in finding clues about Caderyn's whereabouts."

Ivy grins. "You want me to spy on my mother? I thought you'd never ask."

Rhona shakes her head. "What a scatterbrain."

Belthair lifts his three right hands. "Hold your ships. Ivy's life will be in danger the second she goes back to the Marauders."

Ivy shrugs. "I am in danger just by being with Lilla." A hint of worry shines in her eyes that her joking can't hide.

"Remember what a good general does," Rhona reminds me.

Not that again. I've heard enough of it in the spirit realm. "Ivy is our best asset to get proof one way or another. Especially since we are in a hurry. Simply put, we *need* her help."

Callum positions himself next to me, glaring at Belthair. "I agree."

"She won't do it," Belthair insists with his six hands raised in fists.

"I'll do it," Ivy says at the same time, "but I have to act right now, before the dowager queen suspects anything."

She steps toward the exit, but Belthair blocks her way. "Are you sure?"

Ivy pats his top right arm. "Don't worry about me. Spying is one of the ways of the Marauders that I happen to excel at." She leaves just as Ragnald returns.

"I found nothing with my magic," the mage says.

May I speak through you, dear?

I nod and relinquish control to Moira, ignoring the strange sensation of not being in control of my own body.

"Lilla was gracious enough to let me speak through her," Moira says, and my friends turn their attention to us. "We are at the precipice of disaster and must act with haste. It's urgent we find Caderyn. Without his tight control, the conquered worlds will revolt against the Teryn Praelium until an intergalactic war breaks out among them. We cannot afford such a conflict, not when the Era War is upon us, and the Archgod of Chaos and Destruction is gathering His army. We need to find Caderyn to ensure the Teryn Praelium stays united till the end."

Thank you, dear, Moira says and gives me back control. I shiver as all the sensations return to me.

Silence falls.

Belthair crosses his top two arms. "These conquered worlds deserve their freedom. Don't you think?"

We nod in agreement.

Belthair opens and closes all his fingers as he looks at us. "We've experienced firsthand what a tyrannical monarchy does to its citizens. Caderyn is no better than the ma'ha, Lilla's father who was a dictator. The praelor just has a better excuse as to why he oppresses people. It does not make it right."

"You are correct. It doesn't make it right." I understand what Belthair means. After all, he, the twins, and I joined the Uhnan rebellion against the tyranny for this very reason. "You are correct. It doesn't make it right."

Before I can say more, Isa says, "We concur." Bella adds, "But don't forget all the good the Pax Septum Coalition offered its members—economic stability, tourism, and safety from the attempts of other worlds to conquer them. Many planets would not have survived on their own for long, including ours, Barbal. It never even occurred to our president to set up a substantial protection against a possible invasion. We were fortunate the coalition found us first and not the Teryns."

Ragnald turns to Belthair. "I agree with you as well. My home world, Raghild, paid the price of oppression and was forbidden from returning to the coalition. Then the ma'ha offered me a position, opening diplomatic channels with Raghild once again."

Glenna frowns at the mage. "That's a bit of an oversimplification of the Magical Cleansing Wars. The mages deserved what they got—"

Ragnald raises a hand. "This is not the right time for a historical debate. As I said, I agree with you, Belthair, but not at the expense of billions of innocents who will die if we lose the Era War."

In the end, that is what we all have to consider—the cost. There are no simple answers here. "The sad truth is we cannot win the Era War without Caderyn and the Teryn Praelium. The Seven Galaxies need them." If I want to keep my promise to my mom to protect the innocents, then I need them too.

CHAPTER 26

Belthair makes a grimace. "What can I do to help you?"

"First, we need to make sure no one enters Sawney's or Caderyn's room," I say, thinking through what needs to be done.

Callum glances at Teague. He shoves the last bite of the spikey orange fruit into his mouth. "I'll take care of guarding the rooms. No one will get past me."

"That will help prevent anyone from finding out what happened tonight," I say, "but it's not enough. We also need a 'praelor' for the duration of our stay." I turn to the twins. "Can you make a disguise that allows Callum to look like Caderyn without anyone being the wiser?"

Isa and Bella perk up. "We've never built such a device, but we can't wait to try." With excited squeals, the twins run out of the room.

Callum clasps my hand. "I don't like the idea of leaving your side. When you embarked on your quest for the Heart Amulet, I couldn't follow you. I didn't know if you were safe."

I squeeze his hand. "This is different. It won't be all day long, just enough to make an appearance, walk around brooding, and look threatening for a few hours."

"That does sum up Dad," Rhona says, then sighs. "I hope we find him in time."

"We will find him," Callum reassures his sister, then turns back to me. "Still, the idea that I have to separate from you again . . ."

I touch his face, his stubble scraping my palm. "We won't separate, not ever again, but I need to know that you have my back."

Callum lifts my hand to his lips and kisses the back of it as he learned when he first came to Uhna. "Always."

Clearing my throat, I look at Rhona. "If it's not the dowager queen, who else could benefit from hurting your family?"

She considers this briefly as she tugs on a few strands of hair. "It could be those conniving Brainiacs."

Callum nods. "They have the motive as they've been pushing against the Ground Rules for decades, trying to erase them, but the praelor managed to hold off any changes."

The warriors live and die by these Ground Rules, which care nothing for nonmelded Teryns or outsiders. I've experienced firsthand how ruthless the rules can be. It's no wonder that the Brainiacs, I mean consuasors, want to get rid of them.

Rhona scoffs. "That's because they always envied our strength, since they failed their trial and could never experience meld."

I don't correct her that she never melded either. "That would be enough reason to kill Sachary. A political assassination."

Rhona's head snaps up. "I thought Callum told Dad that Sachary was killed because of his temper."

Callum puts an arm around his sister's shoulders. "Lilla and I didn't want to upset the praelor any more than necessary; we told him a partial truth."

Rhona pushes away from Callum. "What is the full truth then?"

Callum explains what happened with the killer. How we found corruption on the disguise device and the tiny purple rocks. "Because of the rocks, we knew we had to come to Pada, but the praelor insisted on joining us."

Rhona fists her hands. "Dad came to Pada, where most of the Brainiacs are for the check-in summit. He may have walked into their trap, all because you and Lilla decided to keep secrets from him."

Callum grinds his teeth. "We acted on what we thought was best. Look what he did to that space station when he was calm. Imagine what he would have done if he knew his son's killer was somewhere among the guests."

Rhona exhales bitterly. "I guess you're right. But you shouldn't have hidden this from me."

I feel horrible for the hurt this has caused her, but I'm not sure I would have made a different decision. There was more at stakes than Rhona's hurt feelings. "The truth is, we don't know who kidnapped Caderyn, killed one of his sons, and attacked the other. It could be the Marauders or the consuasors or someone else altogether. Hurting Sawney and Sachary could be a different crime from kidnapping Caderyn. We simply don't know much at this point. What I do know is that we must act as if nothing's happened. We won't play into their hands or raise an alarm, as they would expect. Hopefully by doing this, we can trigger whoever is behind these offenses to make mistakes and reveal themselves." Because we don't have anything else to work with.

Isa and Bella enter the room, holding a shoulder, holster-like contraption made of black leather. Isa hands it to Callum. "Try it on." She is all but dancing on her feet from happiness.

Callum pulls the holster on.

Bella shows him a small button on the side of the holster. "Press it once to activate it, twice to deactivate it."

Callum presses the button, but nothing happens. "Are you sure this works?"

Isa slaps her forehead. "Oh. I forgot to tell you that you must be in constant motion, or it won't work. Also, you can't touch anything or anyone, nor can you eat while wearing the disguise. Crumbs are a nightmare for the wires." Bella adds, "Don't touch it or fidget with it either; it's very fragile."

"I'll try to remember," Callum grumbles, then strides outside. Right before he steps out into the dark, he presses the button.

We follow him but stop in the doorway.

Callum paces around, looking like Caderyn with gray hair and a well-kept beard.

I can't believe the twins have engineered such a great disguise in such a short time. "You've outdone yourselves."

Isa beams. "We tried."

Bella adds, "One more thing, we couldn't find a battery strong enough to operate it longer than three days."

CHAPTER 27

Callum deactivates the disguise. "Three days is not enough time."

Buckets of fishguts! We'll never find Caderyn in such a short time.

We head back into Sawney's living quarters and out of the cold. Glenna checks on Sawney, then shakes her head.

My fingers curl into my palm. Sawney is dying from Acerbus poisoning and there is nothing we can do about it.

All we can do, dear, is find whoever is behind these crimes, bring justice to Callum's brothers, and save Caderyn before it's too late. Everything else must wait till then.

You're right.

I turn to the twins. "Is there anything you can do to add one more day?" That would still leave enough time to get back to Cathal as The Lady ordered.

"It's the best we could come up with in such short notice," the twins say in unison.

Glenna touches my arm in comfort. "It's better than nothing, sweetie."

I make a grimace. "True. Now that we have our 'praelor,' we need to accelerate our investigation and find out who supplied the Acerbus-infused technology."

Arrov scratches his chin. "How are we going to achieve these feats in just three days?"

Ragnald clasps his forearms in front of his chest. "I don't see us having a lot of options. We must search the monastery without attracting notice, while Callum, as Caderyn, masquerades and distracts others. Hopefully we'll find more clues."

Arrov shakes his head. "There's a lot of uncertainty around these crimes. I don't like the odds."

"We shouldn't have come to Pada," Glenna mutters, a manic fever in her eyes. "Now the whole Teryn empire is in peril. All I want is to burn down this whole . . ." her voice trails off when Ragnald channels Fla'mma magic into her. After a moment, her expression clears, looking like her old self again.

Everyone gets quiet, trying not to look at Glenna.

Dear, I don't understand why Sawney got infected with corruption, when DLD attacked both Callum and Teague in that battle that I saw in your memory, one that destroyed so much of your home world, including the Crystal Palace. The new and melded Teryns have significant magical immunity, thanks to their spirits. Sawney should not be affected like this. Especially since DLD had no luck turning my people in the previous Era War.

I consider this for a moment before replying to Moira. *First, I think there is a significant difference between the magical immunity of the original Teryns and the new Teryns. Second, Sawney was stabbed with a blade coated in Acerbus, which led the corruption to enter his blood, compromising whatever magical immunity he had. Otherwise Glenna could have healed him. I also suspect that Sawney's actions opened him up for corruption. The Acerbus stain sought out seeds of corruption and took advantage of them. The same thing happened to Glenna when she tried to poison Ragnald; she created an opportunity for DLD's corruption to take hold. Then when DLD blasted my friends with Acerbus in that battle, she got infected. Arrov was lucky he only turned into an A'ice giant as a consequence and not worse.*

The pain in Callum's eyes that flashes every time he looks at Sawney nearly breaks me. I wish we'd never come to Pada too. But the chain of actions started long before we arrived here. Someone killed Sachary. "It's too late for regrets now. We cannot change what happened; we must move forward."

"With luck this will be over soon," Isa says and Bella nods.

Rhona scoffs. "I've never believed in luck. It's nothing but an illusion and an excuse the weak-minded use."

Belthair scratches the stubble on his face with a thoughtful expression. "Even if the attacks on Callum's brothers and Caderyn's kidnapping are connected—which we cannot know for sure—our chance of success is still bleak."

I nod. "That's why we need more help."

Sawney groans in pain. Silence blankets the room as we stare at him, willing him to feel better.

Rhona frowns at me. "Didn't you say to keep what's happened a secret? Or have you changed your mind already? That's not a good characteristic of a great general."

A muscle jumps under my left eye. "I *did* say that. What I mean is, we need someone suitable to help us."

Callum strides out of the room before I can stop him.

Rhona paces up and down the small room. "Where is my brother going?"

Maybe he is running away from his sister's temper, Moira says wryly.

Rhona raises a hand, not letting me answer her. "You know what, don't tell me. You've wasted my time long enough. I know in my heart that it was the Brainiacs. They must have concocted the political assassinations and the kidnapping."

What has gotten into Rhona?

Arrov scowls. "Correct me if I'm wrong, but I thought you blamed the Marauders."

Rhona waves a hand in dismissal. "I've changed my mind, okay? The Marauders are not smart enough to execute an elaborate plan like this. They are nothing but blunt tools. No, these crimes required utmost precision and thorough planning. Guess who is great at these skills. The Brainiacs."

Moira flashes white fangs. *For someone who is so judgmental about changing an opinion, she sure is going from one extreme to the other.*

"That makes sense," Belthair says, then points at me. "Which means you've sent poor Ivy away for no reason."

She is not the only one who is judgmental. "Rhona, it's not like you to vacillate so haphazardly. What is really going on with you?"

Rhona shoves Belthair out of her way. "I'm tired of being powerless. I had enough of talking. It's time for action."

You can't let her leave, dear.

I jump in front of Rhona with both of my hands raised. "Don't do anything hasty without—"

She pushes at my shoulders. "Get out of my way!"

Arrov steps to us. "Rhona, relax. Just take a few breaths."

Rhona looks from Arrov to me. "You can't stop—"

Behind me the door opens.

"What is the meaning of this?" I hear a vexed male voice followed by footsteps.

We turn to see Callum holding a man in his forties, with curling and rune-like tattoos on his right cheek—Devotee Zorion.

Oh, that's why he left so abruptly. "I'm glad you read my mind, but I wasn't expecting you to drag him here in the middle of the night." Then I turn to Rhona and add, "We need *his* help."

Devotee Zorion extracts his arm from Callum, then crosses them over his dark blue ceremonial robe with a short, silver ruffled cape that ends just under his broad shoulders. Two sashes run down the front of his chest, one sky-blue for A'ris and the other ruby-red for Fla'mma—the two elements he is expert at using. "Why are you all up so late?" His brown gaze takes in the crowded room.

I step to block the monk's view of Sawney. "That's a long story. Thank you for coming here—"

Devotee Zorion extracts his arm from Callum. "I did not have a choice now, did I?"

I smile at the irritated monk. "Yes, uh, apologies for bothering you. We require your assistance in an urgent matter. Someone has attacked Colonel Sawney and kidnapped Praelor Caderyn."

Devotee Zorion blinks in shock. "That cannot be possible."

Callum gets close to the Pada monk. "Are you implying that we're lying?"

"I am afraid it is true," I say in a hurry before the situation can escalate. "We must find the praelor before anyone learns about this."

"Not to mention the culprit of the attacks," Rhona adds.

Devotee Zorion studies us. "There were multiple attacks?"

I wave a hand, dismissing the monk's question. "That's not important." I don't want to divulge all the information to him until I know with certainty that he is trustworthy. "We don't have much time. Can you help us?"

Devotee Zorion wipes his brow. "I have to think about this. Meet me at dawn and we can discuss it more. I'll send a disciple for you." With a curt nod, the Pada monk leaves the room.

CHAPTER 28

DAY 2

"Please close door after you," Devotee Zorion says when I enter the spacious and bright room the next morning. Last night, after everyone had dispersed, I had a restless sleep. Worry kept me up. Everything depends on whether this monk will agree to help me or not.

I comply, then I hesitate. I wish Ragnald could be here, but the note I received from the disciple was adamant that I come alone.

The rising sun paints the shiny surface of the hardwood floor in orange hues. Dust motes swirl in the swaths of light that come through the floor-to-ceiling windows. Stone tiles cover the walls. High wooden coffered ceilings complete this cavernous space that could double as a ballroom.

I inhale the dusty air. "Have you thought about my request?"

Devotee Zorion arranges the A'ris blue and Fla'mma red sashes over his blue robe. "I am not sure it is wise for me entangle myself, and the Pada world, in such political machinations."

He can't be serious. "You must be joking."

Devotee Zorion smiles, and the curling runes bunch up on his right cheek. "I assure you, I am not joking. I have given this matter plenty of thought before deciding to stay neutral."

Did he know? "You are already implicated. These attacks happened under *your* watch, during the check-in summit *you* led. You are responsible for the safety of your guests."

Well said, dear.

Devotee Zorion steps to the side and lifts his arms out with his palms facing me, a stance that looks ready for an attack.

"What are you doing?" I ask, and step back, reaching for my bright and pulsing magical orb covered in millions of elemental threads as I prepare to defend myself.

Devotee Zorion lowers his arms. "I thought we could practice magic. We can still carry a conversation, can we not? This would give a good enough reason for why we're spending so much time in each other's company so that the other guests won't get suspicious."

Oh. "Good idea."

"Don't forget to do your warm-up exercises."

My what?

Devotee Zorion sighs. "Has that mage not taught you the importance of warming up your arms before engaging in magic?"

"He, uh, I mean, I am not sure."

"Just follow my lead." Devotee Zorion moves his arms in circles a few times, both forward and then backward. "Just follow my lead."

Following his example, I circle my arms. "You cannot stay neutral in this matter, not when you are accountable for the well-being of your guests. One of those guests is dying and another is missing, in case you missed those facts."

There is no way I accept his position on staying neutral. I don't have time to find another way to solve these crimes. I just have to convince the monk to help me.

Devotee Zorion clasps his hands. "I understand. Truth be told, it is the Teryns who are leading this check-in summit, and thus they are the ones responsible here. We Pada monks are only providing a location for them. Maybe you should try to ask their help first."

I grind my teeth. "I can't do that. If the consuasors learn that their praelor is missing they will try to erase the Ground Rules, which would lead to a bloody civil war with the warriors."

"The inner workings of the Teryn Praelium are not my business. Now enlighten me about what you've learned regarding magic theory and magic application."

I take a deep breath to argue with the monk, but Moira interrupts. *It's best to play along with his magical lesson, dear. He might be more cooperative if you engage him on his terms.*

I am not sure if—

"Please focus on me," Devotee Zorion cuts into my thoughts. "It is crucial that you give this lesson your full attention and not allow your thoughts to wander. The welfare of both of us depends on this. Understood?"

I'll stay quiet, dear.

I nod in answer to both, though I can't say I appreciate his directness. Ragnald was never *this* arrogant.

Devotee Zorion raises an eyebrow and I realize he is waiting for me to answer his previous question regarding magical theory and application. "Ragnald and I focused on the magical elements and the level of affinity I have with them. We even combined the elements into magical minitornado and—"

Devotee Zorion groans. "I've heard enough. I am not shocked at your lack of knowledge and understanding. Mages are infamous for their rash and temperamental magic battles, but they have never been the best educators when it comes to magic. I see I have my work cut out for me."

Moira snorts in my head.

I can't decide whether to be offended on Ragnald's behalf or not.

"It is important for you to learn how the six light elements—A'ris, Fla'mma, A'qua, T'erra, A'nima, and Lume—form an interconnecting web around us. Lume is an element that is largely impossible to use if you are not a god or a Lumenian, but I digress. Using this interconnecting web is how we magic users—whether we be healers, the mages, or the Pada monks—can access the elements and master our efficiency in them. Since you are a Lumenian, all these elements are also in you, making it easier for you to use them. Correct?"

"Yes, that is correct." Using my magic was anything but easy, often resulting in near catastrophes when I lost control. But it's true; I do have that magical sphere where the elements reside somewhere in me. All Lumenians used to have one. "Before we move forward with the lesson, do you know any magical cure for Acerbus poisoning?"

Devotee Zorion raises both of his eyebrows. "Are you referring to the painful process of corruption done by the Archgod of Chaos and Destruction to create more of his dark servants? Or are you referring to an infection with Acerbus?"

Is there a difference? "The latter."

Devotee Zorion nods. "That's what I thought. I am aware of one solution. Death."

Well that's no help.

"Now I want you to look beyond the surface of reality," Devotee Zorion instructs, "and search for the magical elements around us. We call this 'seeing.'"

I turn my head and look more deeply into my surroundings.

The walls and the hardwood floor light up, covered in dark brown transparent hues of T'erra magic threads, crisscrossing with the sky-blue of A'ris.

The tall windows shine with more A'ris magic.

Zorion shimmers with transparent ribbons of ruby-red Fla'mma and sky-blue A'ris magic, enveloping him like layers upon layers.

I lift my hands and gasp. They're encased in thick Lume threads, while the transparent hues of all the other elemental ribbons are there underneath it as well.

Raising my head, I look up into the air around me. Thin threads of all the elements are interwoven, sparkling when they come into focus and disappearing the next second.

The way the elements interconnect reminds me of the magical architecture of the spirit realm that sustains and supports it. Laoise made it first, but when I severed her connection to the realm, I had to use my magic to stabilize the realm and prevent it from imploding. Maybe I was wrong to designate the word *architecture* to what makes up the spirit realm. Maybe it was just a natural formation of elemental magics interconnecting with each other, which I did not understand at the time.

Devotee Zorion smiles. "This is the foundation upon which we are going to build your magical lesson. It is rumored that the Omnipower created the magical and interconnecting web of elements before the two archgods. When we pray to any of the gods—be it a guardian or one of the archgods themselves—we sacrifice a minuscule amount of magic that we've gathered for our own use. We give it up to the gods so they can get stronger. Many Pada elders dispute this legend, but that is beside the point. Now that you know the basics of elements, I want you to create a clay container of any shape, size, or color that holds crystal clear and drinkable water."

I gape at him. "How would I do that?"

Zorion spreads his arms. "Remember, magic is all around us."

I exhale in frustration. All I have to do is to retrace the steps I made when I formed those minitornados. They were magical creations of a sort.

I close my eyes and search for my magical orb. A hot-and-cold-and-hot-again feeling envelops my body, and my skin glows bright white. I reach for A'ris and Fla'mma threads, holding them with imaginary fingers, trying to combine them.

Zorion makes a *tsk, tsk* sound. "That is the wrong approach, Sybil Lilla. Remember, you must *unlearn* what you know and start fresh."

I have no idea how to "unlearn" and create what the monk wants.

Taking a few relaxing breaths, I release the elemental threads. What is a clay pot made of? From plant life, minerals, and decomposing animals—all the ingredients of soil. So that would mean T'erra, A'nima, and . . .

"Sybil Lilla, you keep going back to what you know. I want you to relax and follow your instincts."

"I am trying to relax." But he keeps interrupting and confuses me.

You can do this, dear.

If Devotee Zorion wants instincts, I'll give him instincts.

With an exhale, I imagine putting both of my hands over my bright magical orb. Threads of T'erra, A'nima, A'qua, and A'ris rise to my call. In my mind, I combine the first three magical threads and shape them into a round clay bowl, then add A'qua ribbons to it until the imaginary pot is filled with cool water.

Then I open my eyes and gasp.

CHAPTER 29

In front of me, dozens of round clay pots, full of sloshing water, cover most of the hardwood floor.

"Devotee Zorion glances around the roomful of clay pots. "You got carried away a little bit, didn't you?" Devotee Zorion says as he glances around the roomful of clay pots.

My feeling of accomplishment deflates at his words.

"One of the most essential lessons a magic user must learn is to take their ego and temper out of the magic equation. Acting hastily can cause serious harm. It's best to keep this in mind for next time, hmm?"

Ego? "I wasn't trying to show off."

"Maybe not." Devotee Zorion dips his curved fingers into the bowl closest to him. He lifts the water to his lips and sips, swishing the liquid in his mouth, tasting it. "The fact remains that you allowed annoyance to take hold of you and, well, you've overused your magic. Remember, I asked for one clay pot of clean water."

"I don't think I overused my magic." I dip my fingers into a bowl and taste the water. It's refreshing and clean. I don't understand what I did wrong. "I don't think I overused my magic."

Devotee Zorion steeples his fingers in front of him. "That is where the danger lies, Sybil Lilla, for any undertrained magic user. The temptation to use a lot of magic—clumsily, I might add—intensifies until the magic user ignores the warning signs that indicate they are close to misusing their magic. Then they'll have to pay the price, of course. This is one of the biggest threats to us all, one we learn during the first magic lesson. I wonder why that mage never discussed with you what happens when a Lumenian overextends her magic."

I am not sure what Devotee Zorion means. I recall Glenna telling me how healers or mages who overdo their magic become Turned. The archgod often unleashes them to cause the most devastation possible. No one can reason with them. No one can stop them. Just one Turned can eradicate a whole city on its own.

"I don't know what happens when a Lumenian overuses her magic." I sure would love to avoid it.

Devotee Zorion purses his lips in disappointment. "I find this lapse imprudent. As a Lumenian, you have a tremendous amount of magic, but little skills or knowledge of how to apply it. That mage never should have allowed you to exercise your magic without teaching you the critical failsafe points: the warning signs to keep in mind; the last burst before it's too late; and, of course, the—"

A polite knock sounds.

A petite disciple enters and steps to the side, waiting.

Devotee Zorion nods toward the disciple, then turns to me. "Now I see the importance of my assistance in your endeavor that we talked about earlier. It is abundantly clear to me that you are in desperate need of my expertise in many areas, including magic. I have decided to aid you." He strides toward the exit.

"That's great, but you were saying about the price of—"

Devotee Zorion looks over his shoulder. "Do not engage your magic. We shall have more lessons, then we'll talk about other matters as well. I shall see you at breakfast. Please don't be late."

CHAPTER 30

"How did your talk go with the Pada monk?" Glenna asks when I join my friends at our table in the Banquet Hall.

Most of the faction guests are already seated at their tables that are replete with yellow silk tablecloths and matching chairs. The hum of conversation echoes between the stone-tiled walls. A fresh breeze brings the scent of pines through the open balcony doors above us, mixing with tantalizing scents of bread and pastries. A dozen chandeliers with Fla'mma-infused candles sway unlit in the room full of bright sunlight.

"He decided to help us. After a confusing magic lesson." I scratch my cheek, which burns as if someone is staring at me.

That is an understatement, dear. That monk is too proud for his own good.

I turn to the right to see Ivy glowering at me. She wears a black dress of torn strips of material. Next to her the dowager queen eyes me. The queen swipes strawberry blond locks from round shoulders covered in red leather that struggles to contain her ample bosom. Cunning green eyes glint with callousness in her wrinkled, round, and pale face. Long black-colored nails drum impatiently on the tablecloth.

When a disciple passes near her table, the dowager queen thrusts her foot out, tripping the monk. Plates and mugs shatter with a loud clang. Food scatters on the floor. The disciple engages a thin transparent ribbon of A'ris threads, shaping it into a broom, and cleans up the mess, then scurries away.

The dowager queen turns to the others at her table, thug-like men in black leather outfits, and laughs.

She preys on the weak and abuses her power, Moira says. *A queen should never behave like that.*

My gaze lands on the two empty seats across from me, and I search for Callum, who in full Caderyn disguise, strides past me. His blue gaze lingers on my face for a moment before glowering at others. The guests quiet down as he passes them, their gaze following him.

Glenna pats my hand. "It's for a short time, sweetie."

"It works," Isa says in a hushed tone, and Bella smiles.

Belthair leans back on his chair, balancing on its two legs. "For now."

Arrov looks around the busy hall. "One or more of these guests are who we're looking for. They pretend to be innocent, thinking they've gotten away with their crimes."

The mood turns bleak.

Rhona puts her elbows on the table while holding a sharp knife between her two forefingers. "I can't wait to punish them until they regret—"

I touch her arm. "Let's not plan vengeance just yet."

"I concur with Rhona," Glenna says with a flushed face and frenzied look in her dark red eyes. "I will help teach them a lesson they'll never—"

Ragnald puts a hand over Glenna's shoulder, channeling Fla'mma magic into the healer, stopping her rant.

Glenna blinks, looking like her normal self, and rubs her face with both of her hands. "I, uh, meant to say that Sawney's condition was, uh, unchanged this morning."

We fall silent.

Ragnald looks at Glenna. "Your condition is getting worse. We need to petition the Academia of Mages for assistance. They are the absolute experts when it comes to—"

Glenna snaps, "I've told you I'd rather die than ask those charlatans for help."

"That will happen sooner than you think," Ragnald mutters, earning a piercing glare from Glenna.

Belthair turns to me. "Do you know what Zorion is planning to do to help us?"

"Not really." I just hope the monk's help will be in our best interest.

A throat clears, loud enough to cut through the noise of conversation.

The guests turn toward the half-moon-shaped platform at the back of the Banquet Hall. On it, Devotee Zorion stands with his hands clasped. "Breakfast will be served momentarily, but I wanted to make an announcement first."

Cold runs through my spine as if someone has dumped a bucket of iced shrimp over my head.

My friends and I exchange a worried look.

Arrov leans close to the table. "The monk wouldn't dare betray us, would he?"

Belthair straightens his chair with a thump. "Get ready to stop him before he can say anything compromising. Just in case."

We push our chairs back.

Devotee Zorion smiles. "In light of the recent developments—"

Belthair and Arrov jump to their feet.

Devotee Zorion claps. "I love the enthusiasm, but before you jump in with two feet, no pun intended, let me expand on my surprise. As you all know, this check-in summit makes the seventy-fifth one and as such I thought we should celebrate by trying something different."

My friends and I exhale in relief and the two men return to their seats.

Devotee Zorion smiles jovially. "We are going to leave the monastery and spend a whole day, twenty-six hours, in the embrace of nature. We will engage in cooperation-building exercises that will facilitate better communication and, well, better cooperation between the Tier One worlds and the Teryn Praelium. Isn't that exhilarating?"

The Teryn warriors burst into obnoxious laughter as the stunned Tier One delegation members stare at the monk. Then a man with slicked-back hair gets to his feet. "The Industrial Conglomerate wants none of this 'cooperation-building.'"

The dowager queen slams her hands on the table. "Not in a million galaxy time."

Other members of the Tier One worlds join in declaring their dissent.

"Quiet!" Callum's voice booms, deeper than usual to match Caderyn's tone.

A frustrated silence blankets the hall.

"You will leave the monastery and follow Devotee Zorion's instructions," Callum/Caderyn says, "or pay the price."

Multitudes of chair legs scrape over the ground as the guests get to their feet in a hurry and clear out of the hall without a word.

CHAPTER 31

"I don't want you to go," Callum says, holding my face in his hands. After skipping breakfast, we all returned to our rooms, with Callum following me into mine.

With his disguise deactivated, I take in his tanned face, framed by short black hair, and his intent blue gaze. My heart feels ready to burst. I never thought I could love so deeply as I love Callum. "I don't want to go either."

"If you keep looking at me like that . . ." He leans down and kisses me. He pours all his desire into that kiss, taking my breath away. His fingers trail my jawline, then my neck and down my arms.

I return his kiss with the same longing and passion. I can't get enough of him. I kiss his lips and the corner of his mouth, trailing a path under his jaw.

Callum groans and slides his hands over my back, caressing it. The he reluctantly lifts his head. "We promised never to separate again." With a deep exhale he pulls me into an embrace, his steel arms bracketing my back and holding me tight to his strong and warm body.

"We did make that promise." I hug his neck. My fingers play in the short hair at his nape. I don't want to let go of him either. I don't want reality to intrude, shattering this precious moment together.

Callum mutters a curse. "We should run away. Get married and forget about anything else."

I snort and slide my hands down to his chest, marveling at the hard and defined muscles. "Tempting, but you would regret it five minutes after we ran away."

Callum tightens his fingers around my waist. "They would be the best five minutes of my life. Worth every second."

I laugh and he steals another kiss from my lips, taking my breath away.

The door bursts open.

Rhona strides in. "It's time."

Callum leans down until our foreheads touch. "Promise me you'll be careful."

"I will." And I will miss him every second he is not with me.

He brushes his lips over mine, then activates the disguise and leaves with Rhona.

With a sigh, I pick up the large bag filled with clothing for the trip and head out, too.

I pass many guest rooms with open doors, revealing a flurry of activity as the others pack and curse or curse and pack.

I look at the courtyards on my right. In the first few are disciples finishing up their Second Light Prayer. Ragnald explained to me that the Pada monks have eight prayer sessions, named after the light and time of day. Each session lasts twenty minutes out of their twenty-six-hour day, complete with a form of magical practice. They do this seven weeks a month and eight months a year. I admire their commitment to their religion and magic. No wonder their guardian god became so strong or how efficient the monks are with their magic.

The other courtyards are full of busy disciples who harvest, plant, or tend to various animals.

Then I see an empty courtyard with long grass where Fearghas paws the ground with fierce purpose.

I stumble to a halt and drop my bag.

"Fearghas, what are you doing here?" I step over the low wall of the corridor to enter the courtyard. I look around for a disciple, but no one is nearby.

Fearghas bobs his head whinnying, then paws the grass again. Already a small hole is forming in the dirt.

Just how long has he been doing that?

The more important question, dear, is why *is he doing that?*

I wish I knew. "Shouldn't you be in the stable with the other nice animals?" I pet his thick black neck.

Fearghas whickers in response, impatience pouring off of him.

I try to lead him away from the courtyard. "Come on. Let's head back to the nice and comfy stable with lots of straws—"

The battle horse rears on his hind legs.

I raise my hands, backing away. "I take that as a no."

Fearghas bobs his head and paws the ground.

Fine. "If you want to stay, then stay." There is plenty of grass available and hopefully he won't hurt anyone else.

Shaking my head, I climb back over the corridor wall and pick up my bag, continuing my trek. When I exit through the front doors of the monastery, I find groups of guests gathering outside. On the right, my friends wait fidgeting.

I wave and head toward them.

Belthair drops his large knapsack on the grass, almost hitting Arrov's feet. "We should search the living quarters."

Putting my bag down, I shake my head. "You know we can't do that." I look around to see if anyone else is paying attention to our group, but no one is.

The wind, scented with pine and snow, picks up. I pull my light gray cloak with faux-fur lining at its neck closer, then pick strands of my long hair out of my mouth. I miss Ivy and her complaining when it comes to camping. She hated it with a passion.

Ahead of us, at least a hundred Teryn warriors stand still in a square-like formation. The Teryn consuasors mingle among the Tier One factions, making it hard to guess their numbers. But it couldn't be clearer how the two Teryn groups avoid each other even if they'd shout it from the top of their lungs. The only time I've seen a warrior mingle with a consuasor was Teague—whom Caderyn adopted—and his husband, Steaphan, when they came to have lunch at the praelor's house. Even then Caderyn wanted to hear nothing about the consuasors and treated Steaphan as if he were a warrior himself.

Belthair crosses his six arms. "You can't deny the fact that it would be more effective."

Arrov nudges Belthair's knapsack away from his feet. "It would also attract a lot of attention. Then we would have to answer questions such as, Why were you inside? or What were you doing while all the guests were participating in the cooperation-building exercises?"

I look at him. "Aren't you going to be cold?" He looks dashing in his white short-sleeved shirt.

Arrov chuckles. "This weather is like a typical summer on A'ice."

"Questions are never good," Isa agrees, looking fresh in her long flowery dress with a red cloak over it.

Bella, wearing a similar outfit, adds, "Unless we're the ones asking them."

I watch the last group of guests, the Marauders, waltz out of the monastery. "We are sticking to the plan: Rhona and Callum will stay behind and look for any evidence they can find. They will rejoin us later. The rest of us will play along and get close to the factions to ask questions."

Flanked by six disciples, Devotee Zorion joins us on the grass. "Welcome, guests, to the most remarkable adventure of your life. This is a perfect winter morning to start our cooperation-building exercises with a trek through the forest. Embrace nature around you and pay attention to your surroundings. Don't hesitate to rely on each other for assistance, since we are building toward that cooperation. Now follow me."

CHAPTER 32

We trek down the hillside and follow the lazy river over a rocky bed before entering the thick evergreen forest.

Devotee Zimon joins our group. "How are you feeling this marvelous morning?" His smile is radiant in his oval face. His dark brown eyes shine with excitement. The red robe the monk wears hangs loose on his tall thin frame. He fidgets with one of the two sashes, straw-yellow A'nima, and trips over his own feet.

The wind rustles the monk's short dark brown hair as he nods at a disciple, who hands each of us a fabric-covered plate.

Lifting the cover, I marvel at the hand-size fruit-filled pie on the black plate. I take a bite of the still warm pastry. The sweetest and tastiest boomberry-flavored filling brings tears to my eyes.

Devotee Zimon looks worriedly at me. "Is it not to your liking?"

I chew and swallow the bite. "It's not that. My dear head chef and friend used to make boomberry-filled pastries before she, uh, passed." DLD killed her to be more precise, trying to corrupt her into a dark servant and killing her in the process. "The taste of my favorite fruit brought back memories." I wipe the moisture from my eyes.

Devotee Zimon pats my shoulder. "Grief takes time. We must allow it to pass at its own speed."

I pick up another pie. "What about your parents?"

Devotee Zimon smiles politely. "I never knew my parents. None of us do."

How can that be possible? "I don't understand."

He points to the far distance, where the top of a tower can be seen among the trees. "We are born in the Haven. Our parenting donors are carefully selected based on magic or other biological compatibility, but that is the height of their contribution. The Breeder Elders raise us until we are ten years old. Then we are sent to one of the monasteries to embark on our own magical journey. When it's time to procreate, the Matron will send for us. She is the only elder who knows our lineage. This is all designed to maximize our engagement with our magic and with our guardian god."

I gape at him. "I cannot . . . there is no dating . . . how, um, underwhelming, I mean interesting."

More like horrifying, dear, but don't tell the poor oblivious soul.

Devotee Zimon nods, then cringes. "I forgot that I wasn't supposed to share this with anyone who is not from Pada. Please don't tell Devotee Zorion."

"I promise I won't." I take another bite of the pie.

Belthair wipes his top two hands in the fabric cover that serves as a napkin as well. "I was expecting something more along the lines of bread and cheese."

Arrov sighs wistfully. "Maybe some bacon or onion with it. Or sausage."

Devotee Zimon chortles. "We wanted to make this trip as pleasurable as possible." He offers his hand to me when we reach a bunch of twisting roots, helping me step over it.

"It was surprisingly filling, too," Isa says, and Bella nods as we duck under low-hanging branches.

The disciples collect our plates and use magic to return them into T'erra, A'nima, and A'ris threads.

"It's because we use special whole grains to make our flours. But that's not all." Devotee Zimon smiles with pride, practically bursting at the seams to share more.

Arrov gestures with his hand. "Please go on."

"I'd love to," Devotee Zimon says with such excitement that I'm surprised he's not clapping his hands. "The secret ingredient is a hint of cocoa."

Belthair makes a disgusted face. "Really?"

Devotee Zimon bobs his head. "We cherish it so much that we add it to almost all our meals. We grow the cocoa in our basement, and it thrives in that dark and damp place."

I shiver. The last time I was in a basement, DLD turned it into His personal dungeon, full of dark servants.

Glenna's eyes glint with interest. "Like fungus? How unusual. I thought cocoa grows on trees."

Devotee Zimon raises his forefinger. "These are ground-dwelling cocoa plants we cultivated with our magic. There are more than three hundred varieties of them just in this monastery. It's more valuable to us than any other currency."

Arrov wears an expression that is a mix of wonder and slight repulsion. "Do you add cocoa to the seafood dishes?"

Devotee Zimon's smile disappears. "Even to those dishes. Though I am not sure if I was supposed to share this with all of you. Devotee Zorion warned me not to chat too much with the guests, but you are such great listeners. I'm sure it's fine."

The twins giggle.

I hide my distaste at the sound of fish combined with cocoa. I've never liked seafood.

You grew up on an oceanic world, dear, and you can't stand it. Why is that?

I've choked on so many fish bones that even the smell of fish causes a strong aversion in me.

What about the others, dear? Shrimp? Lobster? Clams?

Shrimp is an acquired taste that I've never acquired. Lobsters are too much trouble. Clams just look like snot in a shell. No, thank you.

Above us, a disciple flies with arms outstretched in a horizontal position, going faster than the green birds in the sky. A complicated network of A'ris magic ribbons cling to the monk, propelling them and keeping them afloat.

Arrov points up. "Did you see that?"

We glance up just as more disciples fly by.

Interesting mode of transportation, dear. I am envious.

Isa puts a hand over her eyes as she gazes up. "How is it that no one can see up their robes?"

Devotee Zorion glances at Ragnald. "We learn the magic skill of flying at a young age so that we can travel easily between monasteries. Surely the mages have their own method of flying?"

In response, Ragnald narrows his eyes at the monk.

We follow a dirt path out of the forest and begin climbing another hill that's covered in short green vegetation frosted with snowflakes.

Devotee Zimon studies the sky that has a few grey clouds in it. "I am glad we are taking advantage of the mild Season of Initiation."

We reach the top of the hill, and I exhale in relief. "Season of *what*?" The other groups are already resting on blankets, stretching their legs, and drinking from clay mugs.

A disciple places blankets for us on the ground, and my friends and I settle down.

In the distance, more monasteries, clustered in groups of six, are visible, at least a dozen.

Devotee Zimon puts his hands inside his wide sleeves. "Oh, it's what we call winter. It describes the start of the year, often a trial for the living to survive, and a forthbringer of spring or the Season of Emergence. During this period, we plant just as nature comes alive, hence the name 'emergence.' After that comes the Season of Tolerance, where we spend most of our time outside, tolerating the heat and enjoying the longer days. Then we gather what we planted during the Season of Harvest and make our famous pies, parcel our cocoa, and bottle our wines. It is also when we make a lot of jams and engage in canning all the fruits and vegetables. In essence, we're getting ready for the Season of Initiation."

Interesting names for seasons. "I thought you plant and harvest in the courtyards."

Devotee Zimon nods. "We have fields beyond the monastery, hidden among the forests, where we plant most of our food. What you see in the courtyards is extra—our pantry staples. Each monastery specializes in different types of fruits and vegetables. We even make our own spices and often trade them with each other or with other worlds."

Teague sits on our blanket. "That's fascinating. Do you have anything more to eat?"

Arrov frowns at Teague. "Aren't you supposed to be with the other Teryn warriors?"

Teague winks. "They ran out of food."

I hide my smile. More likely he ate all their food, and they sent him away.

Devotee Zimon beams and waves at a disciple who conjures plates with magic, then serves finger-long cakes, pastries filled with cheese and dried meat, sugar-coated flowers, and mugs full of refreshing water with minced fruits in it.

For a few minutes we are busy eating and drinking our share. Then the disciple gathers our empty plates and mugs, and deconstructs them back to their magical elements.

Isa discreetly wipes her lips. "This is like a walking buffet. Literally."

Bella adds, "I ate so much I'm stuffed."

Devotee Zorion, standing across from the seated guests ahead of us, claps his hands. "I hope you've enjoyed your snacks. Please try not to lag behind."

I have a feeling the monk means our group. "Where are we going?"

"Are we far?" Isa asks, and Bella adds, "Please tell me we are not far."

"I'm more worried about what happens when we get there," Devotee Zimon mutters.

CHAPTER 33

"Behold the Pilgrimage Circle," Devotee Zorion says as we stop at a glade with a half-circle- shaped, six-foot-tall wall that has runic writing on it.

My friends and I make our way toward the wall, stepping around gawking guests. When we reach it, I realize it's made from a large chunk of smooth black metal with writing carved into it in an elegant and organized way. The top of the wall looks jagged, and wires stick out of it. The air around it smells metallic.

Devotee Zimon bows his head toward the wall with his hands clasped in front of him, murmuring words under his breath.

I touch the cold surface of the wall. "Can you translate what's written there?"

Devotee Zimon wrings his hands. "No outsider is allowed to have the knowledge of the Pilgrimage Circle. Frankly, I am shocked that Devotee Zorion brought everyone here. He was not supposed to let outsiders into our most sacred place. What will the elders think if they learn about this?"

Devotee Zorion gestures toward the wall next to him. "Behold the Site of Warning. Isn't it the most stunning memorial you've ever seen?"

The dowager queen crosses her arms. "Is that a wall from a spaceship?"

A hefty Teryn warrior tilts his head. "That looks familiar, but why?"

Other Teryns mutter in agreement.

Devotee Zorion frowns. "None of that is important. What matters is the rich history that is embedded into these writings that—"

"I think Site of Arrival would be a better name," a man from the Industrial Conglomerate faction says. The wind tries to rustle his slicked-back hair to no avail.

Devotee Zimon's eyes go wide, and he covers his mouth with his right hand. "We are not supposed to talk about that."

The other faction guests and many Teryn warriors turn to Devotee Zorion, peppering the pale-looking monk with questions.

"We are dying to know what those runes say," Isa pleads, and Bella adds, "We really, really do."

Devotee Zimon lowers his hand. "I find your enthusiasm for knowledge so refreshing, but I really shouldn't—"

Isa and Bella clasp their hands in front of their chest. "Please!"

Devotee Zimon sighs and glances around to see who's watching, then gestures for us to lean close. "I, uh, I guess I might be able to explain the gist of it now that the Fla'mma ball is out of the magical bag, so to speak. What could be the harm?" He points at the first section. "Behold the Site of Warning. This meadow is the first place my ancestors set foot on this planet. They felt the importance of conveying their history and the knowledge of their arrival by using their magic and transcribing it into this wall."

Belthair gestures to the middle. "What about this section?"

Devotee Zimon wipes his mouth. "I, uh, am not sure—"

Glenna smiles sweetly. "We're all ears."

"Fine, fine. Only because you insist," Devotee Zimon says. "It essentially talks about how fundamental magic is to us, and how it was our downfall before we got to this world. We were not strong enough in our magic then. We tried to fit in with our cousins so much so that we neglected to practice it. We even kept our magic hidden from them, but to no avail. They found out. Then we were separated from them and sent away. Families were broken up all because of having magic. This section cautions us that suppressing our magical skills to fit in better will hinder our progress. They encourage us to devote our whole lives to study magic until we can rise to become specialists in one element and reach the rank of elder, which we have done ever since."

Moira shakes her head. *Maybe they embraced their magic a bit too zealously.*

Bella asks a question about Devotee Zimon's robe, and I tune out their conversation, thinking about what the monk has said about their arrival.

What is it, dear?

Something about this Pilgrimage Circle sounds familiar. Also, Guardian God Patra'ch mentioned the monks' duality. I feel like I've stumbled on an important piece of the puzzle, but I do not know where it fits. Yet.

It's best to leave the past in the past, dear.

I wish I could, I say to Moira, trying hard not to think about my cousin in order to prevent that tragic memory from resurfacing again.

Devotee Zimon turns to me with a concerned look on his face. "Sybil Lilla, are you okay? You look so sad."

I didn't even realize how true that was until the monk mentioned it. "It's nothing."

Your cousin was the young girl, dear, who appeared in your memories when you saw Sachary's body, wasn't she?

Yes. Her name was Be'trice. She would often visit with her parents, staying at the Crystal Palace for the whole summer.

But? I sense a but, dear.

I sigh. *But her jealousy of my station made the time we spent together miserable. She wanted to be a princess so desperately. She despised my lack of appreciation of the court and would bicker with me about it. Which, in turn, would get us into trouble all the time.*

"We demand answers," the hefty Teryn warrior shouts, breaking into my conversation with Moira.

Devotee Zorion shakes his head. "That is enough for today. Clearly the significance of this hallowed site is lost on many guests, including our Teryn sponsors. I should have known better than to expect anything else. What a way to ruin our Ancestor Day of all days."

Devotee Zimon winces. "I pity poor Devotee Zorion. He really tried his best to impress the guests. It's just, um, this visit . . ." He trails off, searching for words.

"It turned into the worst crash in the history of spacefaring," Belthair says, helpfully.

"It was worse than an avalanche," Arrov injects.

"Or worse than getting infected with troll leprosy," Glenna adds.

Devotee Zimon nods. "All of the above, I'm afraid."

CHAPTER 34

"It's time to mingle," I say to my friends as we head out, leaving the Pilgrimage Circle behind. "Let's see if we can find out who had a motive for kidnapping Caderyn, whether they had the means to carry it out, or if they know anything about who could be behind the crimes."

The wind picks up and dry leaves shower my hair. I wipe them off and glance up. Dark gray clouds float in the sky. The last thing we need is a storm to make this day perfect.

I turn my head in search of the lanky Devotee Zimon. I find the monk assisting Devotee Zorion at the front of the crowd, allowing my friends and me to carry out our investigation without prying eyes. I suspect that Devotee Zorion didn't involve the other monk, especially seeing how Devotee Zimon cannot keep anything to himself.

Isa steps forward. "We'll talk to the Industrial Conglomerate." Bella adds, "They seem like inventors; we'll have a lot in common as such." The twins hurry ahead in the forest, approaching a group of men with slicked-back hair and wearing expensive black suits.

"I'll take the Marauders Syndicate," Belthair offers. "I want to make sure that Ivy is doing okay." He glares at me for a second before rushing off.

I watch him disappear among the thick tree trunks covered in patches of red-striped mushrooms. If he thinks he is the only one worrying about Ivy, he is sorely wrong.

He'll come around soon, dear, I'm sure.

Arrov nods toward a group of young men and women with long shaggy hair and four ears. "I can handle the Merchants Verde and the Free Traders Consortium. I'm sure they're each other's competitors. All I have to do is use that against them." Whistling, he strides toward the merchants group.

"I'll talk with the Miners Coalition," Glenna says, then glances at Ragnald. "You can come with me if you'd like, as long as you don't bring up the Academia of Mages."

Ragnald stares at her. "I don't understand what you mean."

I try hard not to smile, but fail. "She's got you there. It's always Academia this or Academia that."

Ragnald pulls his black mage robe closed with a sniff. "I did not realize my pride of where I came from bothered the two of you so much."

Glenna rolls her eyes.

"We love hearing stories about your time with the Academia," I say and elbow Glenna until she mutters, "Sure."

Ragnald's face lights up. "Is that so? Did I tell you about the time the Academia sent me to take care of a fire goblin infestation at—"

"Later, mage," Glenna says and grabs Ragnald's arm and drags him away.

That leaves the Farmers Partnership—the faction that had their space station destroyed by Caderyn the night when we arrived on Pada.

CHAPTER 35

Picking up speed, I wade through the forest, trying to think about what I'll ask of the Farmers Partnership delegates. Will they even talk to me after what Caderyn did to them?

My boots disturb the composting leaves near the roots of the trees. A rotting scent wafts to my nose, making me grimace.

If they didn't have any motive to kidnap Caderyn, dear, after that tragedy I'm sure they developed one.

Let's hope not. I climb a small hill with flat rocks jutting out of it and reach a group of people wearing simple homemade clothing led by an older woman with gray hair. They are not in a hurry; their steps are measured. They must be the farmers.

"I am so tired of seeing one pine tree after another," the older woman mutters. "I miss the golden fields of wheat of home."

It seems she and I have common ground. Especially when I substitute the wheat field for the sparkling water of the Fyoon Ocean. "I'm tired of these trees, too. I am Sybil Lilla."

The older woman glances up in surprise, then bows her head. "May your harvest be plenty and with no drought in sight. I am Elder Fran and can't say I am in the mood to participate in these cooperation-building exercises Devotee Zorion's cooked up. I'd prefer his pies instead. My joints ache painfully in this cold weather."

The other farmers all agree.

A young woman with blond hair reaches for Elder Fran's arm, helping the older woman step over a large puddle.

Elder Fran's face creases with a pleased grin. "This is my granddaughter Young Luiza."

Young Luiza waves in greeting and I smile at her.

Devotee Zorion's voice carries to us from the front of the crowd. "We are taking a few minutes' break."

Elder Fran stops and puts her hands on her waist, groaning in pain as she stretches. "Thank the Archgoddess of the Eternal Light and Order."

One of the men places a pillow over a tree trunk, and Elder Fran lowers her thin body over it. "Young Luiza, where are our manners? Please get some tea for our guest."

The granddaughter hurries away.

I lean a hip on the tree next to Elder Fran. "How are you holding up? What the praelor did was unacceptable."

Elder Fran looks away with tears glistening in her eyes. "Many lost family members or friends who worked hard on that space station. May the Lume accept their souls. We are holding up as expected." She wipes the corners of her eyes.

"My sympathies to all of you."

Young Luiza reappears, holding out two metal cups with steam rising from them.

I accept the steaming cup. "How long have you been part of the Teryn Praelium?"

Elder Fran takes a sip of her tea. "We were occupied after the miners' world fell. About fifty galactic years ago. We knew that the Teryns were coming but had no means to stop such a formidable armada. We live on moons around other planets and rent outposts or space stations from the Coal Miners Coalition or the Industrial Conglomerate, who do not care for agriculture. But it is something we've loved doing, generation after generation, cultivating plant life and harvesting what we sow. It's what makes us who we are—an amicable partnership of millions of farmers united in one goal, helping each other to achieve a successful harvest. We've survived thousands of years like this . . ."

"Until the Teryns came," I finish Elder Fran's sentence. I can't help but wonder whether the Teryn Praelium did more harm than good for the Seven Galaxies with their aggressive approach to handling corruption and forcing others to participate by conquering them.

Elder Fran glances away. "Ever since the Teryns interfered with how we run our partnership, other worlds suffer as a consequence."

"How so?"

"We're responsible for supplying other worlds with grains. But the Teryns demand a tenfold increase of output—one we struggle to meet. Our own people are on the verge of starvation as we take the food from our young'uns to fill our quotas. Of course, the merchants are flourishing under the Teryns, finding interesting ways to meet their quotas, but we cannot fault them for their good fortune. Nor do we want to replicate their methods."

I cannot imagine the hardship they must be going through. Lost in thought, I raise my cup, inhaling the flowery scents of the tea. I blow on the purple liquid and am about to sip from it when Moira says, *Do not drink it, dear. I don't like the smell of this tea.*

I lower the cup so quickly that some liquid sloshes to the ground.

Elder Fran gestures toward me. "Aren't you going to drink your tea?"

"Uh, maybe later."

"You should try it, Sybil Lilla. This tea is our specialty. It's relaxing and great against insomnia, among other ailments. Unfortunately, we are not allowed to export it, due to the restrictions the Teryn consuasors force on us, but we still enjoy its exquisite taste."

Is this tea poisoned? I ask Moira as I smile back politely at Elder Fran.

Let me smell it again, dear.

Lifting the mug to my nose, I inhale. "It does smell wonderful."

I don't detect any poison, dear, but there is something wrong with it. The scent of it makes me feel a bit woozy.

Elder Fran locks her gaze on a group of Teryn warriors far ahead of us. "I just wish someone could stand up to the Teryns. They are nothing but bullies who think they can get away with their actions. I don't know how long we can keep going like this."

Devotee Zorion claps his hands at the front. "It's time to continue our trek. Please follow me."

CHAPTER 36

With a courteous bow, I leave the Farmers Partnership and head back to my friends.

I would not be surprised if the farmers had a hand in the kidnapping, dear.

They may have been through a lot, but they don't look like the type who would resort to violence as revenge.

Moira scratches her furry cheek. *Anger can make even the most peaceful person do hasty and illogical acts.*

I push a branch out of my face and go around a thorn-covered thicket. *I just don't see the frail Elder Fran participating in such a heinous crime.*

You are forgetting what happened to your healer friend, dear.

I exhale, and my breath leaves a puff of air in front of me. I did not forget what happened to Glenna. How she went from being a peacemaker to almost poisoning Ragnald due to her prejudice against the mages. Granted, her family's history, a true tragedy, had more than given her the reason to try to act vengefully. Luckily, Ragnald survived without a scratch.

Stopping in front of a wide trench, I look both ways, unsure of which direction to take. On the right, I recognize a tree covered in red-striped mushrooms. I decide to head toward it.

Glenna is different. It's true that she can be unpredictable, but her personality leans toward empathy and helping others. That incident was a fluke, not a regular occurrence.

The truth is, dear, we don't know what any one of us thinks or how they truly feel until it's too late.

I stop by the mushroom-covered tree and catch my breath.

That is true, I say, and look around. Where are the others? There is no sign of my friends—or anyone else, for that matter.

I bite my lower lip. Have I gone back too far?

A loud crack sounds.

Watch out! Moira shouts.

CHAPTER 37

Dropping my bag, I whirl around to see a large tree falling toward me.

Before I can move, a black blur tackles me.

Callum cradles me to him. One hand protects the back of my head, pressing my face into the hard muscles of his chest. His other hand brackets my back as we land on the ground, with him curling protectively around me.

A tremendous crash sounds near us. Clouds of dust and dirt shower over us.

Callum lifts his head, scanning our surroundings. He pushes up onto his elbows. "It's clear."

With my heart beating in my throat, I look to my right. A twenty-foot-tall tree lies broken on the ground not a few feet away. Jagged splinters stick out of the gnarled brown trunk.

If Callum had not appeared when he did, I would be the one lying under that tree. Crushed.

He did come at the best possible time, dear.

Saving both our hides. No pun intended.

I look up into his clear, blue eyes. "Where did you come from?"

A smile lifts the corner of Callum's lips. "Is that how you show gratitude for me saving you?"

I push at his muscular shoulder. I can't even budge him an inch. "How do I know it wasn't you who arranged this whole scene of saving me?"

Callum moves one of his arms to encircle my head, his fingers playing in my hair. "Why would I do that?"

"So you can be my hero?"

Callum snorts. "I don't need such petty plans. I know I am your hero."

Unable to resist, I touch his face. "Are you now?"

He turns his head to the side and presses his lips on my wrist, making my skin tingle. "All I need now is a token of your gratitude."

Smiling, I pretend to think about that. "I am but a poor ex-princess. I can offer nothing to you, uh, hero sir."

Desire darkens his blue gaze as Callum says, "You're smart. I'm sure you'll come up with something." Then he lowers his head and kisses my lips. All humor drains from his expression as passion takes over. His kiss turns fierce and possessive. He holds me to him as if he can't get enough of me.

Our breath becomes one. I melt into his kiss, stealing his breath, happy to be alive. Happy to be in his arms. I've missed him so much.

When he lifts his head, both of us pant for air, breathless. He reaches for the front of my cloak.

"We can see you," Belthair's voice interrupt us.

CHAPTER 38

Callum curses. "One of these days . . ."

One of these days, we'll have privacy. Just the two of us. Until then, we'll just have to wait.

I'm sure it won't be for long, dear.

Callum jumps to his feet and helps me up. Embarrassment smarts my cheeks as we face my friends.

Arrov jabs his thumb over his shoulder in the direction of the fallen tree. "What happened here?"

Callum studies the scene, then turns to me. "I'd like to know the same."

I shrug. "Don't ask me. All I heard was a loud crack, then I'm lying on the ground with you, uh, on top of me."

Isa bats her eyelashes. "How romantic." Bella giggles.

Arrov crosses his arms. "The question is whether that tree fell on its own or someone helped it along."

Glenna puts a cold hand on my face. "Are you okay, sweetie? You have cuts on your cheek."

Now that she's pointed it out, I do feel the sting of a few minor cuts. "I'm fine." Glenna hands me a tissue and I wipe off the blood. Then, using a bit of Fla'mma magic, I burn the tissue to ashes. There is no need to leave any trash behind.

Ragnald studies the tree, his hands clasped behind his back. "I can highlight the area of splinters with A'nima magic, looking for anything that does not belong on the tree. That would give us a better understanding of what happened, although A'nima is not an element with which I have much of an affinity."

I have no such problem with A'nima. "Let *me* try it."

Ragnald nods with an impressed expression. "It seems your magic lesson with the Pada monk pays off. I'm glad to see that you are leaning on your magic more. Please, go ahead." The mage takes a pair of yellow glasses from his pocket and steps back to make room for me.

Not sure how to respond to his compliment, I focus on my task. With a deep inhale, I reach for my bright magical orb. Hot-and-cold-and-hot-again sensation overcomes my body as I select a wide ribbon of straw-yellow A'nima and shape it into a net. Then I guide it over the tree until the net encloses the area with the jagged splinters.

For a second, nothing happens.

Ragnald adjusts his glasses on his straight nose. "Maybe you didn't use enough A'nima magic."

Before I can reply, a small red spot appears at the base of the trunk, standing out among the straw-colored magic.

CHAPTER 39

I frown at the red area that seems to be concentrated in one spot, near the splinters. "Does this mean something hit the tree? Like a laser gun shot?" I disengage the A'nima magic, making the elemental thread retreat into my magical orb.

Ragnald pockets his yellow glasses. "I believe this proves without a doubt that the tree did not fall down on its own."

I can't take my eyes off the splintered tree. Just moments ago, I'd been oblivious of any danger as I'd left the farmers group.

Don't let this shake you, dear. You are getting closer to answers that someone is desperate keep you from finding. This is a good sign.

My body shivers as the adrenaline dissipates. *I am having a hard time considering this attack as good sign.*

Callum clasps my hand. "I won't let anything or anyone hurt you."

I manage a smile for him.

Devotee Zorion's voice carries to us. "We must stay together as a group. Do try to keep up."

He must use magic to see so far back.

With a groan, we gather our belongings and resume the never-ending hike through the evergreen forest.

Glenna kicks a small rock out of my way. "Who could have done this attack on Lilla?"

Arrov bumps his head into a tree branch and mutters a curse under his breath. "More importantly, *why* did they attack her?"

Belthair glances at me as he holds three branches to the side, letting us women pass by him. "It's clear that the Marauders can't stand the Teryns. That also includes you, Lilla."

"The Industrial faction is not a fan of the Teryn Praelium either," Isa says, and Bella nods as they lower their heads to avoid dry, low-hanging vines that are full of creeping insects.

Arrov swipes pine needles off his midnight-blue hair. "Same with the Merchants and Free Traders, though they also consider all the other factions a problem and competition."Ragnald holds his elbow out to Glenna to help her step over a small stream. "The coal miners were quite open about their dislike of the Teryns," she adds as she accepts help from the mage. "They had a lot of complaints about the quota they have to fill."

Callum rubs his thumb over the back of my hand, and I smile up at him. "I noticed the same with the farmers faction, though they seemed peaceful in temperament."

"Even after what the praelor did to them?" Arrov asks incredulously.

I nod as we climb up a small hill. "They were understandably sad, but I did not get any vengeful vibe from them."

Moira clears her throat pointedly.

I sigh and say, "Moira wants you to know that she does not buy into their peacefulness."

Belthair shoves a hand into his short dark hair. "All of the Tier One factions seem to dislike the Teryns. We all knew that going into this."

"But now they know we're asking questions," Callum says. "Sooner or later, someone will make a misstep."

I turn to him. "Are you done with the search?"

He shakes his head. "I missed you and asked Rhona to finish up without me. She'll join us once she is done."

I squeeze his hand. "I'm glad you came. Thank you for saving me."

Callum lifts my hand to his lips. "Always, my love and my life."

A rushing noise becomes louder as we reach the gathering guests and stop.

CHAPTER 40

In front of us, a majestic waterfall rumbles into a small lake. Mist blankets the large meadow of short grass and dirt patches. All around, flat rocks jut out from the ground, reminding me of another field, where I'd met Guardian God Patra'ch.

"I can't wait to find out what more is in store," a man from the Industrial faction says without any eagerness as he eyes the waterfall. His dark gray suit has patches of dirt and grass stains on the knees and elbows, while his shiny shoes are plastered with mud. The other men in his group snicker. Their lack of interest is in stark contrast to Devotee Zorion's high level of energy, but it's not just this faction that looks like it wants to be anywhere but here. All the other guests wear exhausted or annoyed expressions of varying degrees.

The Teryn warriors look indifferent, keeping their distance from the other factions and from the Teryn consuasors. They don't even pretend to make the most out of this exercise.

Callum crosses his arms. "I don't like this."

I glance at him. "Do you mean the waterfall or the crowd?"

"Both."

"Don't tell me you can't swim," I joke. I learned to swim before I could even walk.

Dear, you've probably forgotten, but the new Teryns' planet has been desolated by DLD, and their lake is unsafe for swimming.

I grimace. *I did forget.*

I turn to Callum to apologize, but Devotee Zorion's announcement interrupts me. "Welcome to the next cooperation-building exercise—trust fall over a waterfall. It's going to be a wondrous experience."

All the guests groan, including us.

With a frown, I study the thirty-foot-wide, hundred-foot-tall waterfall. "Is this even safe to do?"

Devotee Zimon appears, but when Callum glares at him, the lanky monk stops a few feet from me. "It is more than safe, Sybil Lilla. Two disciples will use their A'ris magic to assist the fall of a volunteer guest—who will be at the top of the waterfall—based on instructions of the other guest, who will stay by the lake. They will guide the volunteer guest safely down from the height of the waterfall all the way to the grass. The point of this exercise is to make each faction work together."

He claps his hands in barely contained exhilaration. "Devotee Zorion is brilliant, coming up with such a delightful practice. It will feel like flying, then setting down safe and sound. I can't wait to see how this exercise will strengthen the relationships among the guests."

"I hate it," Callum growls.

Arrov, Ragnald, and Belthair agree.

Glenna smiles encouragingly. "I'm sure it will be over quickly." When she studies the waterfall, her smile disappears.

Isa's eyes shine bright. "Sounds like fun." Bella adds, "I want to go first."

"I don't like those boulders in the lake," I say, and point to the left—to a group of sharp, serrated rocks sticking out of the churning water at the base of the waterfall.

Devotee Zimon eyes them with an oblivious look on his face. "Those shouldn't be a problem. The goal here is to avoid the lake. I can assure you; no swimming or other preparation is needed. We would not recommend swimming anyway. The lake is full of giant eels that attack anything that moves."

I am not sure I like this, either, dear.

"How does this exercise facilitate cooperation," I ask, "if the disciples have to do all the maneuvering with their magic?"

Devotee Zimon clasps his hands in front of him. "It facilitates cooperation because the two disciples will be blindfolded and will have to follow the guest's instruction of when to engage their magic and how to guide the other guest down. It's going to be marvelous!"

Devotee Zorion looks around at the assembled group. "Who wants to try it?"

Silence falls over the crowd. Only the reverberating sound of water crushing down into the lake can be heard.

Devotee Zorion walks into the crowd with a jovial expression. "Don't be shy. We're all going to participate sooner or later." He looks at each guest, then his gaze lands on me and adds, "Sybil Lilla, will you do us the honor of going first?"

CHAPTER 41

All eyes turn to me as I stand rooted to the spot, staring open-mouthed at Devotee Zorion.

I point at my chest. "Me?"

Devotee Zorion nods with a patient smile. "Is there another Sybil Lilla here?"

The guests laugh.

"She is too scared to do it," the dowager queen's voice from the Marauders Syndicate booms.

Of course I'm scared but I'd rather die than let the queen know that. I step forward, faking courage. "I'm not scared. I'll do it."

Callum grabs my hand. "Are you sure? There is no shame in—"

Yes, there is but I have no other choice in the matter. I squeeze his hand before letting it go. "I'm sure." There is no way I'll show any weakness to this crowd. They are worse than the Uhnan courtiers, who were nothing but scavengers, ready to strike when you were at your most vulnerable.

You are a lot braver than you think, dear.

That may not add up to much, I'm afraid.

My friends watch with worry as I make my way to Devotee Zorion. "What's next?"

The monk gestures with his hand toward the guests. "Now you'll need a team."

Closing my eyes, I hope he won't pick *her*.

"Marauders faction. Dowager Queen Sheela of the Two Guns and a Dagger House, please follow the disciple to the lake."

Buckets of fishguts! I open my eyes with a silent groan. The Marauder Queen is the last person I want to do any sort of trust exercise with.

Queen Sheela laughs and shoves Ivy to the side, making her daughter stumble in her high-heeled boots. Ivy finds her footing and pulls down her short faux-fur jacket over her black minidress.

When our gaze connects, Ivy looks away and pretends to laugh with the other Marauders. "She'll take the coward's way, just you wait," she says with a slanted look toward me. The others laugh even more loudly at her words.

Devotee Zorion steps back politely. "After you."

The crowd parts in front of us as we make our way through the slippery mud that becomes more prevalent the closer we get to the cascading water.

Devotee Zorion and Devotee Zimon engage their T'erra magic, forming thick, transparent dark brown ribbons into stairs.

After they anchor their magic to the ground, the three of us climb the makeshift stairs.

Reaching the top, Devotee Zorion builds a magical, square platform about fifteen feet wide, one that bridges the top of the waterfall, all the way to the edge of the surging water.

Devotee Zorion waves at the hovering platform. "All you have to do is stand at the edge with your back to the crowd. When you're ready to jump, just yell 'Go!' Your team will catch you and take care of the rest."

I put a foot onto the platform. It sways a bit to the side, like a boat.

Buckets and buckets of fishguts!

Stifling a yelp, I jump onto it, holding my arms out for balance. Sweat breaks out on my forehead and on my hands. My vision blurs for a second.

The last thing we need, dear, is for you to develop a fear of heights.

Too late.

With muscles trembling, I put my hands on my knees to look over the edge of the rushing water. In an instant, the spraying mist soaks my clothing and hair.

Below, all the guests and my friends gather around the lake, gazing up at me. The dowager queen and a petite disciple stand close to the rocky outcrop, with the queen smirking up at me.

There is no point prolonging this ordeal any longer than necessary, dear. Let's just get it over with.

Easier said . . .

I make eye contact with the queen, and she nods with a smirk.

"Here we go," I mutter and turn my back to the roaring waterfall that makes the platform vibrate.

"Go!" I scream and jump backward with arms spread, letting my body fall.

CHAPTER 42

For a millisecond, I soar weightless in the air. The wind brackets my body, plastering my cloak to me, and blowing my hair into my face. It feels as if I am flying.

Then reality kicks in. I plummet, with a cry stuck in my throat.

My surroundings blur.

A furious bellow sounds.

Steel-like arms slam into me as Callum catches me out of the air. "I've got you." He locks his arms around me.

All I have time is to thread my arm around his neck, then we plunge into the lake, sinking fast.

Piercing cold hits like a crashing tide, squeezing my lungs and robbing me of air.

Callum holds me tightly as we submerge under the water. Thin lines of air bubbles escape from his nose and mouth. He struggles to get back to the surface but to no avail—his heavy uniform and black boots weren't meant for swimming.

I try to make him release me, so I can help, but he won't let go of me.

The surface of the water becomes a one-way mirror, impossibly out of our reach, getting farther and farther away.

Something moves below us in the murky and churning water. The impossibly long, slimy body of a giant black eel—with a triangular head full of sharp teeth—wraps itself around Callum's right leg. It proceeds to drag us down.

Callum's body jolts. More air bubbles escape his mouth as he grimaces in surprise. He grabs a dagger from a leather holster at his waist. He stabs at the eel.

Another eel wraps its thick body over his right arm. It twists until Callum's fingers open, dropping his dagger.

Then another one swims at us, wrapping its thick body over my legs, constricting painfully until my bones feel like they will break from the unbearable pressure. My lungs struggle as the pressure builds. I will run out of air soon.

Everywhere I look, giant eels rush toward us from the bottomless depths of the lake.

Suddenly, iridescent wings twenty feet long burst behind Callum. A humongous head with tiny antlers and long whiskers appears. Large green eyes glint with mischief and intelligence, taking in the scene.

Magical green vines whip around us and cut into the eels. Screeching, they release us and swim away in a hurry.

Then we shoot up from the water, trailing huge bubbles, and land on the grass near the lake.

The szyrilla retracts its wings and blinks out of view before I can say a word.

Callum leans to the side, throwing up water. Coughing, I gulp in air. Shivers rack my body as I pat his back.

Glenna elbows the noisy crowd to the side and drops to her knees next to us. "Are you okay?"

With chattering teeth, I nod.

The guests push too close, blocking us in. My eyes widen as my claustrophobia rises to the surface.

"Give them some space!" Glenna yells.

Arrov and Belthair shove the crowd back with the help of Isa and Bella until the muttering guests retreat, leaving behind trampled mud.

Callum wipes his mouth, his lips blue-tinted, his eyes livid. "Where is that idiot monk? I'll kill him for this."

Ragnald approaches us. His hands form two Fla'mma threads of lattice network, roughly in the shape of a blanket, which he deposits over Callum and me. Our clothes dry in a matter of seconds. "What happened?"

Someone tried to kill us, that's what happened, Moira says, sputtering.

Feeling warm and dry, I search for the dowager queen. I find her not far from me, on my left, laughing so hard that tears run down her round face.

A muscle jumps in my jawline. "She failed to catch me." I know she'd seen me when I'd looked at her right before the fall. She'd even acknowledged it with a nod. Yet she chose not to do her part. The question is, why? Was this her attempt at revenge on me for taking Callum from Ivy? Or was this her attempt to kill me because I'm trying to find Caderyn?

Or was this her attempt to finish what she started with the tree, dear? But why do it in such a public way?

In any case, it's clear she wants me dead.

"How did you survive that fall?" Glenna asks, sitting back on her heels. "Both of you were under the water for such a long time. Arrov was getting ready to jump in after you." She gestures toward him. He holds his shirt in his hands as he stands barefoot in the mud.

Frowning I wonder why she asks. "Didn't you see the, uh, huge magical creature with iridescent wings?"

Callum and the others look at me in surprise. "No," the twins say in unison. "What creature?"

"Never mind." I know I hadn't imagined her. She was the same szyrilla I'd met when I'd talked to Guardian God Patra'ch, though she'd been much smaller then and had no wings.

Glenna checks my forehead with her A'ris magic. "I think you have a fever."

Devotee Zimon strides to our group. "My apologies, Sybil Lilla. I don't understand what went wrong."

Callum jumps to his feet. "You trusted a Marauder to do the right thing, that's what went wrong."

"What are you going to do with the Marauder queen?" I ask and stand up.

Devotee Zimon cringes. "There is nothing we can do. According to Queen Sheela's recollection of the events, she did not hear your signal and thus could not react in time. I'm afraid it was an unfortunate accident."

CHAPTER 43

We sit on pillows placed around a welcoming fire trying to get warm as the sun slowly makes its way toward the treetops.

The trust fall exercise continued for a few more hours after my "accident" without any further incident. Lunch was served as we walked away from the waterfall, meat pies and other savory pastries with hot spiced wine. We hiked through the forest until early afternoon, then made camp in a large pasture at the foot of a small mountain.

I cross my legs over the red pillow and sip a mugful of water with minced fruits, then I bite into a crispy cocoa-flavored biscuit just as Rhona joins us.

"Is everyone comfortable?" Devotee Zorion asks as he walks around the circle with Devotee Zimon in tow.

Many guests nod or mutter a response. The Teryn warriors just glare at the two monks while sitting in one cluster at the far right. They couldn't be more defiant if they tried. I'm not sure why they even came along.

Devotee Zorion smiles as he stops in the center of the gathered assembly, near the fire. "I'd like to invite you to an icebreaker exercise—"

"You mean a fire-warming exercise?" Arrov asks, interrupting the Pada monk.

"We call it a 'coal-off exercise,'" a miner with dark brown beard says. "Get it? Like 'cool off.'"

"It's a free-for-all," the dowager queen says.

Belthair's forehead creases in a frown. "That's just robbing."

Devotee Zorion claps his hands and assumes a forced smile. "Whatever it is called, the point is to engage in conversation. So please chat and enjoy your snacks."

The guests look at each other. No one is willing to go first.

Devotee Zimon folds his robe under his knees as he kneels in one fluid motion. "We should all introduce ourselves again."

The factions mutter in disagreement.

Devotee Zimon raises a hand. "We could make it interesting by adding one strength, one weakness, one thing that you are proud of, and something nice about the, uh, Teryns, our patrons."

That's one way to put it, dear. Is that what we call tyranny these days? "Patrons"?

"My name is Elder Fran. As many of you know, I am the lead farmer in the Farmers Partnership. Our strength is cultivating plants in the harshest environments; our weakness would be that we are too kind."

Cheers sound from the nine other farmers wearing homespun and pastel-colored clothing. Many of them raise their mugs full of tea, while a few, such as Young Luiza, lean on other farmers and openly sleep.

"We are proud of our peaceful nature, and, uh, lastly, the Teryns are . . ." Elder Fran pauses as she searches for words before adding, "They are, um, . . . decisive."

The Teryn warriors on the far left hit their fists to their chest, their way of clapping, while the Teryn consuasors, sitting among the factions, pretend to ignore the warriors' antics.

How Elder Fran stays so civil after what Caderyn did is beyond me.

She is a wise leader, dear. She might be biding her time for a strike.

I still don't believe that Elder Fran would do such a thing.

I didn't believe Daryhna would do what she did, but here we are, dear.

I have no response to that. I know how much Daryhna's betrayal hurt Moira. One that Moira did not see coming. One that almost lead to a coup.

"I would have chosen a different word," Belthair mutters, "to describe the Teryns if I were the farmers." He glances at Rhona. "No offense, but feel free to take some."

Rhona snorts. "That's what Ivy always says."

Isa and Bella giggle.

"Besides," Rhona goes on, "I don't care what anyone thinks of us. The Teryn Praelium's control is ineluctable."

"What does that even mean?" Glenna asks Ragnald.

The mage replies, "Inescapable, I believe."

"Then why didn't she just say that?" Glenna grumbles.

Belthair crosses his top two arms. "Because Walking Dictionary likes to show off."

Rhona shakes her hand in a fist. "If you call me that one more time—"

"Enough!" Callum snaps just as Teague joins us, munching on a dried meat strip.

"We are the Free Traders," a portly man says. His white shirt, with food stains all over it, stretches to its limits over his bulging stomach. Dark strands of greasy hair cover the top of his balding head. His round, ruddy face with a double chin has a haughty look on it. Behind him, two hulking androids tower, covered in shiny gray plastic. "I am—"

A zap sounds, interrupting the large man.

An Industrial faction member puts away a small black device, just as a hulking android crashes to the ground.

CHAPTER 44

The Free Traders, all fourteen men, try to jump to their feet, but they cannot pull their legs under their bulging stomachs quickly enough. Their leader, the largest man, points at the Industrial faction. "Stop that!" he shouts. "It will damage it, and then I'll have to pay to repair it."

A man in a suit spreads his arms with an innocent smile. "Trader Pecker, it's just a harmless interfusion inhibitor. You know well that it will wear off in a short time."

Trader Pecker, with a purple face, stammers for a moment.

Isa's eyes glint with excitement as she says, "How splendid!" Bella bobs her head and adds, "Whatever they used was strong enough to take out a functioning android in an instant. We need to get our hands on that tech."

Glenna shoots a long-suffering look at the twins. "Tech this and tech that. That's all you two can talk about. There is more to life than technology and invention."

Isa retorts, "Says the woman who goes from obsessively tending to injured animals to anger outbursts." Bella nods curtly.

Glenna does a double take. "What does she mean by 'anger outbursts'?"

Ragnald waves it away with a flick of his wrist. "Don't worry about that. I took care of everything."

"Trader Pecker," Devotee Zimon says once the guests quiet down, "please continue."

The other Free Traders instruct the functioning android to pick up the fallen one and take it away.

Trader Pecker makes a *harrumph* sound. "You all know me, so I won't repeat my name. Our strength is our brains."

Many guests boo his words, but the trader ignores them.

"Our weakness is that we are too lenient."

The dowager queen guffaws. "I'd rather we never see your 'lenient' side." Many other factions snigger, too.

A delusional trader. What a stereotype, dear.

Trader Pecker glowers, his beady eyes practically disappearing under the drooping folds of his bushy eyebrows. "All I can say about the Teryns is that they don't know how to treat valuable partnerships."

Many guests concur, but the Teryn warriors don't even acknowledge the jab.

"My name is Miner Gregry," a man with black hair and pale skin says, showing off white teeth. Next to him sit nine dark-haired men and women, wearing similar gray shirts and pants. One of them removes a few knapsacks from a hovering platform packed high with bags and other belongings of all shapes. The bags tilt to the side, unbalanced, but the platform shifts shape to accommodate the missing weight in an instant, preventing them from falling off.

Isa gasps. "Those bags must weigh a ton." Bella places a hand on her sister's forearm as she adds, "I want to know how that platform changed shape so intuitively."

I poke my oversized bag. "We could have used something like that to carry ours."

Callum leans toward me. "I carried your bag without complaint."

"That platform is overrated," I mutter with heat climbing up my cheeks.

"Our strength would be our perseverance," Miner Gregry continues. "Our weakness would be that we tend to overwork ourselves."

The other miners nod their agreement.

"Last, we think that the, uh, Teryns are, uh, ruthlessly committed to their goal of fighting in this Era War."

That's why Laoise chose them, dear, to replace my people. The new Teryns are nothing if not committed to eradicating corruption.

The other guests grimace while the Teryn warriors cheer again; this time Rhona's voice joins the shouting. Callum and Teague wear blank expressions, staying silent. I touch Callum's hand. He threads his fingers with mine and lifts my hand, placing a kiss on the back of it.

"I am Factory Leader Ia'an from the Industrial Conglomerate," says a man with slicked- back hair. Eight similar-looking men smirk at the other guests. All their bags are laid out in a neat row next to them, like a wall that separates their faction from the Marauders. "Our strength is that we always deliver our quota. And we are very proud of the quality of our products."

The other guests jeer Factory Leader Ia'an, but he continues, "Our weakness is that we are maximalists."

The eight men yell in pride, managing to smirk even more.

"As to the Teryns, they are brutes, running the Teryn Praelium without any mercy."

The Teryn warriors shout their appreciation, along with Rhona.

"That sums it up pretty well," Arrov says and Teague nods.

"I am Dowager Queen Sheela of the House of Two Guns and a Dagger, from the Marauders Syndicate." Twelve men wearing leather outfits and six women in skimpy dresses, including Ivy, let out an ear-piercing whoop.

My gaze connects with Ivy's. She pushes her tongue out at me and shakes her fist to the sky with the others.

A reverberating boom sounds and a blue-gray blur flies above us in the sky, leaving behind a white streak.

I glance up. "What on Uhna was that?"

"That was our pride and one of the fastest ship in the Seven Galaxies," Queen Sheela says. "We are best at delivering goods on time."

"Space pirates," a guest yells, and many laugh outright.

"We have no weaknesses," the dowager queen continues, ignoring the laughter as she lifts her chin. The other Marauders cheer even louder.

Glenna rolls her eyes. "They are so humble."

She will keep trying to kill you, dear.

Oh, I have no doubt she'll try again. But she will *fail.*

"The Teryns better be careful with their senseless games," the queen says in a low voice, "or they might upset the wrong world."

Callum glares at her. "That sounded a lot like a threat."

The Marauder queen spreads her hands. "Just a bit of wisdom I like to dispense."

"I am Chief Merchant Kristofer," a young man with shaggy brown hair says. "From the Merchants Verde." Around him ten men and women gather, wearing expensive and fashionable clothing in vivid hues of blues and reds. Their four ears twitch as they listen to their leader. Their oval faces, with light green skin, wear cheerful expressions. Many have plates piled high with food, or trinkets in front of them, engaging in a game.

I don't smell anything on two plates, dear.

When a man points at a plate, the other deactivates a hologram to show it is, indeed, empty.

Isa claps her hands. "Oh, hologram tech." Bella smiles. "We adore holograms."

Chief Merchant Kristof flicks one of his ears. "I'd say our strength and pride is our ability to detect valuables. Our weakness would be that we like to play games too much."

"I bet," the dowager queen says with an obnoxious chuckle.

"We think that the, uh, Teryns are going to make a, um, difference in the Era War."

"Boot-lickers," the dowager queen says, loud enough to be heard over the Teryn warriors' boisterous racket.

Devotee Zimon gestures toward me. I open my mouth to introduce our group when Queen Sheela cuts in, "Don't bother with your introduction, silly girl. We all know who you are."

The Marauders hoot.

The dowager queen grins. "You have no strength other than hiding behind the Teryns. Your weakness is that you are too stupid to know when to get out of the way of others. You've never learned the consequences of what happens when you take something that's not yours. But I'll teach you."

CHAPTER 45

Red descends in my vision as the queen's words echo in my mind. Anger chills my skin. Hot-and-cold-and-hot-again feeling blankets my body. My skin glows as thick ribbons of Lume rise from the pulsing and bright white orb, ready to be used.

Callum places a hand on my arm. "Don't do it. You'll only give her an excuse for violence."

The Lume magic thread wraps around my hands, taking up the shape of vines with sharp thorns. Fury drives my magic, the silver tattoo on my back amplifying it. The temptation to release the magic vines is nearly impossible to fight.

I glare at the dowager queen. I am done with being on Pada. I am done with the crimes. And I am done with the Marauders and their games. The queen tried to kill me twice, but now she'll pay the price.

The magical vines thicken, the thorns growing longer on them. It would be so easy to release the vines. To make the Marauders understand that I did not take anything from them. Callum and I fell in love. Not for politics or for alliances. All we need is time to get married.

The wind picks up, blowing the hair around my face as more Lume vines flow to my arms, branching out in front of me, questing. Dirt from the ground lifts into the charged air, hovering in front of everyone like a curtain made of rocks. The flames of the Fla'mma-infused campfire brighten to a blinding degree. The clouds speed up, and birds burst to the sky, escaping.

The faction guest stare at me with various degrees of fear and shock.

Devotee Zorion waves a hand in front of his face. "There is no need for such a dangerous magical display, Sybil Lilla. Please put your magic away."

Callum holds my arms with both of his hands. "Wait for the right time."

The dowager queen will win if you engage her now, dear. You are playing right into her hands.

Glenna grins and her eyes glint with a wild light. "I'm right there with you. Let's show the queen who's a coward!"

Ragnald places his yellow glasses on his nose, then winces when he sees the Lume vines floating around me. "What Glenna meant to say is that you should listen to Callum. Please, Lilla. I've never seen you release so much power before. I am not sure I can mitigate the damage." Then he turns his attention to Glenna and channels Fla'mma magic into her. She shivers as the feverish light drains from her gaze, then she leans on the mage for support, looking dazed.

"Don't do it, Lilla," Teague implores.

My friends all say encouraging words.

"You are better than this," Callum says, looking into my eyes as his grip tightens on my arms. "You are better than she is. Come back to me, my love."

Callum's words cut through the fog of wrath. He is right. I cannot fight the dowager queen. Not here and not now.

The red curtain recedes from my vision.

I blink at him. He smiles with relief and sits back. "There you are."

With a deep exhale, I retract my magic.

The dirt falls back to the ground and the brightness of the fire dims. The wind dispels, and the clouds drift lazily again. Even the birds return to the trees.

A collective sigh echoes from the guests and conversation picks up again.

"What a coward!" Ivy yells over the chatter. "The dowager queen was right. All the pathetic ex-princess can do is hide behind the Teryns."

The glow dissipates from my skin. "I, uh, I'm not sure what got into me." I wipe sweat off my face with shaking hands. Humiliation makes me look away.

Something bumps my side. I find the szyrilla curled up next to me, asleep. I thread my fingers into her fur, the vines around her tiny body silken to my touch. "I've never thanked you for saving us." Her whiskers twitch as her ears turn toward me.

When I glance up, Devotee Zorion shakes his head in disappointment, while Devotee Zimon gapes at me with a horrified look on his thin face.

I cringe. I cannot believe how carried away I've gotten. I should have known better. "I'm sorry for losing my temper." The two monks acknowledge my apology with a regal nod.

CHAPTER 46

Lying on my back, I stare up at the ceiling of the gray wool tent that balloons out from the cold wind whistling through the forest in the darkness of the late night. The szyrilla drums her leg in her sleep, then stretches her slender body out by my arm with a soft sigh.

After the disastrous icebreaking exercise the guests dispersed into their tents, eating dinner away from my contingent. Embarrassment presses down on me as the events of the magical incident replay in my mind.

I am not surprised, dear.

What do you mean? I listen for noise in the night forest, trying to discern any footsteps. The dowager queen is not the only one who can bait a trap. Before I went to sleep, I made sure everyone knew that I would be alone, hoping to trigger an attack from whoever is behind the crimes. By now all our questioning should have made the culprit nervous that we are onto them. All they have to do to silence me is to come to my tent, while my friends lie in wait, ready to assist at my signal.

Moira yawns. *You had a lot of things happen to you—the postponement of your wedding, Sachary's death, the attack on Sawney, Caderyn's kidnapping, and two attempts on your life. Any one of these would have been enough to drive a person mad, but put them all together . . .* She makes a booming sound.

That may be so, but it does not change the fact of what happened. You heard Ragnald. He didn't think he could lessen the magical damage. He had to do just that twice on Uhna.

A branch rustles against my tent and I hold my breath, listening.

Nothing happens.

I rub my eyes to rid them of sleepiness. It's getting harder to stay awake after the trying day; I feel exhausted both physically and mentally.

What if it's another attack from the Marauder queen, dear?

Shoving the blanket off my body, I turn to my side. The little szyrilla scoots closer, practically burrowing into me.

Then I'll have a chance to ask her some questions.

A loud crack sounds.

The front of my tent quivers.

CHAPTER 47

Sitting up, I clutch a sharp dagger with a jagged blade. Callum gave it to me right before we retired to our tents. I check for the szyrilla, but she is already gone.

Get ready, dear.

I pretend to snore loudly, which is the signal to my friends, and wait for the intruder to enter my tent.

Muttered curses sound. The front flap of the tent is shoved to the side.

Gathering my legs under me, I hold the dagger out.

More muffled cursing sounds.

Callum shoves the hooded intruder into the tent. Then he jumps on the invader and presses his forearm against the other man's throat.

"Get off of me," a hushed voice says, "you imbecile."

Callum snarls, "Identify yourself."

"For godssake. It's me, Ivy."

Callum lets her loose and then sits next to me.

Ivy pulls the hood from her blond head and glares at him. "You almost killed me," she says, massaging her throat.

Callum snorts. "Then you'd be dead. I don't do anything halfway."

"Are you okay, Lilla?" Arrov asks, bursting into the tent. The others follow. Rhona scoots in last and closes the front of the crowded tent. Meant for two people, it's now full with eleven of us.

Teague pulls out flower petals covered in sugar and points at Ivy. "I was expecting someone else—your mother to be precise."

"What are you doing here, Ivy?" Belthair asks, then winces when Isa and Bella kneel on his two lower hands on either side of him.

"You're crushing me," Glenna snaps at Ragnald when the mage tries to drape an arm over her shoulders.

"My apologies," the mage says, and scoots back a few inches.

The others shift, trying to get more comfortable, pressing close to me.

Sweat breaks out on my body.

Callum pulls me into his lap. "Back away from Lilla."

"Oh," Glenna says and moves closer to the tent wall with Ragnald. The others follow her example until the triangular tent looks like a round orb, with the tent walls stretched to their limit.

Ivy points to my right. "That's a quite a cute little creature. Where did it come from?"

I look down at the szyrilla, who has reappeared again. She gazes back innocently, munching on a stalk of grass. "You can see her?"

Teague shoves another sugary petal in his mouth. "We all can, love."

"What's her name?" Isa asks, and Bella adds, "She is adorable."

The women make crooning noises.

"I am not sure if I have the right to name her . . ." My voice trails off when a name appears in my mind, S'affi, and I know it's her chosen name. "Hello little S'affi, nice to meet you."

Callum clears his throat. "Ivy, who sent you and why?"

Ivy crosses her arms, elbowing both Arrov and Belthair on either side of her. "No one sent me. I am here to report to Lilla, since that is my job as a spy, no?"

Rhona puts a hand over her eyes. "You just ruined our trap."

Ivy looks at Rhona, then at me. "What trap?"

"Never mind that," I say and pet S'affi. One of her vines twirls around my finger before letting it go.

Ivy tugs on a long blond strand. "There is something afoot. All the factions were acting strange and—"

Rhona chuckles. "'Something is afoot'? That's your professional report?"

Ivy throws her hands up. "I don't know how else to say it, okay? I knew I should have poisoned you when I had the chance."

Rhona narrows her eyes at Ivy. "You spoiled little—"

"We don't have time to bicker," Callum says and Rhona quiets down, pursing her lips.

Ivy shrugs. "Poisoning is the Marauders' way. No offense, but feel free to take some."

Moira taps her chin. *If poisoning is the Marauders' way, then would they try to kill you with a tree?*

They could use other tactics just to cover their tracks, while making everyone believe they would not resort to those types of attacks. Great misdirection if you ask me.

"How are they acting strange?" I ask Ivy, trying to make sense of her jumbled report.

She shrugs her shoulders. "I don't know. The factions were either too polite toward each other, even to my, uh, the dowager queen. Or avoided eye contact altogether, going out of their way not to engage in conversation. Very atypical behavior—it's what we, Marauders, call 'suspicious.'"

Callum drapes an arm in front of me as he brackets my legs with his. "That proves nothing. After what the praelor did, they must be distressed and overly cautious. Probably trying to avoid any unwarranted attention."

Teague wipes the sugar granules from his mouth. "Did you hear anything about a planned attack on Lilla?"

Ivy shoves long blond tresses off her shoulder. "No, but that doesn't mean anything. The queen has her inner circle, and I am not invited since I 'broke her heart' by befriending Lilla."

Wind rustles the tent flaps, and we listen in quiet for a few seconds. No noise comes after that.

Belthair smiles encouragingly toward Ivy. "You did great, but now you better go, before anyone realizes you're here."

Ivy wiggles her fingers in good-bye. "I'll let you know if I hear anything else." She crawls out of the tent, followed by the others, except for Rhona.

I put my head back on Callum's chest with a sigh. Ivy's so-called report was useless. My trap failed. We are no better off than we were before these godsforsaken co-operation building exercises began.

Callum kisses the top of my head. "It wasn't helpful, true, but it also wasn't a waste either. The pressure will get to the culprit. Sooner or later, they will make a mistake."

"How did you know I was thinking about that?" I ask him.

"I know how you think, love."

I look at Rhona. "I didn't have a chance to ask you, how did your search of the rooms go?"

She grimaces. "Did not yield a single thing."

CHAPTER 48

DAY 3

The sun wasn't even up when we took down the tents and headed back to the monastery. The guests were grouchy as we ate breakfast along the way. After a few hours of hiking, we were back in the monastery. Most of the guests headed straight to their rooms. I had no such luck. Devotee Zorion decided that I needed another magic lesson.

Covering my mouth, I yawn until my jaw cracks. After Callum and Rhona had left my tent, I hadn't slept well. I kept waking up from dreams of falling to my death, or eels attacking, or the forest coming alive, trying to crush me.

"Sybil Lilla, please answer my question."

What question? I glance around the familiar, spacious room. Sunlight pours through the tall windows, bouncing off the shiny hardwood floor and the stone-tiled walls. They hold no answers for me.

"Uh, could you please repeat it?"

"I understand that it's early morning, but a seasoned magic user cannot have any excuse for being unprepared."

You are not unprepared, dear, just tired. Don't worry, I'll stay quiet and won't distract you during this lesson.

"I, uh, understand." At Devotee Zorion's impatient gesture, I begin the warm-up exercises with the arm circles.

"I asked, where are you with your investigation?"

Oh, that. "Still gathering information. One thing is for sure, none of the factions like the praelor."

"That is to be expected. Frankly, I thought that by providing you with the opportunity to search the monastery undisturbed, you'd be farther along. I should have assisted you, but I assumed you and your friends could handle it. Clearly, I was wrong."

There is no need to rub it in. I know we are running out of time. One more day left before the disguise device runs out of power.

"The last time we practiced magic, you mentioned something about the price of overusing it. What is it?"

Devotee Zorion looks at me as if I've grown lobster claws. "You should already know what that price is. Please don't waste my time with such a banal question."

A muscle jumps in my jawline. I bet he has no idea.

"Now that we've got the chitchat out of our way, it's time to focus on your magical training. One of the most important lessons is to understand the limitations of your magic. Relying on magic makes you vulnerable and can easily result in depleting it. Then what will you do, left standing without any means to defend yourself?"

That's a strange question. "Run away?"

Devotee Zorion waves a hand in dismissal. "Yes, that is an option, but what if you can't run away? Then what will you do? How will you fight back?"

"Uh, shape whatever magic I have left into a weapon?"

Devotee Zorion presses his lips into a thin line; even the rune-like tattoos on his right cheek look disappointed. "Now you are thinking like a Teryn warrior, reaching for brute force when there are other and better solutions. Your best strategy, when it comes to fighting with magic, is to disable your attacker right away, especially if they are magic users themselves. Every second you hesitate or overspend your magic is a chance for your opponent to kill you."

The Pada monk does have a point. "Disable how?"

Devotee Zorion steps with his right foot forward, leaning on it, while balancing on his back leg. "First, you assume the magic fighting position like me." He lifts his hands in front of him, with his right leading. His position reminds me of sparring.

I mimic his stance. "What's next?"

"It's easier to show. Please attack me with your magic, any way you want."

Thinking, I reach for my bright orb. Hot-and-cold-and-hot-again feeling makes my skin glow golden. I gather multiple elemental threads to me. The silver, magical tattoo on my back heats up, like the engine of a spaceship starting up, but I shut it down. I do not want to amplify my magic and risk overextending it.

"Sybil Lilla, you might want to stop telegraphing your moves."

Fine. I let go of all the threads except for the Fla'mma one. I shape it into a fireball and lob it at the monk's head.

He pivots out of the way like a dancer, weightless and fast, then moves his hands in a circular motion.

The hand-size Fla'mma ball falls apart inches from him.

I gape at the monk. "How did you do that?"

Devotee Zorion's dark brown eyes glint with pride. "This is decades of magical practice in the making. You are not advanced enough to achieve such techniques, but we all have to start somewhere. Even if it's at the beginning, as you're doing right now."

It's not like I have a choice to skip magic levels, no matter how I wish I could.

"Now I'm going to attack you, Sybil Lilla. I want you to try to intercept or dismantle my magic attack. Rely on your instinct and try not to overthink it."

"How? I have no idea what you did with my Fla'mma ball."

"Please try to focus instead of complaining." The mage pulls his right arm to his body, curving his hand inward, then flicks his wrist, as if sending a disc in my direction.

My eyes track dozens of A'ris threads flowing around his fingers that the monk forms into thin needles.

Time slows down as the magic needles hurtle toward me.

I step out of the way while throwing a thick Lume ribbon, like a whip, at the needles, trying to intercept them.

The Lume whip misses them. The needles graze my right arm in multiple places, cutting through my yellow tunic's sleeve, and leaving behind thin, bleeding lines.

"You are doing it wrong, Sybil Lilla. You must remember that the elements exist together in harmony. Counterattacking A'ris with Lume is the equivalent of throwing rocks at a snowball. It is not very effective, is it? You need to start thinking about how the elements complement each other, and finally how they can neutralize each other. For example, if I had thrown Acerbus at you, then using Lume would have been the right choice."

I nod as if what he said makes sense. Sweat breaks out on my palms, and I wipe them on my silver tunic. Beads of sweat roll down my back, gathering at the waistband of my black leggings. I am in way over my head.

I take up the magical fighting stance. "Let's try it again."

Zorion flicks his hand. More A'ris needles sail toward me.

What counteracts A'ris?

Hesitating, I miss my chance.

New bleeding lines appear, this time on my left arm.

I grind my teeth. "Again."

I try to block the A'ris needles with T'erra rocks and miss. Rips open at my collarbone and shallow wounds drip blood.

"Again."

Miss.

"Again."

Miss.

"Again!"

Miss. Miss.

Dozens of new cuts bleed on my sides as I bend down and put my hands on my knees, panting, with sweat dripping off me.

I wipe my face, impatient. Nothing I've tried has worked against the A'ris needles. What am I doing wrong?

I straighten and motion to Devotee Zorion to try again.

The monk raises an eyebrow. "I appreciate your eagerness, but we shouldn't overburden your magical muscles. It is important to reflect on each lesson. I recommend you do that, so you can gain enlightenment."

I need to know what he did. "But—"

"Don't let this discourage you. It takes at least eight decades of practice for disciples to achieve devotee status. Of course, I did it in six, but I was an exception. No one can hurry the process of learning. Not even you, the sybil to the Archgoddess of the Eternal Light and Order. In time, you'll gain a better comprehension, akin to what the disciples have."

Devotee Zorion bows his head and leaves.

Limping, I step through the doorway. I couldn't deflect, let alone intercept, a single A'ris needle.

CHAPTER 49

Outside I run into "Caderyn."

Callum grabs my arms and pulls me into a nook, out of sight. He scans the surroundings, then disengages the disguise. He slides his hand into my hair and leans his head down to kiss me. His lips, warm and inviting, move with impatience on mine. His arms close around me and he pulls me to him. "Gods, I've missed you."

Threading my arms around his neck, I pull his head down for one more kiss, drinking in his scent of sun, sand, and that masculine scent that's uniquely his. "How could you have missed me? The lesson took no more than an hour."

"Every second away from you is excruciatingly painful. How did your lesson go?"

I make a face.

"That well?" Callum asks, then notices the multitude of bleeding cuts on my body. "You're hurt. We must go to Glenna right away—"

"It's nothing," I insist and put my hands on his chest, tracing the shape of his pectoral muscles.

Callum groans, his eyes glinting with desire. "Don't tempt me."

Smiling up, I let my fingers slide down toward his hard stomach, unable to stop touching him. I've missed him too. "Are you telling me you can't resist me?"

Callum grasps my hands, lifting them above my head as he presses his body close to mine. "Truth is, I never could, my love."

His blue gaze studies my flushed face for a moment, drinking in my features as if he hasn't seen me for years.

Losing my patience, I rise on my tiptoes and steal a kiss from his lips.

He tilts his head to get better access, pressing his thigh between my legs. He transfers my hands into his right one, while his left hand skims down my arm, down my side. He grasps me by my waist.

Rushing footsteps sound from behind him, making me bump my head on the wall. "Ow."

Are you done, dear? I don't want to intrude.

Um, yes.

More hurrying footsteps pass us by.

Callum releases me and looks around. "What's wrong with everyone?"

Dozens of guests rush by.

I grab Callum's hand and pull him after me as I follow the crowd. "Only one way to find out."

CHAPTER 50

Callum and I reach a corridor crowded with Teryn warriors, consuasors, and with Tier One faction guests gathering near the edge of a courtyard, snickering.

Callum cuts a path through the crowd until we reach the low wall separating us from the stone-tiled courtyard.

Through the arches a mostly empty courtyard comes into view, with two weapons racks in its corner, and a tall, dark-haired man striding around, shadow sparring. His tanned face sports a well-kept goatee. His black sleeveless shirt and loose pants emphasize his athletic body's defined but not bulky muscles. He holds a long, thin-bladed sword, thrusting it in the air with purpose. Each time he "attacks" his invisible opponent, loud and mocking cheers sound from those gathered, especially from the Teryn warriors.

Rhona comes to a stop next to Callum. "What's going on?"

Callum gestures toward the courtyard. "Chief Consuasor Graeme decided to practice in public." He watches the other man lunging and pivoting around the courtyard with humor glinting in his blue eyes. The warriors around us laugh even more loudly. Rhona joins them.

"Keep up the good work, Brainiac," an older warrior says from behind us. "You're doing great against your imaginary enemies."

The others snigger. Rhona even slaps her thighs in mock hilarity.

Many consuasors eye the warriors with scorned expressions.

"Shouldn't we do something?" I whisper to Callum.

"This is nothing out of the ordinary," he says, but the humor drains from his expression.

"Graeme deserves our scorn," Rhona adds without bothering to lower her voice. "He is never going to be a warrior, no matter how much he 'practices.'"

"Especially since he uses a toothpick as a weapon," the older warrior comments behind Rhona.

The warriors around him guffaw.

One of the consuasors in a red and green silk shirt bristles on my left.

"General Crane, are you jealous?"

The consuasors burst into contemptuous laughter, while the warriors glare back with stern expressions.

General Crane pushes his way to the front until he stands in front of the consuasor, who has to look up. The older man sports wide shoulders that could double as battering rams in a pinch. "I have not failed my trial, as you did Staan, or Graeme here. There is nothing for me to be jealous of."

The other warriors snigger while Staan gulps but doesn't back down. "There is more to being a Teryn than your trial, Ground Rules, and honor."

General Crane crosses his arms, making his huge biceps stretch his military jacket to its limit. "Like what?"

Staan lifts his chin up even higher. "Like diplomacy, managing interstellar political connections, or—"

General Crane dismisses the other man's words with a flick of his wrist. "Yes, yes, yes. You Brainiacs do love your talks and words. Blah, blah, blah. But when it comes to maintaining order, you beg me to take care of it. I find that ironic."

"Me too," Rhona says. "Only the weak try to justify their failure. Explanations do not change the facts."

Many warriors agree, raising their fists to the sky.

The tension between the warriors and the consuasors rises to a new height. I glance at Callum, who frowns, watching the exchange.

Moira shakes her head. *They are a hairbreadth from a violent civil war with neither side willing to respect the other.*

"Well," Consuasor Staan sputters, "you won't have the protection of those stupid Ground Rules much longer. Chief Consuasor Graeme will—"

"We don't need the consuasors," Rhona cuts in, and the warriors cheer all around us. "We are the ones with honor."

"What are you doing?" I hiss at Rhona, but she ignores me.

"In fact," Rhona says, "we should erase the Senatus altogether."

An ear-piercing cacophony erupts from the warriors, while the consuasors cry out with indignation.

"What is the 'Senatus'?" I ask Callum.

"It's the governing body made of Brainiacs. They even have their own building, guards, and rules."

Consuasor Staan's face turns purple. "You are insane, General. Where is your honor now? Where is—"

General Crane grabs Consuasor Staan's shirt at the neckline, bunching it in his huge fist and lifting the consuasor off his feet.

CHAPTER 51

"What did you just say?" General Crane booms as he holds Consuasor Staan with one arm, dangling him in the air at shoulder length. The general's arm doesn't even shake from the effort. "We allow you babbling Brainiacs to think that you lead the Teryn Praelium through your precious Senatus, but everyone knows that without us, there is no empire."

A tall blond man approaches the general. "General Crane, there is no need for any hasty actions that you may come to regret." The man's silk shirt, with blue and purple colors, emphasizes his well-built shoulders. His immaculate blue trousers, tucked into shiny knee-high black boots, shows off well-defined quads. "The person you are holding is not a warrior, and there is no portable fight circle set up to sanction the ground for a fight per Ground Rule number three, addendum seventeen, subsection two hundred one. I would recommend you let Consuasor Staan go before he runs out of air. I would hate to see your case end up in front of the Senatus. There is only so much I can do to support the warriors, but even I cannot overlook murder."

General Crane mutters a curse under his breath and drops the blue-lipped man. The consuasor gasps for air as he backs away from the general.

"Consuasor Finigal," General Crane says to the blond man, "perfect timing as usual. You better talk sense to your fellow Brainiacs and educate them on the dangers of picking a fight with a warrior."

"I'll keep that in mind, General."

General Crane raises his chin and leaves the courtyard. The warriors follow him, clearing out.

Graeme's gaze tracks the general's withdrawal without missing a beat in his sparring routine. Then he twirls a few times, swinging his sword and slashing in front of him.

Finigal nods at Rhona. "I was expecting better from you, Colonel Rhona."

Rhona raises an eyebrow. "General Crane is my superior. Nothing I could have said would have made any difference."

Moira shakes her blond mane. *Rhona participated of her own accord.*

Finigal shakes his head. "That's not what I meant, and you know that. You should have become a consuasor after you failed your trial. Your talents are wasted among the warriors."

Rhona makes a disgusted noise. "Never going to happen."

Finigal lifts a hand up in a placating motion. "Don't worry, I won't poach you from the warriors. I would never hear the end of it from your father. By the way, where is the praelor? He was pacing around the monastery all morning; I could not stop him for even a second."

Callum and I exchange a look.

Rhona clears her throat. "You know how he is. Busy, busy."

Finigal studies her. "Is that so? Well, I hope the praelor will rein in his warriors before they start something with the consuasors they won't be able to finish. They tend to underestimate us until they regret it."

Rhona narrows her eyes at the consuasor, staring him down.

Finigal turns to me. "I am surprised you're still here, Sybil Lilla. I thought now that you recruited the Teryn armada, you would be off fighting corruption in a faraway world and not tiring yourself to death on Pada with politics. I heard you had an unfortunate accident during yesterday's cooperation-building exercise. Those Marauders cannot be trusted."

Maybe I should talk to the Marauders next, I say to Moira. *Shake that fishing net until something falls out.*

I like how you think, dear.

Callum growls, and it's a lethal sound that raises the hair on the back of my neck. Finigal takes an involuntary step back.

"As you can see, I am fine. Water under the ship."

Finigal glances at Callum, then at me. "The Era War has already started. Shouldn't you be in a hurry to win it?"

"The Archgoddess of the Eternal Light and Order is the one who tells me where to be. Until then, I do as I please."

"I meant no offense, Sybil Lilla," Consuasor Finigal says, "but if I were you, I would hurry." He tilts his head toward Chief Consuasor Graeme, who glowers at us. "There are many who do not wish you to control our formidable armada, not even for the Era War. The tide of support can turn in an instant."

CHAPTER 52

Consuasor Finigal bows his head and leaves the courtyard.

I whirl to Rhona. "What's gotten into you, riling up the warriors like you did?"

"I did no such thing. I simply voiced my opinion. Unfortunately, you don't understand what's happening on Teryn. A reckoning has been coming for quite some time now." She storms off with an indignant air.

Callum eyes the dispersing crowd. "This is a sensitive topic for my sister. She'll cool off in time. I better continue my 'pacing.' What are you going to do?"

I grimace. "It's time to visit the dowager queen." I'd rather eat a bucket of day-old squid than talk to the Marauder queen.

That may not be good for your health, dear.

Nor is the dowager queen.

Callum steals a kiss from me. "Please stay safe and assume the worst." Then he leaves.

With a sigh, I head toward the Marauders' living quarters.

I'm running out of time, I say to Moira.

Let's see what the dowager queen has to say.

A courtyard becomes visible through the arches, with large trees full of round, pinkish color fruits. Petite disciples harvest the fruits into woven baskets at their feet.

I watch them work, envying them. Their life is so different from mine. I had no idea what I signed up for when I agreed to be The Lady's sybil. I did not think that I'd be a tool and nothing else.

For a second, I let myself daydream, imagining a life where Callum and I live together, somewhere far from wars, gods, politics, and magic. Just us and our growing family.

I miss my family, Moira says, lost in thought. *I hope you'll get your wish, dear.*

One of the disciples near the low wall notices me and offers a few pieces of fruit from a woven basket.

I take two, and smile in thanks.

Biting into the soft flesh of a fruit, I marvel at the sweet taste and resume my trek. Then I hear a familiar neighing sound.

A grassy courtyard comes into view, with Fearghas in the middle of it, digging feverishly. The sunshine makes his black hide look glossy. Dirt and grass cling to his webbed claws. Near him are two buckets, one full of feed and the other with water.

I enter the courtyard. "Fearghas, look at the damage you've done."

The grass, much shorter than before, lays trampled around my horse, the hole looking more substantial than the last time I saw it.

I offer him the second piece of fruit.

Fearghas plucks the fruit from my hand. He chomps on it a few times, then gulps it down.

"This has gone on long enough. Let's—"

Fearghas rears up, clawing the air.

Not again. "Whoa there." He has not been this temperamental since he was a foal.

It seems the monks have placed food and water for him, dear. Surely that's a sign they don't mind him staying.

That might be so. "You are making a scene. I don't fathom your fascination with this spot."

He snaps his fangs at me in response and rears up again.

I back away so quickly that I stumble on my own feet and land on my bottom. S'affi appears in my lap out of nowhere. Her whiskers twitch as she takes in the scene. Then she disappears, only to reappear dangerously close to Fearghas's claws. She studies my black horse with intelligent green eyes.

"No, S'affi. He'll trample you."

Fearghas whinnies and rears up.

S'affi sits back on her haunches and twists her lustrous squirrel-like tail around her vine-covered body. She touches a paw to Fearghas's back leg.

From one instant to the next, Fearghas calms, nickering.

Getting to my feet, I comb my horse's mane with my fingers. "Maybe being on a different world is affecting you in an unexpected way. If you like this courtyard so much, then stay. Just promise me you'll behave."

CHAPTER 53

They will be fine, dear, Moira says as I leave S'affi and Fearghas behind.

I hope so. I take a corridor on my right.

I meant to ask you, dear, what is that prophecy I saw in your memory?

Oh, that. I am not sure. The Saage women from the Aak world mentioned something about a prophecy when I was supposed to marry their crown prince thanks to an arranged marriage contract. Thank the ocean that fell through. Anyway, they didn't go into details. All I know is that my stubbornness and willfulness matched something in their prophecy, and they considered it a sign. I can't say I'm convinced that it was about me.

Don't sell yourself short, dear. For one, you are the last of your kind and look nothing like a typical Lumenian.

Don't start on that. I've heard that from almost everyone I've met. All I know is that I look like my mom, with my dark violet hair and eyes.

I'm not trying to offend you, dear, but have you ever thought about why you and your mother are so different from the rest of the Lumenians?

Not really. I'll check my mom's journal when we get back to the Teryn world.

The journal is my one keepsake from her. I didn't want to bring it with me and risk something happening to it.

One more thing, dear. Have you ever wondered why The Lady puts all Her eggs in one basket?

You mean all the shrimps in one barrel?

Moira waves a hand. *Yes, that.*

I bite on my lower lip. *No. Why?*

If you think about it, it's only you against DLD and His vast army. Yet The Lady is sending you on all these missions, risking your life in the process.

I frown. *I don't think The Lady has anyone else to do these missions. I am the last Lumenian, so I must do them. She cannot get involved in these matters, remember?*

That might be so, dear, but the question remains, why is She risking you so carelessly? She does want to win the Era War, doesn't She?

I shrug, getting closer to the living quarters. *I don't know the answers to your questions. All I know is that without my Lume magic, She can't defeat the fully corrupted dark servants and dark fiends. Which means that She needs me.*

For now.

Then, in your opinion, what is Her true motivation?

To keep you busy? To let you die? Maybe both? We don't know what She is doing when She is not here. Her missions don't seem that urgent, now do they?

Before I can respond to Moira, a black blur materializes right next to me, and shoves me to the side just as something clatters to the ground by my feet.

CHAPTER 54

"What on Uhna?!" I yelp. My heart beats in my throat, trying to burst free.

A flickering "Caderyn" turns to me, glances around, then disengages the disguise to reveal Callum.

He points at the ground. "Someone doesn't want you to visit the dowager queen."

My gaze follows where he points.

A throwing knife with a dark gray substance smearing its tip lies on the stone tiles.

Callum and I scan our surroundings but detect no one.

Leaning forward, I study the knife. There is nothing special about it, no markings to differentiate it from any other throwing knife with a leather hilt.

I would not touch it, dear. It could be covered in poison.

Callum squats next to me. "It's not Teryn in origin. We prefer daggers that have jagged blades."

"Do you recognize the style as one of the preferred weapons of the Tier One faction?"

Callum tilts his head. "Both the Marauders and the Free Traders like using throwing knives, but only one of them would cover it with poison."

"The Marauders."

I reach for the knife to pick it up. Painful repulsion makes me snatch my hand back immediately.

Callum's blue gaze snaps to me. "What is it?"

"That's not poison. It's Acerbus."

Callum swears.

"We must take this knife and show it to Ragnald."

Callum nods. "I'll pick it up—"

The throwing knife implodes into a puff of black smoke, dissipating in the air without a trace before Callum's fingers can touch it.

CHAPTER 55

Callum mutters another curse under his breath as he gets to his feet. "There goes any evidence we had."

I straighten. "All the more reason for me to talk to the dowager queen."

"I'll come with you," Callum says, as we turn right, striding down the corridor. "She has gone too far this time."

"What I want to know is where she got her hands on the Acerbus. We have Acerbus-infused technology and Acerbus-poisoned weapons. DLD is busy spreading his corruption and gaining allies in unprecedented places."

How will I win against DLD's vast resources? He is always a few steps ahead of me, while I'm scrambling to keep up with Him.

Callum threads his fingers into mine. "He won't win this Era War."

There he goes again, reading my mind.

We take a left turn when something across the courtyard catches my eye.

Pulling at Callum's hand, I make him stop.

He scans our surroundings. "What is it?"

I point across the courtyard. "Do you see them?"

Three hooded feminine figures converse with a man who looks a lot like Chief Consuasor Graeme, although it is hard to tell as I only glimpse a colorful tunic underneath a hooded cloak.

Callum lifts an eyebrow. "I do. What about them?"

"Don't they look like the Teryn Wise Women? What are they doing on Pada?"

"I doubt they would be here. The Wise Women never leave their cave on Teryn."

This makes no sense. Why would the Wise Women be here, on Pada, talking to Chief Consuasor Graeme of all people?

Who knows what Laoise is up to, dear? She always had more plans than I could count.

I still remember Laoise's threat when Guardian God Patra'ch and I fought her off: *"I will come back and kill you, Sybil Lilla. Then my children will be the new Lumenians."*

"Something is off," I mutter. When I look back, the group is gone.

"We should keep going."

We take a few right turns, when we run into a crowd of Teryn warriors, consuasors, and Chief Consuasor Graeme, blocking our way.

CHAPTER 56

Callum and I stop.

"Make way," Callum says.

Chief Consuasor Graeme raises a hand. "I'm afraid I cannot do that."

I have a bad feeling about this, dear.

"Is that Brainiac bothering you, General Callum?" General Crane asks in a booming voice. Rhona, Teague, and my friends push through the crowd, to the front, by the burly general.

"More like blocking my way," Callum responds, "but I'm sure it's a misunderstanding."

Chief Consuasor Graeme lifts his chin. "General Callum a'ruun, I have received disturbing evidence of your insubordination. I am here to arrest you." He gestures and six Teryn men wearing uniforms like the warriors but in a dark blue color step forward. "Please don't resist the Senatus guards."

Angry shouts burst from the warriors.

"On what charge?" Rhona and I ask almost in unison.

"On the charge of treason," Graeme replies, "by hiding signs of corruption on an assigned world, and betraying the sacred Teryn truth to an outsider." Finished, he nods at the guards to take Callum.

"Belay that order," General Crane yells but the guards don't obey him. As two of them grab Callum's arms the general asks, "What proof do you have?"

Chief Consuasor Graeme bristles. "As I said, I have plenty of proof, General Crane, including two reports of these actions."

At the word *reports*, realization hits. This is what Callum talked about when he said, back on Uhna, that someone had sent the reports of the corruption to Caderyn behind his back.

"No!" I cry out.

Callum makes no move to resist the guards. "General Crane. I don't dispute the charges. They are true."

"This is the Brainiacs' way to retaliate," Rhona says with a snarl. "You must fight them, brother."

With my eyes, I beg Callum to escape.

Callum looks at Rhona, then at me, and shakes his head. "I won't do that."

Buckets of fishguts!

"It's time I paid the price for my actions. It's the honorable way."

My vision blurs and sobs lodge in my throat. My world is falling apart and there is nothing I can do to stop it.

Glenna and the twins hug me, cooing comforting words. Rhona, with her hands in fists, shakes from her rage as moisture wells in her eyes.

Callum looks at Chief Consuasor Graeme. "Lead the way."

Graeme nods and turns to the consuasors gathered around him. "It is also time that I invoke an emergency meeting at the Senatus about other matters. I expect to see all of you on Teryn shortly."

The other consuasors mutter in agreement and join their chief.

The warriors fall silent as the consuasors stride away, with Callum as their prisoner.

Arrov, Belthair, and Ragnald refuse to step out of the way of the group.

"Just say the word, Lilla," Belthair says, and the other two men nod. Ragnald lifts his hands, covered in Fla'mma magic.

"You can't fight this," Callum says to Belthair, but his eyes are on me.

I shake my head at Belthair, with tears rolling down my cheeks.

Callum wipes the tears off my face. "I love you, Lilla." Then he nods at the guards.

"I forgive you," Callum adds as he passes Teague.

CHAPTER 57

My gaze lands on a shocked Teague as Callum's words replay in my mind.

A horrible notion builds. "What did Callum mean when he said he for-gives you?"

Teague gulps. "It was me, who . . ." his voice trails off as he looks around at my friends, then at me, seemingly unable to finish his sentence. Rhona, who stands with the other warriors, doesn't even pay attention to us.

"It was you who sent those reports," I say.

"I had to," Teague insists. "Sachary and Sawney captured Steaphan and blackmailed me into—"

"That doesn't change the fact that you did it," I snap, feeling empty and cold inside. My mind cannot process what's just happened. Callum's arrest. Teague's betrayal. If this is a nightmare, it's the worst I've ever had. "You were always there for us. How could you do this to your best friend and brother?" I cover my mouth to keep from saying anything else I might later regret. Holding on takes all my effort. I cannot fall apart and give in to de-spair.

I'm sure . . . Callum will be . . . There, there, dear.

Teague opens his mouth, but Arrov shakes his head. "Just go."

Belthair crosses all six of his arms. "Or we'll make you."

With a shaky nod, Teague turns on his heels and leaves us.

"Should we tell Walking Dictionary?" Belthair asks, eying the oblivious Rhona.

I sigh. "There is no point. It won't change anything." All it would achieve is to make Rhona more upset.

Arrov gestures at Rhona to join us, but she shakes her head and raises a hand at the dispersing warriors. "Are we going to let the Brainiacs take my brother?"

General Crane turns back to Rhona. "You heard General Callum."

Rhona's eyes glint with anger. "Doesn't matter what my brother said."

I elbow the warriors to the side and step in front of her. "What are you doing?" She shoves me back by my shoulder in answer, then she strides to the low wall on our right and jumps on it.

Rhona faces the warriors. "We cannot let the Brainiacs do this to us. We've allowed them to play their political games. They think they know everything better than we do, but we warriors, are the ones who deal with their predicament when their flowery words fail. And this is how they show their gratitude?"

The warriors shout in anger.

General Crane folds his muscular arms over his chests as he watches Rhona.

Rhona shakes her fist to the sky. "We've tolerated their arrogance long enough. We've given them plenty of leeway, but the Brainiacs have abused it."

The crowd rumbles in agreement.

"Rhona, please stop this," I say to her.

She ignores me. "We've suffered the Brainiacs' subjugation long enough. They mock us every chance they get. They look down on us as if *we* are worthless. Honorless. Enough is enough. They cannot keep pushing us without consequences."

The warriors roar.

General Crane snaps his fingers, and everyone quiets down.

Rhona continues, "I say it's time to teach them who's in charge."

Chills break out on my body.

Crane lifts an arm and makes a circle in the air. "You heard the Colonel. We are leaving now." He marches away. The warriors, including Rhona, snap to attention and follow the general.

I pull at Rhona's arm when she nears me. "Don't fuel this civil war between the consuasors and warriors. This will tear the Teryn Praelium apart."

Rhona wrenches her arm out of my grasp. "It's time for a change. The Brainiacs want to erase our Ground Rules, our way of life, but we will erase them in turn. I will save my brother." Then she strides away.

Arrov grimaces. "This does not bode well. Now that 'Caderyn' cannot be here, it's only a matter of time before the factions realize that the praelor is missing and buck against their short leashes."

Moira had warned me of this very thing.

I shake my head as I say, "Then an intergalactic war will break out between the Tier One factions and the Teryn Praelium that's already neck deep in a civil war, paving the way for DLD to win the Era War." There will be no life left once DLD is done corrupting the whole Seven Galaxies into His dark servants and dark fiends.

"They will be back on Teryn in less than twenty hours," Isa says, and Bella adds, "That's all the time we have to prevent the Teryn Praelium from imploding."

That's not enough time. "How will we even do that?"

Belthair looks at me. "We must find the praelor. Only he can stop this."

CHAPTER 58

"We should separate and search the monastery one more time," Arrov says. "If they haven't moved Caderyn, they will try to do it now that the warriors and consuasors are leaving Pada."

"Unless they are planning to kill him," Belthair says.

"Don't be so pessimistic," Glenna says.

Belthair spreads his top two hands. "I'm just saying it is an option to consider."

Ragnald drums his fingers on his cheek. "If they wanted to kill the praelor, they would have done it by now."

"He raises a good point," I say. "In fact, they would have done it in a public way to get the most out of the horrid act and to create chaos."

That is a useful, albeit ruthless tactic, dear, but I concur.

Isa says, "Which means the praelor is still alive somewhere around here." Bella nods.

I look at my friends. "Please search the monastery and the spaceports again. I'll have a long-overdue conversation with the dowager queen."

Glenna puts a hand on my shoulder. "Watch your back, sweetie." Then my friends disperse.

With an exhale, I turn right and head toward the Marauders' living quarters for the third time.

The dowager queen won't want to talk to you, dear.

I huff. *That's her problem.*

Moira chuckles. *That's the spirit. Pun intended.*

I take the next turn in the corridor when I run into five hooded men blocking my way.

CHAPTER 59

I take a step forward, but the closest man raises a hand, halting me. "You cannot pass," he says. He must be the leader of these "fine" thugs.

This is getting old.

I study the five men. They all wear nondescript black cloaks with hoods that cover most of their faces, except for their shaved chins. They seem to be conscious about good hygiene. Four of them are more than six feet tall, with burly to thin body types. The last one, a head shorter than the others, stays behind. I don't detect any weapons on them.

I raise my hands. "Then I'll just go back to where I came from." I can always make my way around the monastery.

The hooded man takes a few steps closer. "We cannot let you do that either."

Is that so?

Before he can reach me, I kick out.

My kick lands in the middle of his chest, propelling him back into the others.

We need to transfigure.

Moira nods. The shimmering cloud begins to form over me when one of the men zaps me with a small black device.

The transfiguration dissipates with a reverberating whiplash that blinds me for a second.

Buckets of fishguts! This is the second time that something has prevented our transfiguration.

Swaying on my feet, I blink to clear my vision. Splitting pain bursts in my forehead. A tickle of warmth emits from the sybil talisman, but it's not nearly enough to take the edge off the agonizing pain.

The leader gets back to his feet and pulls a dagger from his cloak. The others follow his example. They move to encircle me.

Moira bares her fangs. *Do not let them surround us.*

Lifting my knee up and stretching my arms out, I step forward while slamming my hands together.

The Saage women's energy manipulation trick bursts out of me with such force that chunks of the stone-tiled wall fly at the attackers.

The energy wave shoves the thugs off their feet. Debris hit them on the head as they slam into the corridor wall with the air knocked out of them. They fall to the ground, gasping for air, and bleeding from cuts on their necks.

Best to tie them up with your magic, dear, before they can get back to their feet.

With a nod, I reach for my pulsing magical orb, letting the hot-and-cold-and-hot-again feeling wash over me as I select multiple thin threads of A'ris, shaping them into ropes.

My skin glows as I tie the A'ris ropes over their hands and feet.

One of them opens his mouth to shout, and I grab more A'ris ribbons, shaping them into patches. I paste them over the thug's mouth before he can make a sound, then proceed to do the same with the rest.

When I reach the smallest one, he shoves the hood off his head with his bound hands.

Ivy glares up at me. "Is this *really* necessary?"

Hiding my surprise, I release my magic and untie her from the A'ris ropes. "I should have known it was you. What are you doing here?"

Ivy rubs her wrists and ankles, then gets to her feet. She looks around at the ground, ignoring my question. "Where is it?" She proceeds to search the thugs' pockets amid angry grunts and muffled curses. Then she turns the thrashing leader onto his side. "There it is."

Ivy picks up the small black device. "We can't let you make a ruckus, now can we?"

I recognize that black device. It's the same one the thug leader used on me, disrupting my transfiguration. Eerily similar to the one Laoise had used.

"Ivy, please don't kill them."

"This won't kill them, just knocks them out for a spell, since they are not Teryns." Then she zaps each man in quick succession.

The thugs fall back, unconscious.

"I would have used poison to make sure they don't talk, but I left my stash back in my room. I hurried to attack you as soon as I heard."

I can't decide whether she is joking or not, dear.

Best not to think about that for long; that way lies insanity. "Thank you, I guess."

Ivy puts the black device away. "Now you owe me two favors for saving your life. I came to warn you."

"Warn me about what? I already know that your mother doesn't want to talk to me." She'd rather kill me instead.

"It's not that. You'd better hurry. The dowager queen is leaving Pada right now."

CHAPTER 60

"She must be taking Caderyn off-world," I say. Now all those attacks make sense. The queen knew I was closing in on her and she tried to take me out before I could catch her.

Ivy swipes a few strands of hair out of her eyes. "It does seem so." She takes out a finger-long metal rod with a few red buttons and presses the top one, aiming it toward the group of unconscious thugs.

The air quivers around them until they vanish.

The Marauders sure have a lot of interesting technology, dear—preventing transfiguration and a camouflage hologram. These must have come in handy when they executed the attacks on Callum's older brothers and kidnaped Caderyn.

Isn't that interesting? "We must stop the Marauder queen. Every second that goes by, the Teryn empire is closer to its demise without its praelor."

She pops a piece of purple gum into her mouth. "We are too far from the spaceports."

"How can you stay so calm?"

Ivy pockets the metal rod. "Since when does worrying ever help?"

I pace a few steps, trying to come up with a plan and almost tripping over a foot, disturbing the holographic cover. I might be far, but the others are closer to the spaceport to stop the dowager queen. Touching my ear, I activate my k'bug. "Arrov? Belthair? Can you hear me?"

Static feedback crackles in my ear.

"Glenna? Ragnald? Anyone?"

No answer.

Ivy chews her gum open-mouthed. "Don't bother. The queen must be jamming all communications."

Buckets of fishguts! "Now what?"

"Don't look at me. I'm fresh out of ideas."

Who else can help us, dear? Think.

I am about to say no one when a thought pops into my head.

CHAPTER 61

"Are you sure he's going to help us?" Ivy asks as I knock on the door.

"Devotee Zorion has access to the spaceport, and he can shut it down. Not to mention his office is closer to us, so we might as well ask for his help."

No answer comes from the other side of the door.

I knock again. Louder.

It is a thick door, dear.

Right. I bang my fist on the door until it shakes.

Still nothing.

Ivy tries the door handle. "It's open."

We enter.

I look around the bright, airy, and empty room. "Devotee Zorion?"

Ivy sashays to the glass armoire that takes up most of the left corner, with shelves full of ancient-looking tomes and scrolls. "Where could he be?"

"I have no idea."

I step behind the large wooden desk with scrolls covering its top. I almost bump into a wooden mug, full of dark liquid, sitting at its edge. The red high-back chair is pushed back as if the monk's just left. I lift a few scrolls, trying to read the scrawled words, but even my genetic translator makes no sense of the runic language.

I drop the scrolls back to the desk.

"Maybe there is a secret passageway. We Marauders have one in every room. As a failsafe against, uh, fire and such."

Moira snorts. *More like a quick escape route.*

"That would be ridiculous . . ." My voice trails off as my gaze locks on a tilted painting on the brick wall to my left.

Stepping to the painting, I straighten it.

Nothing happens.

"Ivy, search that armoire please; I'll look around this side."

She nods and opens the glass door of the armoire. She pulls out random tomes and throws the scrolls to the ground without much care.

I move every painting, metal decoration, and dust-free weapon on the wall, waiting to hear that telltale click.

Ivy wipes her hands on her black cloak. "Nothing."

"Same here. We've looked everywhere."

I doubt there are any secret passageways in the monastery, dear.

That may be so, but my instincts tell me that we missed something, I just don't know what.

Ivy leans back on the desk. Her elbow knocks into the wooden mug, spilling its contents all over the scrolls.

She looks over her shoulder. "It's not my fault. Who leaves a mug so close to the edge?"

I frown at the dark liquid dripping off the edge of the desk. "Didn't Devotee Zimon say that the Pada monks love cocoa?"

Ivy raises an eyebrow. "How would I know? I was spying for you, remember?"

Right. "The Pada monk mentioned it that they grow their cocoa in the basement of the monastery. But neither Callum nor Rhona ever found any trace of this basement. So where is it?"

Ivy scratches the desk with her long nails. "We should grab a disciple or two and interrogate them."

"We don't have time to do that." Not to mention that would be wrong.

We didn't find any clues searching by traditional means. But I haven't tried the magical one. I tilt my head at the wall and look beyond what's in front of me.

Transparent shimmering ribbons of T'erra, Fla'mma, and A'ris magic cling to its surface. I notice an unusual concentration of A'ris magic at a spot waist-high. "I wonder . . ."

Ivy comes to stand next to me. "What are you muttering about? I don't see anything. We might as well leave to search somewhere else."

Ignoring her, I reach for my magic orb and pull a thin thread of A'ris, forming it into a needle. A hot-and-cold-and-hot-again feeling pricks my glowing skin as I push the A'ris needle at that odd spot on the wall.

A loud click sounds and a wide section of the wall, like a jagged door, swings backward, revealing a dark passageway.

CHAPTER 62

Ivy and I exchange a look.

She grins. "I told you there is a secret passageway."

I roll my eyes.

Together we enter the narrow pathway with stairs descending, barely wide enough for two people.

After two steps the wall section closes, taking all the light with it.

Cold sweat breaks out on my body. My lungs struggle for air. The urge to *flee!* to *run!* almost overwhelms me.

"I despise the dark," Ivy mutters. "Although your skin is glowing, it's not enough to light our way. Can't you do something about it?"

Panting for air, I reach for a thick ribbon of Fla'mma magic and shape it into an orb floating in front of us. Its bright light illuminates the stairs and twisting tunnel.

I wipe my hands on my leggings and fight to breathe in more air.

Ivy glances at me and her eyes widen. "We better get going since no one knows we're here."

"If . . . that's your . . . way of . . . distracting—" I gasp out the words just as blackness intrudes at the edge of my vision.

I can't faint now.

You don't have to be in this tunnel for long, dear. You can do it.

Stopping, I nod and slow my breath. I count the exhales and inhales of the stuffy air until the claustrophobia-induced panic recedes.

Ivy beams. "It worked, didn't it?" She resumes climbing down the stairs.

Leave it to Ivy to take credit. With a sigh, I follow her.

A breeze ruffles our hair, scented with dust and cocoa.

Ivy wrinkles her nose. "Ugh. I can't stand dust. It makes my throat itchy."

Could be worse. "At least there are no cobwebs here." Which means no spiders.

Ivy shivers. "I am deathly afraid of spiders."

"Who knew we have that much in common?"

Ivy glances at me with a stern expression as we reach a dead end. "Don't fool yourself, Lilla. You had a cushy life while I fought off assassination attempts every single day. We're nothing alike."

CHAPTER 63

"I didn't mean to offend you," I whisper and disengage the Fla'mma light, throwing us into darkness again.

"What are you doing?" Ivy says with a hiss. "You know I—"

"Don't get your sail in a knot. I'm searching for a crack so we can see what's behind this wall. Unless Marauders tend to run blindly into any situation, heedless of danger."

"Some Marauders do do that, but not the smart ones." Ivy giggles. "I said, doo-doo."

I roll my eyes. "Very funny."

Moira chuckles in my head. *She is a peculiar one, isn't she, dear?*

Don't get me started. I turn my attention to the wall until I find a crack on our far right that's wide enough to peek through. I step close to it.

Ivy grabs my right arm with both of her hands and shoves me to the side. "I want to see too."

Together we peer through the crack.

CHAPTER 64

A vast room comes into view. Wooden racks piled with sacks and jars line both sides of the long rectangular space with dark gray bricks. Fla'mma orbs hover near the ceiling, making the windowless room as bright as day. Multiple corridors branch off the warehouse-like basement on each side. Muffled voices drift to us.

A bound Caderyn stumbles into the middle of room, pushed by four leather-clad Marauder thugs. Caderyn's uniform hangs looser on his brawny frame, covered in dirt. A purple bruise darkens his jawline, but his blue eyes glint with fury.

Dowager Queen Sheela, in a white leather pantsuit, sashays into view. She turns her back to us. "Hurry up!" she barks.

Ivy was right. The queen is about to move Caderyn, dear.

I nod and am about to pull back when Factory Leader Ia'an strides into the room. He aims a small black device at Caderyn and zaps him.

I almost do a double take. *The Industrial Conglomerate is working with the Marauders? Sharing technology, but why?*

This is more complex than we thought, dear.

Caderyn's knees tremble. It looks like he'll fall, but he forces himself to straighten. "You'll regret this."

"Yes, we heard you," the dowager queen snaps. "What's taking them so long?"

Elder Fran with Young Luiza hurry in, their homespun dresses flapping around their legs. "No need to shout," Elder Fran mutters, holding a glass pitcher full of light-purple-colored liquid. "We had to steep the herbs, or the tea would not be potent enough."

The dowager queen snaps her fingers at four thugs, and they restrain Caderyn. "Just get on with it."

"Don't you dare," Caderyn says with a growl.

The queen pats his cheek, her long sharp nails close to his eye. "Haven't you figured it out yet? Your orders don't matter anymore." Then she steps out of the way.

Elder Fran's gaze holds a ruthless look. "You only get what you deserve praelor. Especially after that brutal show of—"

The dowager queen rolls her eyes. "Yes, yes, we all know the sacrifice you had to make to get the praelor to Pada. Now quit your whining and do your job."

Elder Fran presses her lips into a thin line, then gestures to Young Luiza. The girl pinches Caderyn's nose until he opens his mouth. Then Elder Fran forces the tea into Caderyn's mouth. "I hope you drown."

Caderyn thrashes, but the thugs restrain him even more. The praelor takes big gulps of the splashing liquid, gagging and choking in the process.

After a while they release the coughing praelor.

Caderyn tries to shake his head but sways dizzily. All the fight seems to drain from him. His eyelids droop and he collapses to the floor.

"That will subdue him for a bit," the Marauders' queen says with a cruel smile.

I told you not to underestimate the gentle farmer's motives, dear.

She sure fooled me. There is nothing gentle left of Elder Fran as she studies Caderyn with a disgusted look. Young Luiza kicks Caderyn's leg. "Just checking to make sure he is out," she says when the older woman glances at her. Then they both burst into obnoxious laughter.

The dowager queen signals impatiently at someone in the left corridor.

"Who else is she waiting for?" I mutter.

Miner Gregry steps into view, holding a hovering three-foot-wide platform with his right hand.

"A little help," the miner says.

Trader Pecker shuffles into the room, followed by two androids. The bulky man snaps an unintelligible command.

One android grabs Caderyn by the armpits, while the other grabs his legs. Together, they haul the unconscious praelor, then throw him onto the platform that reshapes itself to accommodate Caderyn's size in an instant, turning into a hovering stretcher.

Shaggy-haired Chief Merchant Kristofer walks out of the right alley. He pulls a finger-long metal rod out of the pocket and points it at the praelor.

Caderyn blinks out of sight, replaced by an image of piled boxes and sacks tied down with a rope.

My jaw drops. All the Tier One factions are involved in this.

"That will do," the dowager queen says and pats the platform, disturbing the holo-image. "Get the spacecraft ready. We're leaving now."

CHAPTER 65

Ivy and I lean back from the crack.

"We're doomed," Ivy says in a low voice. "They outnumber us. Let's just go back—"

"We can't let them leave." My mind whirls, trying to come up with a plan that won't end with us dying.

The odds of that, dear, do not look promising.

Ivy spreads her arms. "With what army are you suggesting that we storm this warehouse—"

All of a sudden a loud noise sounds, like feet thumping.

We look through the crack again.

The dowager queen stares at the ceiling. "Not with this again."

Bang! Bang! Bang!

Thin lines of dust trickle from the widening cracks between the bricks, raining down on everyone and disturbing the holo-image.

Bang! Bang! Bang!

"What's going—" Ivy asks, then sneezes.

She covers her mouth as her eyes go wide.

Everyone's head snaps toward our spot.

CHAPTER 66

The section of the wall to our right opens outward. Blinding light replaces the darkness.

We shield our eyes against the harsh brightness.

Zorion shakes his head. "Neither of you should be here. Please join us." He gestures to the side.

Reluctantly, we exit the passageway.

Dowager Queen Sheela narrows her eyes on Ivy. "So that's where you disappeared to, you useless—"

"She is a thousand times better than you," I interrupt the Marauder queen.

Ivy looks at me with a shocked expression.

I don't think anyone's ever stood up for that poor girl, dear. I'm glad you did.

The queen raises an arched eyebrow. "Is that so? No matter. She will be dead soon." She sniggers as more thugs rush in, surrounding us.

"How can you kill your only heir?" I ask.

The dowager queen smirks. "I have clones ready to take my place when I see fit. I don't need *her* anymore."

Ivy pales.

I look at each faction leader. "I can't believe you all worked together to kidnap the praelor. Did you also kill his older son, Sachary, and injure his other son, Sawney?"

"That was only a message," the dowager queen says with a leer. "The praelor was too dumb to understand its meaning."

Flames of fury rise at her words, but I push it down. "You are their leader, aren't you?" I ask Zorion.

He smiles and the rune-like tattoos wrinkle on his right cheek. "I simply strive to inspire them."

Still can't give me a straight answer, can he? "Did you 'inspire' them on your own, or are you working with someone else?"

Zorion raises an eyebrow. "I cannot divulge that information."

"You just confirmed it," Ivy says and spits her gum at one of the thugs.

I shake my head. "Why are you doing this?"

Queen Sheela harrumphs. "It should be obvious to you, silly girl. We all want to be free of the Teryns. This monk found a way to achieve that. Who says we can't have a bit of fun along the way? Trying to crush you with that tree and watching you sink at the base of the waterfall were such delightful moments. I will cherish them for the rest of my life."

"As if you'd know the meaning of 'cherish,'" Ivy says.

I scoff. "Your attacks are pathetic; I'm still here. You must be getting clumsy in your old age."

A cruel and satisfied expression spreads on the round face of the queen. "Yet I led you right here. Are you still thinking how smart you are, silly girl?"

I resist the urge to slap my forehead as the chain of events suddenly make sense all the way through to Ivy and me ending up in Zorion's office, seeking the monk's help. I played into her hands.

That might be so, but we have bigger problems. I can see only one possible way for these worlds to get their freedom, dear, and that is if the Teryns give it to them. Someone high in power.

Surprise raises goose bumps on my arms. *This will destroy the Teryn empire.*

A lot of change comes from chaos, dear, and someone is in a hurry to make it happen.

"A respected monk like you should have known better than to commit such a horrible crime," I say to Zorion. Maybe he'll slip up and reveal who is pulling the strings.

Red patches of anger bloom on the monk's face. "Where were you with your righteousness when the Teryns attacked us? Where were you when they forced us to make weapons for their petty war? No one cared what happened to us. As long as the Teryn Praelium is fighting corruption, they can get away with anything. We didn't fight them when they arrived to avoid any bloodshed. We thought we'd be able to influence them and promote an alliance instead of oppression, but the praelor had no intention of listening. Well, I've made him listen now, haven't I?"

"What you've done is wrong," I snarl the words. "You are no better than Caderyn."

"That is where you are wrong, Sybil Lilla. The praelor had it coming. Had he treated us, Tier One worlds, with respect, none of this would have happened."

Zorion waits until the other faction leaders stop cheering. "This is a lot bigger than you think, Sybil Lilla. The Teryn Praelium is already on its way to a civil war, but I had no hand in it. It's time all the conquered worlds separate from the praelium and go free. It's what we deserve. It's our right."

CHAPTER 67

The others shout in agreement.

Who could benefit from all of this, dear?

Then comprehension hits. How Chief Consuasor Graeme wanted to erase the Ground Rules, how he arrested Callum in front of the warriors, all but ensuring that his actions triggered a revolt. The chief consuasor must have promised freedom to the factions, including Pada, to help him with the political assassinations of Caderyn's older sons and the kidnapping of the praelor.

"How can you risk the fate of the Seven Galaxies so selfishly?" I ask the monk, reeling from the depth of the conspiracy.

Zorion smiles proudly as he spreads his arms. "It would have been irresponsible for me to not take advantage of such a rare opportunity. Besides, the Seven Galaxies are better off without the Teryn brutes imposing their will on them. There are other ways to fight in the Era War."

We must stop him, dear.

Gladly. I reach for my magic. "This is not the opportunity you say. This is an atrocious offense."

Zorion laughs. "What makes you think you can do anything about it?"

Bang! Bang! BANG!

The ceiling comes crashing down in the middle of the warehouse, making the others scatter out of the way. Fearghas jumps down. My horse rears on his hindlegs, trampling a group of Marauder thugs as he lets out an ear-piercing neigh.

The dowager queen shouts orders. The faction leaders scramble to move the camouflaged Caderyn away.

T'erra-magic infused rocks form a descending staircase from the gaping hole. Ragnald takes the steps two at a time. "Well done, Fearghas. We couldn't have found the praelor without you."

That's why Fearghas wouldn't leave that courtyard. He must have known

Caderyn was held somewhere underneath him.

Belthair sprints down the makeshift steps, holding a pirate sword in each of his six hands. Arrov follows, shooting crossbolts at anyone who dares approach. Isa and Bella leap off the stairs midway, firing laser shots from their guns. Glenna hurries to join them, holding a slingshot full of rocks, and ribbons of her A'ris magic trailing her.

The faction leaders scream commands. Dozens of men and women flood in, attacking my friends.

Ivy lets out a scream and pulls a few throwing knives from her boots, then wades into the fight.

Zorion steps out of the way of Fearghas, who chases a shrieking Marauder man. Then the monk points at me. "It's you and me."

Following him, I keep my hands loose but ready multiple threads of elemental magic ribbons from my magical orb. I let the hot-and-cold-and-hot-again feeling bring clarity. Then I raise my glowing arms. "How disappointing."

Zorion looks incensed. "You can joke all you want, but you were not able to defend against my attacks during our last magic lesson. How are you planning to survive an actual magical fight with me?" Thick transparent ribbons of A'ris and Fla'mma rise from the Pada monk.

It's a question I hope to find answers to quickly.

Can we transfigure? I ask Moira, but she shakes her head. *Whatever those Marauders used on us, it still hasn't worn off.*

"You should back out before it's too late," Zorion says and closes his fingers into a teepee, turning his palms out. "I will not hold back, whether you are the sybil or not. Do not get in my way or you'll regret it."

I narrow my eyes on the Pada monk. "I will not let you get away with this."

Zorion smiles. "Good. I was looking forward to defeating you, a Lumenian, ever since you stepped foot on Pada." He flicks his wrists, sending out a barrage of A'ris needles.

Shield up, dear.

What shield? I ask but my arm is already shaping a thick thread of A'ris magic into a pair of circular discs in front of me, with Moira's help. The discs deflect most of the A'ris needles, with a few grazing my thighs underneath it.

Pain flickers across my mind, muted by the adrenaline pumping in my veins.

Moira disengages the shields. *I hope you don't mind, dear. You weren't the only one who paid attention at the magic lessons. It helps that I have more battle experiences than you.*

I don't mind at all; I can use the help.

"I see you've internalized our magic lesson," Zorion says. "Too bad it won't help you against a master of magic."

Someone has a high opinion of himself, dear.

I don't have time to react as the Pada monk unleashes more A'ris needles, Fla'mma torrents, cutting A'ris wind, and Fla'mma balls in quick succession.

Again, with the help of Moira, I form a new pair of A'ris shields; then drop them and reach for Fla'mma threads, shaping them into a firewall to deflect the torrent of fire and then disengage them. Then I grab A'ris threads and push against the cutting wind and drop it. And then I form Fla'mma threads into a swirling shield of fire to combat dozens of Fla'mma balls before releasing the last of the magic threads.

My body moves with the grace of a fighter, thanks to Moira. It's as if she is side by side with me, coordinating my movements. It's not like a meld, yet harmonious at the same time.

Time to send our own attack, dear.

I nod and shape A'ris into whips, adding A'qua to form frozen spikes on the air whips. Then I encircle Zorion with a Fla'mma wall, while cracking the ground under his feet with T'erra magic ribbons.

Breathing hard, I watch Zorion deflect, avoid, and jump over each of my attacks with the skills of a true master.

"This is not bad from a novice. You have a tremendous well of power, but your skill is lacking. You should have practiced more." Zorion barely finishes speaking when he pushes with his arms out, releasing an avalanche of A'ris and Fla'mma mixed into a deadly tide of burning gale.

I am too slow to counteract it with my magic. I jump to the side and land on my left shoulder hard. The pain reverberates all the way to my feet as I cover my head, letting the attack stream above me. Strands of my floating hair burn into ash, raining around me like gray snow.

The fiery gale intensifies, robbing me of air.

I'm out of ideas, dear.

Panting, I inhale the charred smell of hair, desperate to find a solution. I realize I still have my Lumenian magic to use.

I reach for a Lume thread, shaping it over me like a bubble to preserve what little air is left, waiting for the magic attack to dispel.

I cannot best Zorion in magic, I say to Moira. *The Pada monk plays with me like Fearghas bats around a sand crab, letting it think it has a chance before crushing it with one of his legs.*

Then we best use what he won't expect, dear.

The fire-air torrent ceases.

Disengaging the Lume bubble, I jump to my feet. I have only one trick left to try. Stepping out with my right leg, I spread my arms out, then bring them close in front of me in a shoving motion. The Saage energy manipulation trick hits Zorion in the chest. He flies off his feet, hovering in midair on his back for a second, but a second is all I need to wrap him with thick Lume magic, shaped into vines, all around his body.

He lands on the ground, bound, and glares up at me.

I study the magical architecture of A'ris and Fla'mma ribbons around him. I wonder what will happen if I dispel the magic he's gathered on his body. With an imaginary hand, I pluck at the elemental strands until they lift off him and disappear.

His magic web falls apart.

"What have you done?" Zorion sputters with wide eyes.

It seems that magic is not integral *in* him, but *on* him. How curious.

Of course magic is not inherent to him, dear; he is not a Lumenian like you.

"I, uh, disarmed your magic," I say. Though I have a feeling it's temporary.

"How dare you use a nonmagical attack in a serious magic fight? You are nothing. You don't understand anything."

"Yet it was this novice who defeated you, the so-called master, and not the other way around. Now be quiet or I'll paste a magic patch over your mouth."

Then I pick up a thin Lume thread and attach it first to the bound Zorion, then to the wall, making sure the monk won't be able to escape.

Finished, I crack my knuckles and turn toward the ongoing battle in the warehouse.

"Who's next?" I shout and stride toward the closest group of Marauder men.

CHAPTER 68

In the few minutes it took to fight Zorion, the factions managed to bring in even more reinforcements.

The windowless warehouse fills with billowing dark smoke from burning crates and wooden racks on both sides. Shouts of anger and pain add to the tumultuous cacophony.

My friends, overwhelmed and outnumbered four to one, fight on the other side of the cavernous room. Green flashes intersperse with red sparks from laser guns and fiery Fla'mma balls from Ragnald. The iridescent six-foot-tall wings of S'affi blink into and out of existence.

The hovering platform with Caderyn on it nears the exit, not far from my friends. The platform is pushed by the two androids and protected by a large group of thugs with laser guns.

Moira hisses in anger. *We cannot let the praelor be taken away.*

With a deep inhale of the smoke-scented air, I engage threads of all six light elements, tying the multihued ribbons to my hands.

My vision blurs for a second and I stumble.

Lilla, this must be one of the warning signs that you are getting close to overextending your magic.

Ignoring Moira, I grind my teeth against fatigue, and shape Fla'mma ribbons into fire balls, hurling them at a group of Marauders bearing down on Ivy. Their clothing goes up in flames and they drop to the ground, rolling to extinguish the fire.

I don't have much choice, now do I? I can't take on all of them without our meld or without my magic.

With weapons flashing and punches flying, I wade deeper into the writhing bodies of the crowd. Something stings my right shoulder, but I pay no attention to it.

My claustrophobia comes rushing at me. Anger burns brighter, allowing me to not give in as I breath through the panic. I have one goal—saving Caderyn.

A five-foot-tall young merchant, with four ears, jumps in front of me and bares his small fangs. He raises a dagger with curving blade to attack, but Moira helps me pivot out of the way at the last second. When the merchant tries again, I shape an A'ris ribbon into a gust of wind and push him away. He slams into the stone wall and goes down, unconscious.

Another wave of dizziness washes over me, and Moira curses. Wiping cold sweat from my face, I force myself to keep going.

One of the androids barrels toward me, blocking my path to the middle of the room. I lift thick Fla'mma threads from my orb, shaping them into a single deluge and unleash it on the plastic giant.

I trip as my vision turns black.

When I look up, a large plastic puddle steams on the dirty ground.

I leap over the puddle, then duck under a jab from a man in a bloodstained suit. I kick out to the side, Moira guiding my moves with dexterity. My kick lands in his side. Something crunches from the force of it, and he tumbles down.

Hurry, dear. They are almost gone.

I can't go any faster. There are more than thirty people blocking my way.

Then make them go away.

With desperate fingers, I reach for all six elemental threads as an idea forms in my head. The elements resist my call, sluggish. I struggle to fuse them into one robust magical vine. I have no doubt I've reached the last of my magical reserves.

If this doesn't work, then I don't know what will.

Lilla, what are you doing? You'll kill us both.

Ignoring Moira, I let the magic vine burst free. It sneaks around the bodies of thugs, fighters, men, and women, unnoticed.

With a jerk of my arm, I ensnare them. Magical sprouts grow out of the vine, wrapping around their bodies in an attempt to bind their arms and legs.

The mass of people struggles against my hold, fighting it, some almost managing to break free.

Grinding my teeth, I drag more magical threads up from my orb that does not shine so brightly anymore. The glow on my arm dims as I strengthen my magic around the group, ensnaring them.

With a shout, I raise my trembling arms and the heavy magic vine, lifting captured faction members off their feet.

Lightheadedness makes the room tilt on its edge.

Panting, I raise the vine higher, all the way to the ceiling. My knees buckle and I land on the ground. A buzzing sound builds in my ears as I tie the magic vine to the wall.

The thirty captured people shout and scream, their voices echoing in the warehouse.

I drop my hands on the ground with head bowed. Sweat pours off me in rivulets, and my stomach roils. I dry heave, then wipe my mouth. My body can't decide whether to shiver from cold or perspire from overheating.

I close my eyes, feeling utterly depleted. It would be so nice to lie down and rest. Just for a little bit . . .

A hand touches my shoulder. "Lilla, are you okay?" Arrov asks.

I open my eyes, only to find myself lying on the ground, with dirt sticking to my cheek. I must have lost consciousness. "I'm fine." I let Arrov help me to my feet.

The room tilts again. My head feels heavy, my muscles sore and aching.

"We were too late," Belthair says as he strides to me, his top arms around a limping Isa and Bella. "They took Caderyn."

CHAPTER 69

W e've lost. The Teryn Praelium will collapse in a bloody civil and inter-galactic war. DLD will win the Era War. Trillions of innocents will die a horrible death. All because of my failure.

My knees give out and I collapse to the ground.

Fearghas clomps to me, nuzzling my hair. S'affi blinks into existence on my lap. She nudges my hand to pet her, and I oblige. "I've failed."

Isa and Bella sit down on either side of me. "You tried your best." Cuts and bleeding wounds cover their pretty faces.

Ivy shakes her blond head. "I told you; we never had a chance."

"It's not your fault, sweetie." Glenna says, then kneels in front of me with a sad expression.

How I wish her words would be true. "Sawney?" I ask, but I already know the answer.

Glenna shakes her head.

Buckets and buckets of fishguts!

We should keep going—

And do what? I snap. *We did all we could and failed. There is nothing left to do.*

A wave of dizziness makes me close my eyes. All my injuries that I didn't notice in the heat of the battle now make themselves known. Dozens of shallow cuts cover my back and side, seeping blood. A puncture wound aches on my right shoulder. Multiple scrapes from laser shots pepper my shoulder and thigh. My sybil talisman spreads its healing warmth but can't seem to keep up with the myriad of injuries and bruises.

Isa glances up at the dangling people stuck to the wall. "Shouldn't you let them down?" Bella adds, "It cannot be healthy to hang like that from the ceiling."

Ivy crosses her arms. "Why should Lilla do that? They wanted to kill us. I think a few hours will give them a chance to think about their actions."

Ragnald gestures upward. "How did you do that?"

"I learned a few things from Zorion." I glance at the bound Pada monk, who sits on the ground a few feet from us, glaring. Then I look back at my friends, all battered and worn. "Thank you for your—"

A manic light glints in Glenna's eyes and red patches appear on her face. "Thank me? How dare you thank me when you ruined my life? I gave up my dream for you."

Glenna takes a breath, not noticing Ragnald squatting behind her, channeling his Fla'mma magic into her with both of his hands. "I followed you to this stupid planet with its stupid pine trees, full of stupid monks who are worse than the stupid mages."

"That's a lot of 'stupid,'" Belthair jokes, but eyes her warily.

Glenna ignores him. "You drag me around the Seven Galaxies without any concern for my well-being. You destroyed everything I ever wanted and all you can say is 'thank you'?"

Suddenly the menacing expression fades from Glenna's face. She slumps backward. Ragnald catches her in his arms.

My heart sinks at Glenna's words. She is right. I did drag all my friends away from their homes, away from their dreams, straight into danger, heedless of their wishes.

I cover my mouth with a shaking hand.

She did not mean that, dear. It's DLD's corruption speaking through her.

"That's not what happened," Arrov insists, looking at me. "There was nothing for me on A'ice. Ever since I joined you, I've had the most amazing adventures. Including turning into an A'ice giant for a short time."

Belthair sits across from Arrov. "You know I wouldn't lie to you, Lilla, not even to spare your feelings. The truth is you did not pressure us into anything. The Era War is more important than any rebellion. We would be fools to sit it out."

"We chose to come along with you," Isa says, and Bella nods. "We have no regrets. You can count on us."

Glenna rubs her face and looks at me. "I, uh, I didn't mean what I said. I mean it's true that I dreamed of being the next Great Healer on Uhna, but dreams can change . . . Lilla, please forgive me." She reaches out to me.

Even though it's DLD's corruption that twists Glenna into this angry bitter person, it's still hard to look past what she's said. Because there is a seed of truth in it. "There is nothing to forgive." I grasp her hand.

"I think it's time to seek help from the charlatans, I mean, the Academia of Mages," Glenna says with a wobbling smile as tears roll down her face. She and the mage get to their feet.

Placing the sleeping S'affi to the side, I stand up as well and hug Glenna. I look at Ragnald over my best friend's shoulder, my eyes pleading with him to take care of her. The mage nods in understanding.

Wiping at the corners of my eyes, I step back and try to smile at Glenna in encouragement.

"I just wish I could stay and help—" Glenna's voice chokes up. With a good-bye wave, she climbs up the makeshift stone steps with Ragnald following her.

CHAPTER 70

A green spark catches my eye on my left. "You can come out now."

My friends stare at me as if I've grown a lobster head.

A green bubble appears near the wall. Teague steps out. "How did you know?"

I snort. "I'd recognize those telltale green sparks of your time-space-displacement pocket anywhere."

Teague shifts his weight from one leg to the other. "When I saw you were in trouble, I—"

I put a hand on his arm. "Thank you for looking out for me."

Belthair gets up and help the twins to their feet. "Enough with the chit-chat. We must go after Caderyn."

"How?" Isa asks, and Bella adds, "They're long gone by now."

Arrov rubs his chin. "We could take Rhona's shuttle. She left it in the spaceport."

Ivy shakes her head. "They probably took the dowager queen's new space-craft. We'll never catch up with them. We don't even know where they're heading."

Belthair points at Zorion. "We should interrogate the monk. I bet he knows where they're taking the praelor."

What is with my friends and interrogation? "There is no need for that. I know the location. They're taking Caderyn back to Teryn. Chief Consuasor Graeme won't waste a second seizing power from the praelor." The Pada monk turns his head away, confirming my words.

Ivy twirls a finger in her long blond hair. "They will be on Teryn in a few hours. Even if we take Rhona's shuttle, we'll need at least ten hours to catch up. But if we take the smaller prototype, which is as fast if not faster, especially if I'm the one piloting, then—"

"You have another fast ship?" Arrov interrupts Ivy. "Why didn't you start with that?"

Belthair rubs all six of his hands together. "What are we waiting for? Let's go."

Ivy raises an elegant finger. "As I said, it's small and only seats two. Lilla should accompany me as I won't let anyone else pilot it."

"Fine. We'll follow you in Rhona's shuttle," Belthair says.

Fearghas neighs and stomps his front feet.

"We'll take you as well," Belthair adds. My horse nickers, and a sleeping S'affi appears on his back.

"I can take Zorion with me," Teague offers and blinks in surprise at S'affi.

"Why isn't Teague the one who takes us to Teryn?" Belthair demands.

"Because I can't take so many of you," Teague explains, then turns to me. "It will take me at least three hours to get there, as I'll have to make multiple stops in between to rest. Try to buy some time until then."

Good to know. I have a feeling I'll need Zorion on Teryn as proof. I look at the monk. "Since you led the factions, you are a vital witness to this crime. I'll need you to vouch—"

"I won't help you," Zorion says, spitting the words as Teague drags him up.

"We'll see about that," I say as I sever the Lume tie from the wall. "Teague, you can take him now."

Teague nods and grabs the monk's arm. Then he engages a green blur around them, using his skill of creating a time-space-displacement pocket. The bubble vanishes.

Ivy claps her hands in excitement. "Off we go!"

CHAPTER 71

DAY 4

Ivy lowers our narrow spacecraft on a flat landing platform on Beware Hills on the Teryn world.

Fighting nausea, I clamber out of the hissing and clanking ship, which has six blue wings. I stumble to the edge of the platform and lean over to throw up bile onto the red sand.

Wiping my mouth, I look around at the desolate red surroundings, with the Mountain of Pain before us.

The early morning sun peeks over the horizon. Two moons, one large and one smaller, dominate the sky. Oppressive heat presses down. Sweat breaks out on my back, plastering my yellow tunic to my skin. Hot wind brings scents of sand and exotic spices.

Ivy grins. "I've told you we'd be fast. I pushed that little ship until it almost fell apart, but we made it."

I point across the shimmering mirage to the foot of the mountain. "We should get going. We'll have to climb that mountain to reach the City of Honor, where the Senatus is. It will be quite a trip."

A small hatch opens to our right and a blond head appears. Steaphan looks up at us. "Glad you made it safely. Now follow me."

Ivy rubs her hands together. "I do love a shortcut."

We enter through the hatch and take the stairs down into a stone- and metal-encased tunnel, barely wide enough for three people. A high metal ceiling, with square lights suspended in its middle, runs in both directions, with no end in sight.

"What are you doing here?" I ask Steaphan as we dash after him.

"Teague sent a message asking for my help. He explained what happened on Pada. Since Chief Consuasor Graeme called the consuasors into an emergency session, everyone is gathering in the Senatus right now. Whatever he is planning, he wants all the consuasors to sanction it right away. You two arrived just in time. I sent the consuasor guards away for a short break, but they'll be back soon. We must hurry."

Steaphan bursts into a sprint, his colorful shirt flapping behind him. Ivy and I follow him, trying to keep up.

We take turn after turn. We climb up stairs and steep corridors as we ascend inside the mountain, nearing the City of Honor. Toward the Senatus.

What if I'm too late? What if the civil war has already started between the warriors and the consuasors?

Let's hope you're not too late, dear. We must prevent that civil war from happening.

We reach a dead end with a thick metal door blocking our way. To the right, a row of metal pegs holds black cloaks with red stripes.

Steaphan grabs two hooded cloaks, then hands one to Ivy and one to me. "Wear this to blend in. Once you are in front of the Senatus, I cannot assist you."

I put on the cloak. "Thank you for your help."

"Nice quality," Ivy says, and smooths her hands down the front of her cloak, which hangs loosely on her thin frame, covering the tips of her boots.

Steaphan arranges our hoods, making sure our hair is covered. "May honor shine on you in this life and the next."

Then he opens the door.

CHAPTER 72

Ivy and I enter a dark hallway, which leads to an open archway with lights visible on the other side. We step through the archway and find ourselves at a side entrance to a half-circle-shaped platform facing an enormous auditorium-like hall. Wide, curving stone steps ascend on all sides, serving both as seats and stairs.

A domed ceiling painted with an artistic landscape catches my eye. It showcases the consuasors engaged in diplomacy and politics, illustrating their superior and divine calling. How humble.

Thousands of voices blend into a loud hum from the gathered consuasors, their volume intimidating.

"I didn't realize there were so many Brainiacs," Ivy whispers.

At the center of the platform the dark-haired Chief Consuasor Graeme waits. His immaculate blue silk shirt, worn over black pants and boots, highlights his fit body. Confidence bordering on superiority radiates from him as he studies the crowd with a patient smile. He has not noticed us yet.

I glance around, but I can't find Caderyn.

"We have gathered here today," Graeme says, "to evaluate the usefulness of the Ground Rules. It is imperative that we decide whether to erase these rules, which I am in favor of, or keep them, which the praelor favors. We all understand the consequences of keeping the Ground Rules—"

Ivy and I march up to him. "Where is the praelor?" I demand.

The consuasors gasp in shock, and the sound ripples through the hall.

Graeme turns to us. "Who are you and how did you get in here?"

I push off the hood of my cloak. "I am Sybil Lilla. I ask again, where is the praelor?"

Graeme frowns. "He is still on Pada. Or have you lost him?"

Laughter patters through the massive hall.

"Enough with your lies," I say. "You kidnapped him and assassinated his two older sons, all for power."

The crowd yells in outrage, their numerous voices rising in strength, like a rolling thunder.

Graeme raises his eyebrows. "The praelor was kidnapped?"

The chief consuasor is either a great actor, dear, or he's genuinely surprised by your accusations.

I can't decide which.

Clapping comes from the left of the platform.

Consuasor Finigal strides out, stopping next to us. Dark brown eyes glint with sharp intelligence in an angular face framed by short blond hair. He lifts an arm out in a theatrical motion. "Chief Consuasor Graeme has been manipulated by our dear praelor. Graeme is too weak. He never would have orchestrated a coup or tried to kidnap our beloved praelor."

Graeme purses his lips. "What are you doing, Finigal?"

"Then who kidnapped the praelor?" Ivy asks, but I already know the answer.

Finigal smirks. "It was me, of course."

CHAPTER 73

The consuasors yell, jumping to their feet, their words getting lost in the discord.

Finigal watches the chaos with a satisfied smile. He snaps his fingers.

Four leather-clad Marauders drag in a struggling Caderyn with bound hands and black tape over his mouth. Rage shines in the praelor's eyes, promising death.

"What are those Marauders doing here, in the Senatus?" Graeme asks.

"They are helping to restrain the praelor, of course," Finigal says, then turns to the hall. "Here is the praelor we know and adore."

The other consuasors quiet down to listen.

"We remember how much he loves mocking us for our efficiency in running the Teryn Praelium."

Graeme frowns. "You cannot do this—"

"I have the right to address the Senatus," Finigal interrupts him. "I called the Senatus in an emergency session *before* you did. I have the right to deliver my speech. Uninterrupted."

"Funny, I did not receive that invitation," Graeme says, then spreads his hands. "By all means speak, so we can get over this nonsense."

Finigal sneers.

Caderyn's muffled voice carries to us.

Finigal pretends to listen to the praelor's muted curses. "What is that you say? You didn't know it is the consuasors who rule the Teryn Praelium? How can you be so astonished? We are the ones who carry out the day-to-day politics, ensuring that this honorable empire runs without a hitch. We are the ones assigning quotas to the conquered worlds, regulating what they deliver to us so that you can run around with your army to bully others, I mean, to fight corruption. We are the ones who finance your battles and allow you to play hero, taking the credit for our hard work. Insulting us in exchange. Showing your appreciation by treating us as the dregs of society. Shaming us for practicing our profession. You encourage your warriors to look down on us, all in the name of honor. But you forget one important fact. Without us, there would be no praelium."

The consuasors cheer and clap, while their chief crosses his arms.

"How many more talented consuasors will have to suffer humiliation and embarrassment for failing their trial?" Finigal asks and the crowd listens in rapt silence.

"We consuasors outnumber the warriors three to one, yet we must tolerate their asinine honor-focused mentality?"

The crowd pumps one of their arms into the air, shouting.

"It's time we get rid of the outdated Ground Rules and replace them with real laws that will govern a prospering praelium. It's time we take our rightful place as true leaders who will make the Teryn Praelium even greater."

The consuasors clap.

Graeme points at the other man. "You mean you'll become our esteemed leader, Finigal?"

Finigal raises a hand. "We must unite against the warriors, who even now conspire against us. They want a civil war. They want to destroy the Teryn Praelium. But we can stop them."

Graeme glares. "You cannot do this—"

"Uninterrupted, remember?" Finigal says, then gestures to the Marauders. The four men shove Caderyn closer.

"We must show them that we can be ruthless like they are to us. We must show no mercy and hold the praelor accountable for his actions that led the Teryn Praelium to this breaking point. It is our job to take the toxic elements from the empire. It is how we stop the warriors—by showing our strength. By showing them that not even the praelor is safe from our justice."

The crowd cheers.

Behind Finigal I glimpse three beautiful and ageless-looking women with hoods around their necks. I recognize them. The Wise Women and avatars of Guardian Goddess Laoise.

I gasp. *It was Laoise all along and not the Marauder queen. Now the "she" makes sense. This is the goddess's revenge. First, on Caderyn for refusing to follow her order when I left the spirit realm, newly melded to you,*

Moira. Second, on Caderyn's sons, since they failed to kill me in the spirit realm. She arranged all of this so she could have a ruler who obeys her orders blindly.

Then it must have been Finigal and not Graeme whom we saw talking with the Wise Women.

I clench my teeth. *I assumed it was Graeme, but I was wrong. The guardian goddess and that arrogant consuasor planned this well. Finigal is the high-ranking Teryn who must have offered freedom to Zorion in exchange for the Pada monk to lead the other six Tier One factions. Then they kidnapped Caderyn and assassinated his two older sons. Through Laoise they had access to Acerbus, which she infused into a disguise device and added to that dagger as poison. All because Laoise is still collaborating with a minion of DLD. We've seen her do that before when she used that Acerbus-infused wand against us in the spirit realm. Since that wand was destroyed, she must have asked for more Acerbus to infuse other tech, which in turn she used to attack Guardian God Patra'ch and me a few days ago, when she escaped from the Lume prison. She must have wanted to test that zapping device on us first, to see if it worked since I am not a Teryn. Once she knew it prevented our meld, she must have informed the Industrial Conglomerate faction to use it on us, so we won't be able to transfigure into our cymmerion battle form.*

I agree. I told you, dear, Laoise does not do anything without a plan. But that's not our biggest problem. If Finigal becomes the new leader of the Teryn Praelium, Laoise can do whatever she wants with the Teryns. Killing you, the sybil, to establish her Teryns as the new Lumenians will help her achieve her goal.

We cannot let Laoise win. Not if we want the Seven Galaxies to survive this Era War.

CHAPTER 74

Caderyn struggles against the men, managing to free himself. He lunges at Finigal, stumbling dizzily in the process.

Finigal sidesteps the attack with ease. The Marauder men restrain the praelor again.

"Our dear praelor is impatient to get his justice, isn't he?" Finigal says to the hall, and the crowd laughs. Then he points at me. "Sybil Lilla has proven herself a true Teryn when she acquired the Heart Amulet and showed a battle form like no other. She may have gained the right to recruit the Teryn armada from the praelor, but she cannot do so without our permission."

My head snaps toward Finigal. "Hold your ships."

Finigal nods at the Wise Women, then turns to me. "It's not too late to show your respect and support to the newborn Teryn Praelium."

My what?

Six consuasor guards in dark blue uniforms stride to the platform, escorting a wounded Callum among them. They stop across from me.

Callum's tanned face bleeds from multiple cuts, with red sand embedded in them. His black uniform is stained with red mud. His knuckles drip blood to the platform.

My gaze locks on Callum's blue eyes. Everything fades, leaving only the two of us. My heart beats faster, love and worry warring with each other.

"What happened to him?" I ask, itching to touch Callum. I take a step forward, but a guard blocks my way.

"He's been in court," Graeme says, looking impressed. "It seems he fought his way to the highest circuit in the shortest time ever, thus earning the right to defend himself. Since the Ground Rules are still in effect, Sybil Lilla is allowed to support one of the men's cases in front of the Senatus. She can—"

Finigal steps in front of Graeme, turning his back on the other man, obstructing my view. "Sybil Lilla has a unique opportunity. Think about this sensibly. You can help just one man. Your words will make a difference. I hope you'll choose sagely."

CHAPTER 75

My stomach plummets as Finigal's words sink in.

How dare he play with us? Moira says with a snarl.

I look at Callum.

Supporting his case would mean saving my love—the man I want to marry and spend the rest of my days with, however many or few they may be. He's the one I want to have a family with. He disobeyed those orders because of me. The first time was when he tried to save me from a horde of attacking and fully corrupted dark servants back on Uhna. He did this by transfiguring into his battle form in front of an outsider, hence betraying a secret he was supposed to kill to protect. The second time Callum disobeyed an order was to buy me time so I could search for DLD. He purposely didn't send his report on the rising corruption levels he'd found in the blood of the corpses DLD deposited on the beach, when the archgod tried to make more of His dark servants, and failed. Callum was obligated to send it to Caderyn right away, but it was Teague who sent it instead, bringing the praelor to Uhna to join my battle with DLD that nearly destroyed my home planet.

How could I fault Callum? How could I let him die for these acts that I feel responsible for?

I look at Caderyn.

Supporting his case would mean saving the empire from a civil war that would tear apart the Teryn Praelium more quickly than a fire destroys a pirate ship. I would save the man who will be my future father-in-law if Callum and I *could* ever get married. A man who is a ruthless leader, who destroyed a space station full of innocents because the Farmers Partnership failed to deliver their assigned quota. A general who won't even let me set foot in his command center. A praelor who stood up against Guardian Goddess Laoise because it was the honorable thing to do, and would not kill me on the spot, as his goddess ordered him to do.

This is impossible. I close my eyes against the moisture that wells up in them.

Moira sighs. *There is only one choice here, dear.*

With a sigh, I open my eyes. "I have made my decision."

CHAPTER 76

Finigal nods. "What is your decision then, Sybil Lilla?"

I force the words out, saying, "I chose Caderyn a'ruun."

The hall erupts into angry shouts.

Caderyn stares at me, shocked.

Callum turns his head away as if I'd slapped him.

It's for the best, dear. He will understand why you did this.

I shake my head, swallowing my tears. *I don't believe that. I've just abandoned Callum, sentencing him to death.*

"You cannot support the praelor!" Finigal shouts. "What is wrong with you to forsake the man you're supposed to love?"

My heart shatters and a sob lodges in my throat. I want to take back my words, but I cannot.

Graeme crosses his arms. "Sybil Lilla can support whomever she wants since the Ground Rules are still in effect. Get on with this charade."

Finigal grinds his teeth and glances at the Wise Women, then turns back to me. "Fine. Help him, for all I care. I can't wait to watch your lover's execution later. But first I will punish the praelor, an inevitable outcome since you will fail in your efforts to help him. Go ahead. What are you waiting for?"

I open my mouth, but no sound comes out. The enormity of the task has taken my voice away.

"All you have to do is to convince the Senatus why they should care to save Praelor Caderyn," Graeme explains in a kind voice. "That is all."

Not helping.

You can do this, dear. The Seven Galaxies depend on you.

How can I save Caderyn when all the consuasors hate him? Caderyn never did anything to gain the consuasors' favor or tried to be cordial to them. He underestimated them. He ignored them. He claimed to be better than them.

Moira opens her mouth, but I continue, *How will I convince the whole Senatus that I am right, and they are wrong? I couldn't even convince my own cousin Be'trix to abandon her petty jealousy of me. We all know how she ended up. Dead. All because she envied my status so much, she dressed up as me and got killed for it. I can't let Caderyn end up dead too.*

Moira nods. *Yes, but—*

I'm not a seasoned politician or a diplomat. My lone experience in politics was when I joined the rebellion on Uhna—a rebellion that failed. What can I say that they have not heard before?

Panic rises and black spots appear in my vision.

Moira chuckles without mirth. *Look at all these "seasoned" consuasors. They are not doing so well now, are they? On the verge of a coup and at a brink of a civil war, misled by their own guardian goddess. They should know better, yet they allowed the situation to get this far. I believe it's time for a new perspective. A fresh start. I believe in you, dear.*

A commotion sounds.

Teague strides onto the platform, dragging a flustered-looking Zorion. The colonel winks at me as he stops on my right, next to Ivy, who polishes her sharp nails with a file.

Taking a deep breath, I face the throng of consuasors. "There has been much hurt between the consuasors and the warriors," I say and then gesture toward Zorion. "Same between the Pada monks and the Teryns; between the conquered worlds and the Teryn Praelium." Just as there was so much hurt between Be'trix and me—all that anger and frustration.

"The warriors have besmirched you," I continue, "for failing your trial. This reckoning has been a long time coming thanks to all this pain, indignation, and mockery. They subjected the Pada monks and many others to the same treatment. There has been so much misunderstanding. So much prejudice."

I glance at Zorion, who glowers back. I can't imagine he likes being compared to the despised Teryns, who avoid anything magical.

What if the Teryns never conquered Pada and other worlds, but made an alliance with them instead? Would we be here today? Would Sachary and Sawney be fine? What if Be'trix and I had never fought but had become friends instead? Would she be alive?

"The truth is that we are not so different from one another," I say and put a hand over my heart, remembering my cousin. "The Teryns from the Pada. The Pada from the Teryns." I recall the Pilgrimage Circle with that wreckage that looked a lot like a spaceship, and Zorion's denial when the Teryn warriors demanded answers to a connection neither side wanted to be real.

"My cousin Be'trix from me, or me from her. We are the same coin, just a different side of it."

"We are nothing like the violent Teryns!" Zorion shouts. "We are better!"

All the pieces fall into place. How both the Teryns and the Pada have an emergence site on their worlds. Both originate from tribes. One tribe had the tendency to go berserk. Another tribe hid their magic from their cousins, trying to fit in. The Teryns don't like magic, while the Pada excel at it. That is why their ancestors warned them at the Pilgrimage Circle to not hide their magic. This is the Pada "duality" that Guardian God Patra'ch mentioned. They were originally Teryns, but they had magic. They were too proud to worship Laoise, so she got rid of them. This is why Zorion is so upset that the Teryns won't treat them as equals when it is their right by heritage, but the monk is too proud to admit that the Pada are related to the Teryns. The monk can deny it all he wants, but the Pada are distant cousins of the Teryns.

I shake my head remembering. "I never appreciated how many things I had in common with Be'trix. Yes, it's true that we got punished a lot for all our squabbling, but I forgot how much fun we had once we spent time together, away from prying eyes. We were more alike than we could understand—just like the warriors are more like the consuasors. Or how the Teryns are more like the Pada than either can comprehend. My own people, whose ancestors were once pirates, formed houses, and they treated each other as if they were different, too. But the only variance was whether their houses had more or less fortune—they were still the same people. All those high-society and low-society houses were the same. Yet it took a failed rebellion to remind them of that fact and force them to change their ways."

The consuasors nod, with thoughtful expressions, as they look to one another, murmuring.

"Lies!" Zorion yells, and Teague covers the monk's mouth with a hand.

"What is she rambling on about?" Finigal asks. "Maybe it's time to—"

"Sybil Lilla has the right to finish," Graeme retorts, "*uninterrupted.*"

Finigal narrows his eyes. "Then I suggest for her to get to the point. Fast."

The truth hurts, doesn't it? "What I do know is that offering freedom to the Tier One worlds without the permission of the Senatus cannot be lawful. That was the trade Finigal offered in exchange for kidnapping the praelor. Not to mention murdering two of his sons. By abolishing the Ground Rules these horrible acts won't be considered crimes. All of this was devised by none other than Guardian Goddess Laoise."

CHAPTER 77

The consuasors jump to their feet, shouting.

Graeme raises a hand to silence the crowd. "Those are serious allegations. What proof do you have?"

The consuasors fall silent, sitting down with their attention focused on me.

Pointing at the three women, I say, "The Wise Women are here, even now, listening and conspiring against the praelor. Since when do you allow Guardian Goddess Laoise to interfere with the day-to-day operations of the Teryn Praelium? Are you her blind zealots now?"

The Wise Women try to back out of sight, but Ivy stops them, holding two laser guns, and escorts them to the middle of the platform.

The Wise Women reach out toward each other, holding hands. A white light envelops them until a giant woman roughly in the likeness of Laoise appears, wearing a flowing and shimmering dress. "How dare you hold me in contempt?" Laoise asks and her voice booms, reverberating in the hall.

We all back away from the humongous feet of the goddess.

The consuasors in the hall stare at the giant goddess, like tiny fish stare at a deep-water shark right before it gobbles them up.

I look up at Laoise. The giant—covered from head to toe in transparent ribbons of A'ris, T'erra, and A'nima—steps to the side, making the stone platform creak and dent under her weight.

Should we transfigure? I ask Moira.

I don't see how that would be helpful against such a divine manifestation, dear. Laoise must be strongest in her avatar form, thanks to the Wise Women's fervent devotion. She can crush us like bugs, with barely making any effort.

"The better question is," I say, "how dare you interfere with your subjects' lives in such a blatant manner? You're supposed to guide them via the Wise Women, but nothing more. You're destroying the balance as we speak."

"I do as I please," Laoise says and bends down, her dark brown hair, infused with light, floating around her large head. "You tried to imprison me, but I freed myself. Your archgoddess did not come to punish me. Nor did She stop me when I cannibalized the magic of those guardian gods. But I'm not surprised. I always knew that the archgoddess was weak. There is no balance in the Seven Galaxies because the two archgods won't do their jobs. I will restore the balance when I am the only ruling power."

There it is. This is Laoise's ultimate goal—galactic domination.

I should have known, dear, that she'd try to grasp for omnipotence at the first chance she got. That is why she never let us spirits move on; it would have weakened her.

Now I understand why she cannibalized the other guardian gods—to become as strong as an archgod.

The crowd gasps, shocked.

I study Laoise. "Did you inform the Archgoddess of the Eternal Light and Order of your opinion?" There is something weblike about how those magical threads connect, reminding me of the magic Zorion stored on himself.

A flicker of doubt, gone in an instant, flashes in Laoise's dark brown eyes. "The archgoddess's job is to govern the Seven Galaxies. Yet She has no idea what is really going on. Why is that?"

I begin to gather the threads from the divine giant's body, pulling them off layer by layer. "How do you know that The Lady does not have bigger plans, and already knows everything that's going on but lets you think you've gotten away with your crimes?"

Laoise straightens. "I've just told you that The Lady does not pay attention . . ." the goddess's voice trails off as she tilts her head to the side. "What is this sensation I'm feeling?" she asks, then looks at me. "What are you doing?"

Instead of answering, I reach for my Lume magic to trap Laoise, then yank off the last layer of elemental magic that covers the goddess, disrupting her giant avatar.

"I won't let you capture me again!" Laoise screams, trying to escape.

I encase her in Lume just as a bright flash of light blinds me.

CHAPTER 78

I cover my eyes with my arm to shield myself from the harsh light.

When the light retreats, I find three dazed and naked women, the Wise Women, lying on the platform. Next to them the flickering form of Laoise lies on her stomach, bound by thick Lume magic. The goddess looks stunned, tied to this reality.

A deafening gong reverberates in the hall.

Everything freezes. The consuasors stay frozen, some sitting, others standing mid-motion. Graeme and Finigal stare at each other, unmoving. Ivy and Teague stand in the corner, reaching for the Wise Women. Zorion's mouth hangs open, in the midst of shouting, yet he emits no sound. No one moves, except for Laoise, who shakes her head, and me, when I take a step back.

What's happening, dear?

I am not sure. The hair stands up on the back of my neck and shivers wrack my body. *Whatever is going on, I have bad feeling about it.*

Suddenly, pressure crushes down on top of me, forcing me to my knees. I struggle to stand up, but my muscles spasm from whatever is pressing me down with such force that my bones creak in protest.

Lilla, what are you doing?

It's not me.

Then the air becomes scarce. I struggle to fill my lungs, gasping. Moira's eyes roll back into her head as she faints.

Laoise groans in pain, struggling against the Lume magic around her. "What have you done to me?"

Before I can answer, waves of love and joy cascade down my spine as something, or *someone*, engages my magical orb, dragging heavy Lume threads out of it. Out of me.

"Stop!" I scream through clenched teeth, but I cannot prevent the magic from rising out of my sybil talisman. It coalesces into thick ropes of Lume, attached to The Lady. She wears Her usual wraparound white dress, Her feet bare as She stands next to me, looking transparent one moment then solid the next.

"This is not my child's doing," the archgoddess says. Her ethereally beautiful face, framed by sunlight-infused, long tresses, wears a stern expression. "Nonetheless, this visit was long overdue, wouldn't you say, Guardian Goddess Laoise?"

Laoise tries to wiggle away, but The Lady shapes the commandeered Lume threads into a spear, then slams the magical spear into the guardian goddess's shoulder.

The Lume spear punches through Laoise, halting the goddess and anchoring her to the platform at the same time.

I attempt to take back control of my magic, but even stronger waves of love and joy crush me. Screams get stuck in my throat that lock up, and I choke, gasping for air.

"Do not dare to interfere, my child." The Lady flicks her wrist and suddenly I can breathe again. The archgoddess turns Her attention to Laoise. "You are wrong to think that I did not know what you've been up to. I couldn't intervene then. For an archgoddess to personally arbitrate with another god or goddess, three crimes must happen in a row: the act or acts that cause imbalance; collaborating with the Archgod of Chaos and Destruction; and lastly, manifesting without permission."

Laoise pales. "I, uh, didn't . . . I mean—"

The Lady waves a hand, interrupting the other goddess. "For these crimes, I judge you wanting. Your punishment is oblivion." The archgoddess wrenches more Lume magic out of me, and She shapes them into spears.

I whimper, feeling helpless, unable to take control of my body and magic again. I try to struggle against The Lady's hold, causing more golden filaments bursting from the sybil talisman to dig and wrap around my spine, keeping me immobilized and supplicant. Tears flow down my face, dripping to the ground beside me.

"No!" Laoise screams with wide eyes.

Dozens of Lume spears blast into her. The guardian goddess bursts into millions of light particles that The Lady sucks into Herself. Then She looks at the three Wise Women who are unmoving, fear locked on their beautiful and ageless faces. "You should not exist either."

The Lady tears more Lume magic out of me, shaping them into Lume spears. She sends the magic spears flying at the Wise Women.

They all burst into light particles that The Lady again collects into Herself. She wipes Her hands. "Acolyte Aisla, join me."

Acolyte Aisla's image appears, wearing a similar wraparound dress as the archgoddess. She looks transparent and flickering as if the petite blonde goddess has trouble keeping her shape. "As you command, my archgoddess," she says and bows her head.

The Lady lifts a hand, placing it above Acolyte Aisla's bowed head. "I assign you to the Teryn world as their guardian goddess." All the light particles The Lady collected from Laoise flow into Aisla, lifting her off the ground.

"I accept," Aisla shouts as her body arches from all the power streaming into her, making her solid for a second.

"You will guard this world and obey my orders," The Lady says. Guardian Goddess Aisla nods and vanishes. Then the archgoddess waves an elegant hand.

A tanned, black-haired woman, wearing a flowing red dress with leather scandals, appears on the stage as if the archgoddess has teleported her onto the platform. "What am I doing here? Who are you?"

The Lady flicks Her fingers, and the woman freezes as if paralyzed. "You will be the new Wise Woman from now on. You will obey Guardian Goddess Ailsa and above all, you will obey me." Then The Lady sends shimmering light particles that She'd taken from the previous Wise Women into the new one.

The new Wise Woman shivers, her body bowing outward as the power floods into her. Then the archgoddess flicks Her fingers and the woman disappears.

A satisfied smile appears on the archgoddess's gorgeous face as she looks down on me. "You did very well, my child. Thanks to you, I was able to take care of the pesky problems Laoise caused. She has been impacting the balance for quite some time, always ensuring she never crossed that final line—manifestation."

The Lady looks away for a moment, lost in thought, then continues, "I thought Laoise would manifest when you came out of the spirit realm melded, but she only used her zealot Wise Women to order your death. I couldn't punish Laoise in the Lume prison, but I suspected she'd find a way to free herself, and the goddess did. I knew it was only a matter of time before Laoise made a mistake. When you took the initiative to head to Pada, I was glad I didn't have to order you. I had a feeling that your presence would be enough to push Laoise to cross the final line of manifestation, and I was right. Now I can focus on winning this Era War once and for all. Don't forget to be back on Cathal with the Teryn armada as I ordered you."

I glare at the archgoddess. Moira was right; The Lady did have an ulterior purpose. She used me to bait Laoise more than once, risking my life in the process. I was Her puppet and nothing more.

From one blink to the next, The Lady disappears.

Suddenly free from restraints, I collapse onto my hands and knees as the Lume magic retracts into my sore body that feels beaten and drained. The glow from my arms dissipates, leaving behind goosebumps.

My mind reels, trying to come to terms with how easily the archgoddess took my magic from me to destroy Laoise and the ex-Wise Women. And there was nothing I could do to block the archgoddess.

A sob tries to break free as I sit back on my heels and hug my middle. I swear to myself right then that I'd rather die than let The Lady ever control me like that ever again. For that to work, I'll first have to find a way to get rid of the sybil talisman.

I curl my fingers into my palms until my nails cut into my skin, resisting the urge to reach back and tear out that fog-cursed talisman, regretting the day I accepted it.

Moira wrings her clawed hands. *I'm so sorry, dear. I couldn't help you . . .*

I manage a nod as I fight the tide of panic that threatens to drown me.

The sybil talisman sends a tremendous burst of healing power. It takes all the physical wounds and pain—including the ones from my earlier injuries—away, as if rewarding me for my "willing" cooperation.

I scramble to my feet to argue when another deafening gong echoes through the hall.

Blinking, I rub my forehead, my mind emptied of all thought.

I look around, confused. "Where am I?" I ask, trying to remember but drawing a blank. My cheek itches. I touch my face, and my fingers come away wet. I stare at my hand. Am I crying? But why?

Moira yawns and rubs her eyes. *I'm not sure, dear. Also, why was I asleep? I can't seem to recall. Let me check your memory.* She pokes inside my mind without waiting for my permission.

Searing pain, like nothing I've ever experienced, erupts behind my eyes, making me go blind for a moment.

Moira, stop! It hurts too much!

Moira obeys and the pain goes away. My vision returns and I face the vast hall, full of people in colorful shirts. Not just any people. Teryns.

The consuasors settle down, murmuring among themselves and looking lost.

Caderyn blinks his eyes with a frazzled expression. Callum glances around, as if reorienting himself. Even the guards holding him fidget, unsure.

Ivy frowns at Teague next to her. "Why are we standing here?"

He shakes his head. "We were . . . we were doing something. Something important, but I can't remember. . ." his voice trails off as he concentrates.

Graeme steps up to me. "I seem to have lost my . . . I, uh, recollect the praelor, you, and the Ground Rules. Yes, and Finigal's betrayal."

Then I recall why I've come here. To save the Teryn empire and the Seven Galaxies.

Finigal blinks, then fists his hands. "You cannot prove my involvement."

Ivy rolls her eyes as she waltzes back to us. "Amateur. He doesn't even know how to deny guilt properly."

The consuasors converse among themselves, sounding agitated.

Graeme clears his throat until the hall turns quiet. "It is unusual for a consuasor to take matters into his hands like this, but this incident does not indisputably prove Finigal's involvement with the kidnapping and political assassinations per se. Do you have any other proof?"

"I do," I say, and turn to Teague who has returned to his place by Zorion, holding the monk by the arm. I gesture for him to come forward. "I have a witness who collaborated with Finigal and who was also an organizer in this offense."

"No!" Finigal shouts and takes out a laser gun, aiming it at the Pada monk.

CHAPTER 79

"Lilla!" Callum roars, struggling against the six guards holding him. "Watch out!

Time slows down.

Moira, we need to transfigure.

A colorful shimmer washes over me. Then our cymmerion battle form emerges, supported by strong dra'agon legs. Three heads—one eagle with black feathers, one wolf with a black mane, and one dra'agon with multi-hued scales—turn toward Finigal. We extend our twenty-foot-long leathery wings to their full length. Our thick and scale-covered tail, ending in a scorpion stinger, flickers into view.

Time restarts.

We slam our tail with the stinger into Consuasor Finigal's shoulder. His arm drops and the laser shot goes wide, missing the pale-looking Zorion. We retract the stinger.

Consuasor Finigal falls backward like a log, his body stiff. Only his enraged eyes move in his frozen face.

Moira.

Fine, dear. You are spoiling all the fun. We make a hacking sound, then bend down from our ten-foot height and spit.

A large gob of spittle lands on Finigal, the antidote of the paralyzing agent. Purple patches bloom on the consuasor's face.

Then we raise our three heads to the domed ceiling, roaring our displeasure. Stained glass shatters in many window frames. We stomp our feet. The already bent platform under our dra'agon feet fractures, fissures spreading far across the stone tiles.

The consuasors stare at us, motionless.

Graeme turns to us. "If you don't mind, Sybil Lilla."

"Sorry," the wolf maw says. We change back in the next second, leaving me stark naked and shivering from the shock of it.

Crossing my arms in front of me, I try to cover the important bits from the Senatus. Hot wind bursts through the open window frames, rustling my hair.

Teague throws me his black jacket. I catch it and pull it on, with cheeks burning.

Moira!

She laughs. *It's not like I can magic clothing on you, dear.*

Zorion clears his throat. "On the way here, I decided not to say a word that would confirm or deny any allegations. However, it seems that I have not anticipated the depth to which Finigal is willing to lower himself for his own protection. I will not take any blame for his actions."

The Pada monk swallows. "I, uh, thank you, Sybil Lilla, for saving my life." He manages to bow his head an inch, the Lume magic around him restricting most of his movements.

"Don't mention it," I say.

"I realize that I have hurt many with my actions," Zorion continues in a solemn voice, looking at the consuasors. "All I cared about was my world's freedom and its fair treatment. I knew about the supposed connection between the Teryns and the Pada, but I did not want to accept it. Frankly, I am surprised that you've figured it out, Sybil Lilla, on your own."

I shrug. "It was in front of me. Literally."

Zorion winces. "I underestimated you, Sybil Lilla. I realize now how I've allowed my prejudice to mislead me from what is right. As an elected leader of the Pada monks, and host to the Tier One factions, I failed many, spurred by my pride that turned me blind."

The monk pauses to swallow, then continues, "I hereby confess to the crime of collaborating with the other Tier One factions, at the behest of Consuasor Finigal, to kidnap the Teryn praelor. I am also responsible for the death of his two sons. I know my words are inept and change nothing, but please allow me to convey how sorry I am for my part in this crime."

CHAPTER 80

Graeme nods at the Pada monk, then turns to Finigal, who scrambles to his feet on unsteady legs. "What do you have to say for yourself?"

Finigal tries to smile, but his jaw muscles won't obey him, making his face stick in a grotesque mask of half grin, half scowl. "I did what I thought was best for the Teryn Praelium. If that makes me guilty, then so be it."

The consuasors boo.

Finigal grimaces. "I had no choice but to act quickly, seeing how the warriors brutalized the Tier One worlds, knowing that an intergalactic uprising against the Teryn Praelium would soon be inevitable. Especially after the praelor demolished that space station with so many people aboard."

I point at Finigal. "It makes me wonder if that was not part of your plan all along—have one of the factions underperform, then watch Caderyn punish them publicly. You achieved two goals at the same time: get Caderyn on Pada so Zorion and the others can kidnap him and prove to the factions that they must break free from the empire before the praelor destroys them. You set up the perfect trap for Caderyn, while ensuring that there was no going back for the factions. I remember the shock on Elder Fran's face when that space station exploded. This is the sacrifice she made; one I overheard the Marauder queen refer to. I bet you promised the farmers a mild punishment, but even you couldn't control the praelor."

Finigal's face falls. "It wasn't like that. I mean, that's not what happened."

"From where I'm standing," Graeme says, "it looks like that's exactly what happened."

Shouts of anger rise in the hall.

I shake my head. "Not to mention, you promised freedom to the Tier One worlds, in the name of the Senatus, *before* Caderyn eliminated that space station. That tragic punishment the praelor meted out was not the cause of your actions, but part of your cold calculation that involved manipulating so many players, including the farmers."

Finigal spreads his hands, pleading with the angry consuasors. "Yes, but at least I didn't transfigure *inside* the Senatus building. That has to count for something."

"It is not illegal to show a battle form—even one as formidable as the infamous cymmerion—inside the Senatus building," Graeme says. "Though it's highly improper."

I cringe. "I'm sorry for breaking those windows."

Graeme turns to Finigal. "I, by the power entrusted in me from the Senatus to act solely in the case of emergency, strip you, Consuasor Finigal, of your rank."

"No!" ex-consuasor Finigal shouts and the crowd cheers.

Graeme gestures to the right. A dozen guards rush in.

"Your punishment for this treason is death," Chief Consuasor Graeme says. "Take these men away. The Senatus will deal with them and the Tier One faction leaders at a later time." He indicates Finigal, Zorion, and the four Marauder thugs who now hold onto Caderyn as if the praelor is their lifeline in the raging ocean.

"No!" Finigal hollers, thrashing in the hands of the guards, next to the calm Pada monk. "This is all the sybil's fault. She will destroy the Teryn Praelium, you fools!"

CHAPTER 81

I watch the men being taken away from the platform and can't help but feel sorry for them. They fought for what they believed in, albeit in the worst possible way.

"Don't mind him," Teague says. He pulls a flat biscuit from his pants pocket and shoves the food into his mouth. "You will not destroy the Teryn Praelium. At least not anytime soon, I think."

I study Teague's face. Here he is, trying to cheer me up even after I pushed him away without hearing him out. Yet he did not give up on me. He stayed and helped, fighting the Tier One factions in that warehouse. Then he used his special skill to bring Zorion to the Senatus, while also arranging for Steaphan to help us get into the Senatus building unseen—even after I'd sent him away.

My gaze scans the platform until I find Ivy standing to the side. She went back to the dowager queen, risking her life as she spied for me. Acting like a good friend, she brought me to the Teryn world at breakneck speed. And she did this even when I was not a good friend to her.

When Ivy notices me staring, she sashays to us. "There are going to be a lot of executions. I was always partial to being thrown out of a spaceport over laser guns. It's a much quicker way to go, and less likely to suffer from misfires."

"She does have a point," Teague says, and wipes the crumbs off his mouth.

I turn to Graeme. "May I say a few more words, please?"

Graeme claps a few times and the consuasors turn to face us. "Go ahead."

I smile at Teague and Ivy. "I have judged two of my good friends unfairly, without hearing them out. I've let them down."

Teague coughs, hitting his chest a few times. Ivy's mouth gapes open.

"I should have been a better friend to both of you. Please forgive me."

Teague waves it away. Ivy manages a nod.

"All these injuries accumulated," I say, turning toward the Senatus, "because each side, the warriors and the consuasors, held onto their resentments.

Both judged the other unkindly and without any compassion. Without empathy, I couldn't understand the actions of my friends."

"Those are sage words," Graeme says. "We heard Sybil Lilla's support of the case of Caderyn a'ruun, our praelor. Without exception it requires a Senatus majority when it comes to any case involving the praelor. What say you of his charges? Raise your right hand for guilty, and your left for not guilty."

CHAPTER 82

The consuasors deliberate among themselves for a minute. Then they raise their left hands—the signal for not guilty—almost unanimously.

Chief Consuasor Graeme nods. "Based on all the evidence presented, and the support of Caderyn a'ruun, we find the praelor not guilty of charges."

The consuasors clap.

Graeme gestures toward Caderyn, and a guard unties the praelor.

Caderyn rips the tape off his mouth. "It was about damn time."

A commotion sounds.

General Crane, followed by Rhona and fifty black-clad warriors, storms onto the stone platform.

"We are here to save the praelor!" General Crane bellows. "Let him go this instant."

Caderyn sighs. "General Crane, there is no need for that. As you can see, I *am* saved."

The burly general glowers. "Are you sure, Praelor? I've got all these good warriors itching to attack the Senatus—"

"I *am* sure," Caderyn says. "Disperse the warriors and do not attack."

General Crane touches his ear, activating his k'bug. He mutters commands, then looks around the Senatus, his gaze snagging on the broken windows and the large cracks in the stone platform. "What happened here?" he asks. When no one answers him, he adds, "If you don't need anything else from me . . ."

Caderyn inclines his chin. "By your leave, General."

General Crane snaps his heels, nods at the other warriors, and marches off the platform.

Rhona crosses her arms. "I was looking forward to looting the Senatus."

Caderyn grunts. "We'll have a conversation about instigating a civil war at home."

Rhona's eyes go wide. "Yes, sir." She hurries out of the hall.

Graeme wipes his forehead. "I had no idea that General Crane was willing to take things so far. I am glad we won't have the praelium face a civil war."

"At least not today," Caderyn says.

I raise my eyebrows. "Praelor, don't you have something *else* to say?"

Caderyn grimaces. "Must I?"

The consuasors watch their praelor, waiting.

Caderyn rubs the back of his neck. "I can see how my actions might have been hurtful to you, Brainiacs, I mean, consuasors. I did look down on you, considered you utter failures for not finishing your trials, and generally disrespected you."

The consuasors gape at Caderyn, including Graeme.

"I cannot change my past actions," Caderyn says. "However, I am willing to make concessions and act differently going forward."

Graeme snaps his mouth closed and nods. "The last item on our agenda is the case of Callum a'ruun, second war general. The charges are treason by disobeying orders twice. You have no one to support your case but have earned the right to represent yourself by getting through the lower circuits of court at an unprecedented speed. What do you have to say for yourself?"

The guards release Callum, and he steps forward.

"I am so sorry," I whisper to him.

A half smile appears at the corner of his mouth. "I now understand why."

"The charges are true," Callum says to the consuasors. "I disobeyed my orders twice. There are no words to excuse my actions. All I have is an explanation. When Lilla, Teague, and I were ambushed on that beach on Uhna, we fought the dark servants, only to realize that they were fully corrupted. They kept regenerating. I transfigured to my battle form to better protect her, knowing that I betrayed our most guarded secret."

The consuasors mutter, but many nod in understanding.

"I also delayed sending the report on the corruption levels I found on Uhna," Callum continues, "because I knew it would bring the Teryn armada to her world. I wanted Lilla to have more time to find the Archgod of Chaos and Destruction."

Graeme clasps his hands with a deep exhale. "I think I can speak for many consuasors when I say that we understand your explanation. However, we are all still bound by the Ground Rules, which dictate keeping the battle form a secret, even from Sybil Lilla, who at the time did not possess the Heart Amulet. We heard Callum a'ruun's defense. I, by the power entrusted in me from the Senatus to act solely in the case of emergency, find you guilty of the charges."

CHAPTER 83

"No!" I shout and try to run to Callum, but Teague restrains me with an arm across my waist.

I am so sorry, dear.

"I understand, Chief Consuasor Graeme," Callum says. "I do not dispute your verdict."

My knees give out, but Teague's hold keeps me upright. "There is nothing we can do, love. I am truly sorry."

They cannot execute him for doing the right thing.

I swipe against the wetness running down my cheeks.

Graeme gestures and two of the guards grab Callum.

Caderyn raises a hand. "Are the Ground Rules still in effect?"

Graeme nods. "They are, though how long is another matter the Senatus must debate, but at a much later time."

"That is all I needed to know," Caderyn says, then turns to me. "Do you want to invoke Ground Rule number six, subsection two hundred fifty, amendment three hundred eleven?"

CHAPTER 84

I blink at Caderyn. I have no idea what that specific Ground Rule covers. I manage a nod while trying to look confident.

Graeme smiles at me. "If you wouldn't mind, Sybil Lilla, would you please verbally acknowledge your choice so that it can go on the record?"

"There is a record?" I squeak, now noticing a consuasor in the front row, writing on a transparent digital tablet. "I mean, yes. My answer is yes."

The consuasors mutter among themselves.

Caderyn rubs his hands together. "As per Ground Rule number six, subsection two hundred fifty, amendment three hundred eleven, do you want the pardon to be extended to General Callum a'ruun?"

I look at Teague. "Uh . . ."

"Ground Rule six focuses on arguments without taking familial ties between the fighter and fightee," Teague whispers. "Subsection two hundred fifty covers all the pardons the praelor can issue—for actions such as saving his life—and when he can't issue any pardon, especially to his own family members. Amendment three hundred eleven allows any pardon issued by the praelor to be extended to a worthy and honorable person of the recipient's choice."

Your future father-in-law is quite cunning, I must say, dear.

"Huh?" Ivy asks. "Translation, please."

"Because Callum is related to the praelor," I say, "Caderyn cannot offer any pardon for disobeying charges, even if there are mitigating circumstances. Since I saved Caderyn's life, he now can offer a pardon to me as a favor, which makes me the, uh, recipient. Those specific Ground Rules allow me to extend Caderyn's pardon to a 'worthy and honorable' person of my choice."

I can save Callum.

"Oh! It's the 'you saved me, now I save you' law with a twist," Ivy says, nodding. "We Marauders had to erase that from our constitution because every thug owed their life to someone else, and no one was punished for their crime."

"What do you say, Sybil Lilla?" Graeme asks patiently.

"Yes! A thousand times yes. Please extend the, uh, pardon to Callum."

"Done," Graeme says. "I hereby dissolve the treason charges against you, General Callum a'ruun. You may return to your rank with no ramifications."

The consuasors drum their feet on the stone steps and clap along as we leave the hall.

EPILOGUE

Callum, holding me in his arms, kicks the door to his room on the Teryn spaceship closed. Through the tall window glass, the orange and vivid green jungle of Cathal is visible in the setting sun's light.

We've returned to Cathal with Caderyn and my friends, including Fearghas and S'affi, in time for The Lady's deadline. Nothing waited for us, just the wild rainforest and even wilder predatory animals and plants.

We honored Sachary and Sawney on their last journey, with their family and fellow warriors surrounding their funeral pyre. It was a somber occasion, but Sorcha and Caderyn held onto each other, sharing their grief and hugging Callum and Rhona as they said their good-byes.

The following evening we honored my Bride's Choice claim with Caderyn officiating in the same meadow as before. It was a simple and blissful ceremony. Caderyn and Sorcha told me that part of their funeral tradition is to follow it up with a celebration of life—and what is a better celebration than a wedding? I missed my family. I missed Glenna and Ragnald, but the ceremony and the dinner that followed, picnic-style on the grass, flew by in a blur. Callum and I couldn't take our eyes off each other and didn't even touch our food. We excused ourselves at the first opportunity. The warriors shouted in jest, but we didn't care as we made our way back to the ship.

"You look so beautiful," Callum says and smiles at me, looking stunning in his form-fitting black uniform, which emphasizes his six-and-a-half-foot-tall muscular body.

I can't look away from his clear blue eyes that shine with so much love and happiness in his tanned face. Excitement sends shivers down my arms, raising goose bumps.

I touch his face. "We're finally together."

Callum holds me closer to his chest. "Just the two of us."

Moira promised to give us full privacy and I have not heard a peep out of her all evening.

Callum strides to the large bed in the middle of his room. Soft pink petals, scattered on the top of the white blanket, scent the air with their sweet perfume.

He puts me on the cover and lays down on his side, next to me. "I have you where I want you."

A blush rises to my cheeks. I can't take my eyes off him, worried that if I lose sight of him, he'll disappear again.

Callum leans over and kisses me, each kiss soft and slow. His hand quests down my arm. His fingers trail over the back of my silver dress until they find the tiny buttons hidden in the soft fabric.

I thread my arms around his neck and deepen our kiss, drinking in his scent and drowning in our love. I never thought I'd feel so happy and free, as I feel right now, in his arms. I never thought I'd find my reason to live. My reason to be happy. With my heart so full of love.

"I will never let you go," Callum says and peppers my jawline with kisses, all the way down my neck, trailing goose bumps as he unbuttons my dress.

"You are all mine," I say breathlessly and push his jacket off his wide shoulders.

Callum laughs and pulls me to his body. "Always and forever."

1 WEEK LATER

Yawning, I wake up. The rising orange sun paints the room in cheerful light.

I move to get up, but Callum's arm tightens around my naked waist. He cracks open an eye. "Where are you going in such a hurry, my love and life?"

I lay back, blushing. "I am not hurrying anywhere." Happiness fills my heart as I look at his handsome face and tousled black hair. How can I love someone so much?

"Good. I have not received a proper morning greeting from you yet."

I laugh. "Is that what you call it these days?"

Callum opens both his eyes and grins. "Your insolence is not appreciated so early in the morning."

"Is that so?"

"Now you must kiss me."

I snort and cover my mouth with a hand. "But I have morning breath."

Callum raises an eyebrow. "I'm still waiting."

I kiss him, just a peck on his lips, but he grabs me by my hips and with a quick move he flips us over until he is on top of me. Then he kisses me, taking my breath away, caging me in with his muscular arms.

Bang! Bang!

Callum pulls back and curses under his breath. He turns his head and glares at the door. I feel bad for whoever has dared to interrupt us. "Go away."

I slip out of his arms and out of bed. From a small closet, I select a silver tunic and black leggings and pull them on. "Aren't you going to see who it is?"

"In a minute." Callum puts on a pair of pants and comes around the bed, stopping beside me. He pulls me into a hug. My hands land on his strong chest. I give in to temptation to run my fingers along his pectoral muscles.

Callum groans. Desire makes his blue eyes darken. He reaches for the hem of my tunic. "There is no need to hide from me."

I slap his hand playfully. "Callum."

"I must say, I am in need of refreshing certain details."

I take a step back. "Is that an early onset of old age? You are six years older than I am, after all."

Callum chuckles, following me. "I'll show you old." He leans his head down and nips my earlobe, sending shivers down my spine. His hands run down my arms, then back to my shoulders.

I can't help but giggle. "Are you going to kiss where you bit me?"

Callum raises his head, his expression full of unabashed need. "Oh, I plan to kiss you everywhere until you beg me to stop. As you did last night."

My breath hitches as I remember how we couldn't get enough of each other. "I was not begging."

Callum nuzzles my neck. "I seem to recall otherwise."

BANG! BANG! BANG!

Callum curses and releases me.

He strides to the door and tears it open. "What do you want?"

A brown-haired warrior gulps. "The praelor requests Sybil Lilla's presence."

I hesitate in front of an inward-angled door that leads to the command center on the Teryn spaceship. Sweat breaks out on my palms, and I wipe them on my shirt. It's been a week since we came back from Pada, and not once have I been allowed to set a foot in there.

I stare, frozen, at the metal door.

"Aren't you going to use it, my love and life?" Callum asks.

"I keep waiting to wake up from this surreal dream only to find your father laughing at me as he slams the door in my face." I turn to the warrior next to me. "Are you sure the praelor asked for *me*?"

"Yes, ma'am," the warrior says, bows his head and leaves, almost running away from us.

"No need to scare the crew," Callum jokes and waves his hand on the right side of the doorframe, over the control panel. The metal door slides open with a swish.

I step through the doorway with Callum right behind me.

Most of the cavernous, two-story room is made of a series of tinted glass panels that show the overgrown, wild jungle in the orange-pink light of dawn.

Metal grates cover the floor, with people working in front of transparent sections of screens, with lights running on their surface.

Behind me, on the second story, narrow corridors run the perimeter, with even more warriors sitting in front of built-in screens. In the middle of the room, on a raised platform, stands Caderyn, looking at three transparent rectangular screens that are five feet by two feet and hovering in the air.

We climb the metal stairs and stop next to Caderyn.

"What took you so long?" the praelor asks when he looks at me.

"I am not sure how to politely answer that," I mutter.

Moira chuckles in my head. *I have a few tips, dear.*

"We were busy," Callum says and folds his arms across his muscular chest.

Caderyn glances at me. "What do you think?"

"Oh, it's, um, a very nice command center. Well put together and, um, organized."

Callum snorts.

"I agree," Caderyn says, and gestures to the three screens showing blue dots around a large orangish planet, Cathal. "As you can see, all my ships are here, waiting. Have you heard anything from the Archgoddess of the Eternal Light and Order about your so-called mission?"

I shake my head. "No."

Counting the dots, I frown. "Those are only five hundred spaceships. The Lady said to bring *all* your ships here."

Caderyn smirks. "Why would I do that, little, uh, I mean, Lilla. I have thousands of ships, fighting the rising corruption levels all over the Seven Galaxies as we speak. I couldn't just order them to abandon their tasks before they're finished. And for what? To stand still over this horrid planet, with all that rain and moisture dripping from everywhere, while they're doing nothing?"

I cross my arms. "But The Lady—"

An alarm sounds above us, and a warrior leans over the balcony and looks at Caderyn. "Sir, this is strange, but—"

Another alarm sounds.

And another.

Soon thousands and thousands of alarms screech in the command center.

Everywhere around us, on every screen, red dots appear, multiplying like spreading mold.

I exchange a look with Callum. "Buckets of fishguts!"

ACKNOWLEDGMENTS

I'm so happy to present you, dear readers, with the third installment in *The Last Lumenian* series. A lot of teamwork goes into creating a book. I would like to thank these wonderful individuals who helped bring this book to life:

Thank you, Matt, for your patience and support. You kept me strong!

Thank you, Mario, for your unrelenting support of this series and me.

Thank you, Leslie, for brainstorming and helping me to clear up a few things.

Thank you, Julie and William, for the amazing editing you both provided. Your professionalism never ceases to amaze me. I appreciate you both very much.

Thank you, Dan and Natasha, from NY Book Editors; it is such a pleasure to keep working with you on this series. I know that my book series is in great hands.

Thank you, Lee and Christopher, from IBPA for all the amazing opportunities you provide for your members. Truly appreciate you.

Thank you, Jane, from Bedside Reading, for your support, enthusiasm, and wonderful ways to promote my book series. Your energy is contagious!

Thank you, RB Aquatic Improv team: Erica, Penny, Laura, Jaycee, Gemma, Suzanne, Jill. You are such talented and amazing ladies. I had so much fun learning the ropes alongside you.

Thank you, Jackson and Doug, for your guidance and expertise in digital media and marketing.

Thank you, Ed and Don, the best PR guys in the whole Galaxy One.

Thank you, Melissa, the best PR director, and friend in the whole Galaxy Two.

Thank you, Clif, the best map illustrator in the whole Galaxy Three.

Thank you, Tim, the best cover artist extraordinaire in the whole Galaxy Four.

Thank you, Lukas, the best illustrator in the whole Galaxy Five.

Thank you, Ray and Abigail, the best web design wizards in the whole Galaxy Six.

Thank you, dear readers, for being the BEST READERS in the whole Seven Galaxies. Your support means the world to me!

Last but not least, thank you, God, for giving me the opportunity to follow my passion and to live my dream.

Family: see dedication page. (I love you but no need to be attention hogs.)

GLOSSARY

A

Aisla, acolyte
She is an acolyte goddess to the archgoddess. She often scowls at Lilla.

A'nima, element
Nature magic.

Ankhar
Right hand, avatar, and general to the Archgod of Chaos and Destruction.

Archgoddess of the Eternal Light and Order
One of the ruling archgods. She is ageless and fights on the side of Light and Order in the Era War. Lilla is her sybil. She is the mother of all Lumenians. Her acolyte is Aisla.

A'ris, element
Air magic.

Arrov, Prince
Seventh son of Queen Amra. He is from A'ice. A great pilot. Very handsome. He can turn into an A'ice giant.

A'qua, element
Water magic.

B

Battle form
This form originates from melding with a spirit warrior and provides superior skills, strength, and a high level of magic immunity.

Belthair
Six-armed ex-rebel who once was Lilla's boyfriend. Now he is an opinion-ated, I mean valuable ally.

Be'trice
A young woman. Lilla's cousin.

Bride's Choice
An ancient Teryn tradition where a woman can claim a man as her intend-ed, which Lilla did. On Callum.

C

Caderyn, a'ruun
An imposing and large, but fit, older warrior who is the emperor of the Teryn empire. Callum's and Rhona's father. He has a well-established beard.

Callum, a'ruun
Second general in the Teryn army. His clear blue eyes tend to glint with intel-lect in his tanned face. He always looks sharp and confident in his black, mil-itary-style uniform, which emphasizes his muscular body. Lilla loves him.

Cathal, planet
Orange-green jungle planet with a peaceful atmosphere. It is the location of Lilla's second mission as a sybil.

Cocoa, plant
Ground-dwelling plants cultivated by the Pada monks. It has more than three hundred varieties.

Compact travel sword, Teryn
Rhona's portable sword, which fits into a black, rectangular box. Very handy.

Consuasor, Teryn
A Teryn title, meaning senator.

Cosmic web propulsion, aka CWP
A Teryn technology that uses the cosmic-web-like space highways for faster space travel. With the help of the beaked salamanders, the Teryns collect space particles, then filter them down to hydrogen atoms to slingshot to their destination, cutting down travel time to a few weeks as opposed to a few lifetimes. One side effect: it tends to push space debris ahead of them.

Crane, General
A burly warrior man with gray hair. He likes to argue with Consuasor Staan.

D

Dark fiends
They are creations of the Archgod of Chaos and Destruction. They tend to be monstrous.

Dark servants
They are creations of the Archgod of Chaos and Destruction. They don't like Lumenians or anyone but themselves alive, to be honest.

Devotee, Pada
Devotee is the second-highest rank among the Pada monks.

Disciples, Pada
Lowest rank among the pada. They are not allowed to speak.

DLD
Shortened version of the Dark Lord of Destruction, a nickname the Archgod of Chaos and Destruction prefers to use. It does drive the point home, if I may say so.

E

Eels, giant
They are impossibly long (twenty feet at least), with a wide and slimy

body. Their triangular head is full of sharp teeth. They live in lakes around waterfalls.

Elements, chaos
There are six chaos elements that are the domain of the Archgod of Chaos and Destruction: Murky A'qua, Black T'erra, Shadowy Fla'mma, Dusky A'ris, Rabid A'nima, and Acerbus.

Elements, light
There are six light elements that are the domain of the Archgoddess of the Eternal Light and Order: A'ris, T'erra, A'qua, Fla'mma, A'nima, and Lume.

Era War, the
A devastating and recurring galactic war between the two ruling archgods that happens when the imbalance of power between them becomes too great. Like now.

F

Factory leader Ia'an
A tall man with slicked-back hair who likes to wear suits. He has a small black device that can zap (and deactivate) androids.

Fearghas, battle horse
Lilla's powerful battle horse. He tends to bite or charge at you for no evident reason.

Fight circle, portable
A palm-size, round, and red device that can create a very useful shimmering yet transparent fight circle anywhere. It is highly customizable when it comes to its borders. Examples: three rows of daggers that point inward, five rows of horizontal laser lines, fire.

Finigal, Consuasor
A blond and athletic man who has a knack for deescalating situations.

Fla'mma, element
Fire magic, one of six light elements. Fun fact: can be formed into fireballs!

Fran, Elder
She is an older woman with gray hair, who leads the Farmers' Partnership. She likes to drink tea.

Fye Island, Uhna
A snow-covered island where once the Crystal Palace stood, half carved into the Piercing Mountains. Then DLD happened . . .

Fyoon Ocean, Uhna
Beautiful but deadly ocean that surrounds Fye Island.

G

Glenna, healer
Petite best friend of Lilla. Talented healer. Has beautiful dark crimson hair with white strands and dark crimson eyes.

Graeme, Chief Consuasor
A tall and dark-haired man in his early thirties who leads the Teryn consuasors in the senatus.

Gregry, Miner
He is stocky man who is the leader of the Coal Miners' Coalition. He carries his belongings on a highly adaptable and hovering platform.

Ground Rules, Teryn
Ten rules with fifty subrules and hundreds of addendums that are very important to the Teryn warriors.

H

Honor ideology
The Teryns always keep honor at the forefront.

I

Intonia Varia Yane, aka Ivy
A blond crown princess from the Marauders' Syndicate. She is a friend of and ally to Lilla. She has a certain preoccupation with poisoning.

J

Jokes, plenty of
There are some good jokes in book 3.

K

K'bug, communicator
Teryn technology. It is a white, button-size insect that attaches to the back of the ear. The thin, long hairs on its leg resonate when pressed on its back, creating sound waves that can reach another bug "device" to far distances.

Kristofer, chief merchant
A young man with shaggy long hair and four ears. He is the leader of the Merchants' Vendere. He loves playing the hologram game: is it real or not?

L

Lady, The
It is the favored nickname of the Archgoddess of the Eternal Light and Order.

Laoise, Guardian Goddess
She is the Teryn guardian goddess. She speaks through the three Wise Women.

Luiza, Young
A blond woman who is granddaughter of Elder Fran.

Lume, element
Powerful magic of light and energy.

Lumenian, legendary
A legendary race that the Archgoddess of the Eternal Light and Order created. There is only one left now: Lilla.

M

Moira
Queen of the original Teryns and melded spirit to Lilla.

N

Nasty beast
Fearghas's nickname.

O

Omnipower
An unknown power that governs the Seven Galaxies with balance in focus.

P

Pada, Galaxy Six
It is the name of the lush, green world and of the monk-like people who reside there. They are mysterious and highly magical. They are also the first world the Teryn Praelium conquered. Without a fight, I might add.

Patra'ch, Guardian God
He is the guardian god to the Pada monks. He is beloved and has his own magical meadow.

Pilgrimage Circle
A sacred site for the Pada monks. It is half-circle-shaped wall that is six feet tall with runic writing on it.

Praelia, Teryn
Title, meaning empress.

Praelium, Teryn
Name of the Teryn empire.

Praelor, Teryn
Title, meaning emperor.

Q

Queen, dowager
Her name is Sheela. She is the ruler of the Marauders' Syndicate, from the House of Two Guns and a Dagger. She is also Ivy's mother.

R

Ragnald, Elementalist Mage
A loyal friend of and ally to Lila. He is a two-hundred-year-old handsome mage who is expert in magic. He has triple elemental affinity in T'erra, Fla'mma, and A'qua elements. On occasion he is known to build stairs for himself out of rubble by using his T'erra magic.

Rhona, a'ruun
She is a Teryn warrior woman who wants to be a general. She is also Callum's sister.

S

Sachary, a'ruun
One of Callum's older brothers from a different marriage. He likes to smirk.

Sa'ffi
A mysterious bunny-squirrel-with-antlers who follows Lilla. She can appear and disappear at will. She is also really cute.

Sawney, a'ruun
The other older brother of Callum from a different marriage. He has a pair of daggers.

Senatus, Teryn
Teryn senators as a group. They have their own building, rules, and guards.

Seven Galaxies
Where this story plays out. It has (you guessed it!) seven galaxies in it.

Sorcha, a'ruun
She is a Teryn warrior woman and empress. Mother of Callum and Rhona. She is a great hostess.

Steaphan, Consuasor
A young, handsome, and Teryn man who is a senator.

Sybil
Right hand, avatar, and general to the Archgoddess of the Eternal Light and Order. Lilla holds the honor of being the current one.

Szyrilla, magical creature
Small red violet-colored animal. It has long ears and a bushy tail, with two-inch-long dark brown pedicles on top of its head. Its rabbit-like body is covered with green flower stalks and white flowers.

T

Talisman, sybil
A talisman that is finger-long, oval, and transparent. It is lodged into Lilla's spine with intricate gold filaments coming from a pair of crab-like claws at each end of the talisman.

Teague, Colonel
A Teryn colonel who has streaks of scarlet, white, and blond in his black hair that frames his tanned face. He constantly munches on something while mischief glints in his dark brown eyes.

T'erra, element
Ground magic.

Teryn, Galaxy Six
Name of the planet and its people.

Tier One factions
Seven worlds that the Teryns conquered first: Pada, Marauders Syndicate, Industrial Conglomerate, Farmers Partnership, Miners Coalition, Merchants Verde, and Free Traders.

Trader, Pecker
A large man with a stained shirt who leads the Free Traders Faction. He has two hulking androids covered in shiny plastic.

Trust fall exercise
One of the cooperation-building exercises done over a waterfall. What could go wrong?

Turned Mages
A corrupted magic user who is bent on destroying everyone and everything in their way. Blood-thirsty and ruthless.

Twins, Isa and Bella
Isa and Bella are twin princesses from Barabal. They are great hackers and friends of Lilla.

U

Uhna, Galaxy Five
The oceanic home world of Lilla. Name of the planet and its people.

V

Very nice!

W

Warship, Teryn
A tremendous, black, and rectangular ship. Its size is so massive it could easily double for a small city. Its jagged surface is covered with world-erasing cannons, space missiles, and energy-shield piercing arrays. In other words, very dangerous.

Wise Women, Teryn
Three black-haired young women who are the vessels for the Teryn Guardian Goddess Laoise.

X

Ex, like ex-rebel or ex-girlfriend/boyfriend. Both can be found in this book.

Y

A letter in the ABC. Also, short for why.

Z

Zimon, Devotee
Dark-haired Pada monk dressed in a red robe with A'nima yellow and A'ris blue sashes on its front. He is lanky and can be a bit chatty.

Zorion, Devotee
He is the leading pada monk with rune-like tattoos on his right cheek. He wears a dark blue ceremonial robe with a silver ruffled cape. He has two sashes that run down in front of his chest; one is A'ris blue and the other is Fla'mma red.

AWARDS

2020 New York Book Festival
Winner: Romance
Honorable Mention: Science Fiction
http://www.newyorkbookfestival.com/

2020 San Francisco Book Festival
Winner: Science Fiction
http://www.sanfranciscobookfestival.com/winners_2020.htm

2020 Annual Best Book Awards
Winner: Best Cover for Fiction
http://www.americanbookfest.com/2020bbapressrelease.html

2020 New England Book Festival
Winner: Science Fiction
Honorable Mention: General Fiction
http://www.newenglandbookfestivals.com

2021 Independent Press Award
Distinguished Favorite: Fantasy
https://www.independentpressaward.com/
2021distinguishedfavorites

2021 Independent Author Network
Finalist: First Novel, Fiction: Science Fiction
https://www.independentauthornetwork.com/
2021-botya-winners.html

2021 eLit Awards
Winner: Science Fiction/Fantasy
Winner: Romance
Winner: Book website for fiction
https://www.elitawards.com/2021_results.php

2021 Eric Hoffer Award - First Horizon Award
Finalist
http://www.hofferaward.com/First-Horizon-Award-finalists.html#.
YIxlnmZKheg

2021 Eric Hoffer Award - Da Vinci Eye Award
Finalist
http://www.hofferaward.com/da-Vinci-Eye-finalists.html#.YIxl5GZ-Kheg

2021 Eric Hoffer Award - Grand Prize
Short List
http://www.hofferaward.com/Eric-Hoffer-Award-grand-prize-short-list.html#.YKRCAH1KgeY

2021 Eric Hoffer Award
Honorable mention: Science Fiction/Fantasy
http://www.hofferaward.com/Eric-Hoffer-Award-winners.html#sci-fi

2021 Speak Up Radio Firebird Award
Winner: Cover Design for fiction
https://www.speakuptalkradio.com/july-2021-winners/
https://www.speakuptalkradio.com/author-s-g-blaise/

2021 Readers Favorite Book Award
Romance - Fantasy/Sci-fi
https://bookawards.com/book-award/the-last-lumenian

2021 Los Angeles Book Festival
Runner-Up: Romance and
Honorable Mention: Science Fiction
http://losangelesbookfestival.com

2021 IAN Book of the Year Awards
Finalist in First Novel over 80,000 words
Finalist in Science Fiction
https://www.independentauthornetwork.com/2021-botya-winners.html

2021 Firebird Book Award
Winner: Sci-Fi Fiction
https://www.speakuptalkradio.com/october-2021-firebird-book-award-winners/

2022 Bookfest Book Awards
Winner: Fiction > Romance - Science Fiction | Fiction > Sci-Fi - Action & Adventure | Fiction > Women's - Fantasy
https://www.thebookfest.com/award_entries/the-last-lumenian/

2022 Independent Press Award
Winner: Best Cover for Sci-fi Fiction
Distinguished Favorite: Fantasy
https://shorturl.at/jLQS5

2022 London Book Festival
Runner Up: Science Fiction
http://www.londonbookfestival.com

2022 Los Angeles Book Festival
Honorable Mention: Science Fiction
http://www.losangelesbookfestival.com

2022 National Indie Excellence Awards
Finalist: Book Cover Design: Fiction
Finalist: Science Fiction
https://www.indieexcellence.com/16th-annual-finalists

2022 International Book Awards
Finalist: Fiction: Fantasy
Finalist: Fiction: Science Fiction
http://www.internationalbookawards.com/2022awardannouncement.html

2022 Independent Publisher Book Awards
Silver: Book/Author/Publisher Website
https://ippyawards.com/167/medalists/2022-medalists--general-categories-59-91

2022 eLit Book Awards
Silver: Best Book Website: True Teryn
https://www.elitawards.com/2022_results.php

2022 Beach Book Festival
Runner-Up: Science Fiction
http://www.beachbookfestival.com

2022 San Francisco Book Festival
Honorable Mention: Science Fiction
http://www.sanfranciscobookfestival.com/winners_2022.htm

2022 NYC Big Book Award
Distinguished Favorite: Fantasy
https://www.nycbigbookaward.com/team-1

2022 New York Book Festival
Honorable Mention: Science Fiction/Horror
http://www.newyorkbookfestival.com

2022 Readers Favorite Book Awards
Finalist: Fiction - Adventure
https://readersfavorite.com/2022-award-contest-winners.htm

2022 IAN Book of the Year Awards
Finalist: Action/Adventure and Science Fiction
https://www.independentauthornetwork.com/2022-botya-winners.html

2022 Best Book Awards
Finalist: Best Cover Design: Fiction
Finalist: Fiction: Fantasy
Finalist: Fiction: Science Fiction
http://americanbookfest.com/2022bbafullresults.html

**KEEP THE MAGIC ALIVE.
IT'S JUST THE BEGINNING!**

THE LAST LUMENIAN

S.G. Blaise

🐦 @SGBlaiseAuthor
f /thelastlumenian
📷 sgblaiseofficial

www.sgblaise.com

To receive exclusive content sign up for the S.G. Blaise newsletter at
sgblaisenews.com